CAN'T BUY ME LOVE

DAN McNEIL

CAN'T BUY ME LOVE

Published by Shubblie Publications, Ottawa, Canada
www.shubbliepublications.com

Back Cover Photo Courtesy of Jeff Radbourne

ISBN 978-0-9877357-2-0
ISBN (EBOOK) 978-0-9877357-3-7

Shubblie Publications Can't Buy Me Love/Dan McNeil

Printed and bound in the United States

URBAN MYTH

February 9, 1964 – 73 million people tuned in to watch The Beatles' first U.S. performance on the Ed Sullivan Show. For many viewers, it was a life changing experience. An urban legend holds that, in the hour that they performed, not a single major crime was committed in New York City.

Or was there?

DEDICATION

For Z:

A writer's confidante and a true friend - your infinite enthusiasm and belief in this story made it all worthwhile.
This is for you.

ACKNOWLEDGMENTS

I began this project with a little bit of trepidation but a lot of high hopes and I'd like to thank a number of people for their help and everlasting support.

First and foremost, I want to thank the love of my life Jes, a brilliant writer in her own right, for helping me be a better writer and an even better person.

I want to send out a big thank you to Ziyada Callender, one of the greatest supporters a writer could ever have. Her enthusiasm for this project was truly inspirational. Her eagerness to see the conclusion of this story was what kept my pen to paper (thanks, Z!).

I would like to give a huge vote of thanks to Lena Robinson, a fellow writer and the best copy editor in the world for her critical eye and spot on suggestions. I couldn't have done it without her.

I'd also like to thank my brother Kevin and my father Joe, two more solid supporters of my literary endeavours and for consistently spreading the word.

I'd like to thank my daughters Richelle and Tess for being the best daughters a dad could ever have.

To Sonya Singh and Taz Boga, thank you for your time, your honesty and your friendship. I appreciate you both very much.

To my cousin (and song writing partner) Steve Casey, thanks for the stellar website design (www.designit.ca).

To Donald Lanouette, a huge thank you for the cover design and all your invaluable help getting it ready for publication.

A big thank you to Ron Barr who saw a writer in me when I first started this crazy pursuit many years ago.

Another big thanks to my pals and fellow band mates Frank McKinlay, Mike Wetmore, Steve Wetmore and Richard Nash for not only allowing me to play with some of the best musicians around, but for taking the time to support my writing.

To the gang at Buster's - Sue and Richard Smith, Eden Windish, Patrick Kilmartin and Curtis Webster - thanks for your endless encouragement.

I'd also like to thank Peter Brown, Adrian Montgomery, Bill Welychka, Doug Hempstead, Melissa Rose-Cornfield (and anyone else I may have left out who stuck with me throughout the years).

To all those in the Twitterverse who have given me encouragement over the years, I thank you very, very much.

And finally, to John, Paul, George and Ringo, thank you for being musical and literary inspirations.

CHAPTER ONE

Thursday, January 30, 1964

If Sonny Carter had a gun that day twenty-five years ago, he would have blown Eddie Bishop's lying, stupid face right off his pathetic excuse of a body. Sonny loathed guns and never used one but sure as hell would have made an exception in that rotten bastard's case.

The bank was theirs for the taking. The plan was fool proof. Every detail pored over, every loose end tied up and any scenario that could have screwed up the heist played out.

Except for one goddamned thing.

For the first five years, it burned a hole in Sonny's gut and percolated his brain. But as time ticked away, the one goddamned thing dimmed until the peptic ulcer it caused was only an occasional reminder. Maybe he couldn't forgive but it was time to forget. It was worth a shot, anyway.

He looked at his watch and cracked a smile, the first real smile in a long time. He slipped his feet into his shoes and began to tie the laces. The banging of a billy club on his cell's bars caught his attention.

"Hello, dirtbag."

Sonny looked up at Officer Hank Hubbard with a blasé stare.

"I understand yer leavin' our little family today, huh?" Hubbard's grin twisted into a sneer. "Can't say we're gonna miss you much, though."

Sonny said nothing and returned to tying his shoes, taking his time. When he finished, he stood up, reached into his breast pocket and pulled out a small, folded piece of paper. Without a word, he handed it to Hubbard. The guard gave Sonny a bemused look and unfolded the note. In small, printed letters, it read, "Go fuck yourself. Hugs and kisses, Sonny Carter."

The guard snorted. "Get yer shit together. Ya got ten minutes." Hubbard punctuated the order by banging his club on the cell bars and continued down the long hallway.

Sonny already had his shit together — a battered suitcase filled with two books, an old photograph and a toothbrush. He packed it weeks ago when he knew he was getting out.

Sonny gripped his hairbrush and stood in front of the mirror over the sink. He stared at his face. He had been behind bars a long time. At fifty-seven, he wasn't exactly handsome in the classical sense, but he believed that he had pleasant enough features. His Roman nose and strong chin had lost some of their chiselled angles, and his cheeks had succumbed somewhat to gravity. Stretching his neck, he tightened the skin, making the soft wrinkles around his eyes disappear for a moment. He smiled but the wrinkles returned so he stopped. As he combed his gray-streaked, dark brown hair, he marvelled at the fact that even at his age, he still had a thick full mane of hair. Once he finished his grooming, he stared at the result. Not quite over the hill…but he was definitely peering down from the top of the crest. He sighed.

Sonny straightened his back standing a full six feet and then some. He was ready to meet the world again.

The mammoth gate swung open with a massive groan and Sonny stepped outside. He paused and looked around. The fetid odor of sweat, shit and despair that was unique to the prison no longer filled his nostrils. It was good to breathe in the fresh, clean air and all the new promise it held.

He noticed a red 1956 Packard parked with the back of the car facing the gate. Sonny recognized the silhouettes of Bernie Miller and Morrie Cooper in the front seat.

With one foot in front of the other, Sonny hit the ground into freedom. The winter air chilled his lungs but it felt great. A light snowfall dusted his shoulders as he strode toward the Packard and his liberty. His movements were sluggish and labored. Yet, he wasn't about to let the guards watching have the satisfaction of thinking that prison broke him.

It hadn't.

As he neared the car, snippets of conversation wafted through the partially rolled down passenger window. He chuckled. Hans and Fritz, the Katzenjammer Kids.

Inside the car, Morrie checked his watch and cleared his throat with a large, wet cough followed by a loud gulp.

"What time you got?" he asked Bernie.

Bernie closed his eyes and ran his fingers in a methodical downward motion over the steering wheel. "Jesus, would you do me a personal favor?" Bernie asked. "If you're gonna make that god awful noise, you wanna do it towards Jersey?"

"I think my watch is busted." Morrie tapped the face of his watch. "How long we been waitin' for?"

"It's about three minutes later than the last time you asked."

Sonny slapped the palm of his hand on the roof of the Packard, interrupting Bernie's tirade. "Hello ladies," he grinned.

Morrie spun his head around and broke into a wide smile. "Holy crap, Sonny. You tryin' to give us a heart attack?"

Sonny was shocked and saddened to see how the years had robbed Morrie's once chubby face, and replaced it with a lined, gaunt mug. Time sure is an unforgiving bitch, he thought.

"Sorry, buddy." Sonny's voice sounded rough to his own ears. "Man, you look like crap."

Morrie shrugged. "Yeah, well, I look better than I feel."

"Then you must feel like shit."

Bernie poked his head forward. "Hey, ya crumb. Nice to see you haven't lost any of your witty charm."

"Up yours."

Morrie flipped the seat and bent his body forward. Sonny squeezed into the back, settling in with a grunt. He tossed his suitcase on top of a mountain of clothes piled up beside him. Bernie put the car in gear and pulled away.

"So what are you two punks up to these days, besides hitting all the all-you-can-eat buffets?"

Bernie looked in the rear view mirror and flipped Sonny the bird. "If you have to know, I got a job in a garage."

"No kidding? You're a grease monkey?"

"Yeah, so? Pay's decent. If you want, maybe I can get you a job there too."

Sonny chuckled. "Only if some sweet young thing is willing to pay for the work without opening her purse." He winked. "Besides, you know I ain't never been too good with cars."

"All I'm sayin' is that I can help you out. Just lemme know."

Sonny studied the interior of the car. "Nice bucket you got here Bern. New?"

"Naw. Had it for a coupla years now. I picked it up practically new a few weeks after I got out. Al dickered the price down and got me a great deal."

"I'm not surprised," Sonny said as he ran his hand over the leather seat. "Al was always good with numbers."

Bernie grinned. "The ladies sure love it."

"Yeah, I bet they do."

"You know they do." Bernie winked. "And the driver too, if ya know what I mean."

"An old fart like you? C'mon. If you get one more wrinkle on that mush of yours, Morrie'll have to carry it in his pocket for ya."

Bernie eyed him through the rear view mirror again. "I still got it, my friend. Never lost it. I had this little dancer - a Rockette no less - who just loved this car."

Sonny rolled his eyes. "Jesus, here we go."

"This doll would get me so worked up just thinking about her," Bernie said. "I always worried about going 'Old Faithful' on her."

"Old Faithful?"

Bernie nodded. "Yeah. You know - pullin' the pitcher? Jackin' the beanstalk? Squeezin' the —"

"Okay, I get it."

Bernie laughed. "One time I actually had to use my sock to — you know — relieve myself before I picked her up."

An uncomfortable Morrie shifted in his seat. "Jeez Bernie," he said. Sonny cast an apprehensive glance at his suitcase on top of the pile of Bernie's clothes. He lifted it a few inches, and with immediate regret, he noticed a pair of dirty socks.

"She was quite an entertainer if you get my drift," Bernie said.

"Hey Bernie," Morrie said. "Remember that Ford Forder you had back in thirty-nine? Boy, that was a beauty."

Bernie turned to Morrie. He shook his head and mouthed the words 'shut up'. "Let's not talk about that stuff, okay?" he said.

"Why not?" Morrie asked.

Bernie jerked his head at Sonny. "'Cause he doesn't wanna talk about it," he hissed.

Morrie gave Bernie a quizzical look and continued. "That was a great car," he said. "It always reminds me of that day at the Hudson." He smacked his forehead with his palm. "Say, that's right. Didja hear about Eddie Bishop?"

Bernie groaned. He caught Sonny's stare in the mirror burning a hole into the back of Morrie's head.

Sonny's eyes narrowed at the mention of Eddie Bishop's name. "What?" he asked in a low voice.

"Jesus Cooper," said Bernie.

"That asshole," said Sonny, his voice tinged with menace. "Did somebody finally cut his throat?"

"Nah. Get this," Morrie said, completely oblivious to the anger in Sonny's tone. "He's president of the Hudson Bank. Yeah, can you imagine? The goddamn Hudson of all places."

Bernie jammed his elbow into Morrie's ribs. Morrie grabbed them and winced. "Geez, Bern, whatcha go and do that for?"

"Would you shut the hell up?"

"Unbelievable," Sonny said, his voice a low growl. "After what that miserable piece of shit did to us."

"It's ancient history," Bernie said. "Let's all forget about it, okay?" He flicked Morrie's ear with his finger. "What's wrong with you, stupe?" he whispered.

Morrie turned around. "Sorry, Sonny," he said. They drove the next few miles in silence.

"We're almost there," Morrie said. "Wait 'til you meet my nephew Gary, Sonny. You'll like him."

Sonny stared out the window, with his thoughts drifting in and out of the past. "Sure," he mumbled.

Morrie continued. "My nephew's a big shot down at the network. At CBS, I mean. He's what you call an 'executive producer.'"

"That's nice."

"Not sure what it is exactly, but it sounds important." He brightened. "Hey, wait a sec. Turn that up, Bernie."

"You turn it up. I'm driving."

Morrie reached over and spun the volume knob. A machine-gun rapid-fire prattle filled the car. "Good afternoon, New York," the voice announced with enthusiasm. "It's all Beatles all the time on your all-Beatles radio station. The countdown has officially begun for the arrival of your favorite recording group's stop right here in New York City. As the day gets closer we'll have live updates on John, Paul, George and Ringo. We'll have our own fifth Beatle himself, Murray the K, bringing you all the Fab Four information that you need to know...."

"Holy cow," Morrie said. "This is what my nephew Gary was talkin' about. It's those Beatles guys. Remember?"

Bernie snickered. "You know, it just occurred to me that your nephew's name is Gary Cooper. That's kinda funny."

Morrie scratched his head. "What's so funny about it?"

"You know. Gary Cooper. 'High Noon'." With a confused expression, Morrie checked his watch.

"Stay tuned to WINS-AM radio for all your Beatle news," the radio voice said. "Coming up after this break, the number one song in the nation...."

"This is going to be a huge deal," said Morrie. "Gary says that they'll have millions watching that show. Can you imagine? Millions."

"What show?" Bernie asked.

"Whattya mean what show? Gary's show. The Ed Sullivan Show. Remember? I told you all about it."

Bernie shook his head. "Naw, ya didn't tell me, Morrie."

Morrie turned around and faced Sonny. "Gary says that these Beatles guys are gonna be huge."

"Beagles?"

"Beatles," corrected Morrie. "Gary'll tell you all about it when we get—"

Sonny leaned back and yawned. "Yeah, I'd rather talk about Bernie's weird sock use instead."

After driving in silence for a few minutes, Sonny asked, "You sure it's okay that I can stay at your nephew's for a few days Morrie? I don't want to be a bother."

Morrie smiled. "Nah, it's fine. Gary and Louise don't mind. They love having me stayin' with 'em. It's all set, so just relax." Morrie turned around to look at Sonny. "Oh, and don't worry. You'll forget all about Eddie Bishop in no time."

"Christ almighty, Morrie," mumbled Bernie.

Morrie turned the radio volume back up. Another Beatles melody reverberated throughout the car but Sonny took no notice. He wasn't the most educated man in the world, but he was well read, he knew what irony was, and it wasn't lost on him either.

The Hudson National Bank and Trust Company.

Eddie Bishop.

Sonny's ulcer began to act up. He rubbed his gut and stared out of the window as the blurry, snow covered scenery whipped by.

CHAPTER TWO

By the time Bernie pulled into the driveway of a beautiful, two-story Long Island home, Sonny's mood had lightened somewhat. He stepped out into the cool dusky night and spied a sleek, late-model Plymouth parked in front of the garage. Being a television executive - whatever must pay pretty damn good.

Bernie rolled down his window and leaned out. "I'll see you guys tomorrow at Finn's. Say around three?"

Warm nostalgia flooded over Sonny at the mention of their old hangout. He tapped the hood of the car. "You bet. Thanks for the lift, buddy."

Bernie gave him a thumbs up and backed out of the driveway.

Morrie's nephew stood at the front door. "You must be Sonny, I'm Gary." He grabbed Sonny's hand, shook it and ushered them into the house. "Welcome. Make yourself at home." He sounded excited.

Gary, in his mid-thirties, seemed to be a gregarious sort of fellow. He had a full head of neatly trimmed, mouse brown hair and pale blue eyes behind thick, black horn-rimmed glasses. He also had one of the widest smiles that Sonny had ever seen. Although his build was slight, Gary exuded a big personality.

"Sonny, it must feel good to leave there. I mean it must be nice to be out of — uh — you know —" Gary seemed to be having trouble finding the right words. "You're probably tired from your — uh—"

"The drive?" Sonny asked. "Or my stay in the clink?"

Gary pointed to Sonny's coat and let out a nervous laugh. "Here, let me have that." Sonny removed his overcoat and handed it to Gary.

"Gary?" The piercing female voice reminded Sonny of the obnoxious lunchtime whistle at Elmira. "Are they finally here?"

"Yes. Yes, they are, hon," Gary responded.

"Well, it's about time. Don't they have clocks in prison?"

Gary let out an awkward chuckle. "That's my wife, Louise. Real cut-up that one. She's got quite a sense of humor." He tilted his head downward and picked off a few pieces of lint from his trousers.

"She uh, had a rough day, but she cooked up a terrific dinner for us."

The aroma of roast beef hung thick in the air. Sonny realized just how famished he was and how much he looked forward to a home cooked meal. Gary directed them into the living room.

"Here you go, fellas. Have a seat. I'll go see how dinner's doing."

With a loud groan and a cough, Morrie settled himself into a stylish, orange sofa. Sonny plopped himself into an overstuffed chair and took in the room. Above the fireplace, he saw some statuettes - awards that Gary won over the years for his work in television. There were many framed photographs on the mantle. They were presumably well-known movie and television stars that meant nothing to the ex-con. His eyes drifted left of the fireplace to a television set, projecting a western movie. At first, he gave it some attention, but it bored him after a few minutes.

A pale boy of about ten, holding a plastic guitar materialized next to Sonny's chair.

Surprised, he said, "Oh. Hello there young fella." The kid had deep blue but vacuous, half-closed eyes. What struck Sonny though was the kid's long hair - the way it crowned his owlish face, hanging down to his eyebrows like a horse's mane. He must have enormous ears, thought Sonny. The boy continued to gawk at the ex-con.

"Who are you?" asked the mop-top in a monotone voice.

"I'm your Uncle Morrie's friend."

"Oh yeah?" He squinted at Sonny. "So, you a jailbird too?"

"This here is Gary's kid, Tommy." Morrie coughed and shifted in his seat. "And you know Tommy, that's not a nice thing to ask a guest."

The boy's face was as impassive as an Egyptian hieroglyph. He went over to a table upon which sat a small box with the word Renzoniphone emblazoned across the front. He lifted the cover of the box and reached inside it. He took a small dark disc out of a paper sleeve and placed the disc inside the box. Within seconds, a powerful, clamorous sound split the air.

With a look of repulsion, Sonny bellowed "Jesus H. Christ, what the hell is that?"

In an even louder voice, Morrie said, "It's the Beatles"

Sonny tilted his ear toward Morrie. "It's the what?"

Morrie cupped his hands around his mouth like a megaphone. "The Beatles," Morrie repeated. "Remember, in the car? They're those musicians from England."

Sonny glared at Morrie and moved to the sofa. He watched the kid bop his head back and forth in time with the beat. "Does it have to be so goddamned loud?"

Morrie shrugged. "I think it's kind of catchy."

"Hey, there." Sonny waved at Tommy, trying to get his attention. "Tommy? Could ya turn it down?"

Oblivious, Tommy strummed the strings of his plastic guitar. He bounced his head from side to side with every "yeah, yeah, yeah" that came out of the record player's felt-covered speakers.

Sonny started to get up again, but Morrie put his hand on his shoulder. Morrie went over to the record player and gradually lowered the volume. As soon as the music stopped, Tommy quit strumming his guitar. Morrie jerked a thumb toward Sonny and mouthed the word "headache" to the youngster. Tommy narrowed his eyes into slits that ran parallel to the bottom of the bangs of his unusual hairdo.

Tommy tossed the guitar aside. "Were you guys in jail together, Uncle Morrie?" he asked.

Morrie grimaced. "Tommy, you know I don't like to talk —"

"It's just a simple question, Uncle Morrie."

Morrie rubbed his scalp and sighed. "Uh — yeah, Tommy — well, no. Actually, Sonny was at Elmira I was at Attica."

It was obvious to Sonny that the kid relished making his uncle squirm. "Did you ever try to bust out?"

"Well, no."

"How about sticking a shiv in a screw's throat?"

Morrie blanched. "Geez Tommy—"

"Ever shank a stoolie?"

"What's the matter with you? Of course not." Morrie shook his head. "Where the heck do you get this stuff?"

"Hmmm." Tommy pulled at his lip and then turned up a sly grin. "Did ya ever have a guy come up behind you in the shower and—"

"Okay, that's enough," Morrie said quickly. He grabbed Tommy by the shoulders and pushed him toward the kitchen. "No more questions. How's about seein' how your mom is doin' with dinner, eh buddy?"

A bewildered Sonny watched the youngster leave. "What the hell was that all about?"

Morrie ambled back to the sofa and flopped down next to Sonny. "Tommy likes to goof around."

Sonny blinked. "Goof around? Where does a ten year old kid get that kind of crap anyways?"

"Gary's brother Donald is a screenwriter in Los Angeles," sighed Morrie. "He writes pictures about hard-nosed detectives, girls with guns, women in jail. You know, real potboilers. He loves to entertain Tommy with that stuff when he's here."

Sonny shook his head. "Jesus Christ."

Morrie shrugged. "Tommy's all right. He's what you might call—"

"A little shit?" Sonny said.

"I was gonna say special, but okay."

"Seriously, what's with the hair?"

Before Morrie could answer, Gary reappeared in the living room rubbing his hands together. "Dinner time," he said. They followed Gary down the hall, the aroma of the roast beef dinner like a siren's song to the ravenous ex-con. Gary directed Sonny to his seat as Louise came through the swinging kitchen doors with a large serving platter. During holidays in the joint, they would serve some leathery gray meat-like thing that they called "roast beef."

This beautiful pink hunk of beef in front of him sure didn't look and smell like that. He eyed it like a lover he hadn't seen in years. He never felt hungrier in his life. Louise plonked the platter on the table with a loud thud, giving the dinner guests a start.

Sonny got a look at his hostess for the first time. She looked to be in her early thirties, but her tired hazel eyes made her look older. Her ashy blonde hair was done up in a bouffant - big on top with flips on either side of the ears. She wore a yellow dress with a deep, rounded collar adorned with bright white polka dots. In spite of all the effort to present herself in an appealing way, the surly scowl anchored to her face sucked away any traces of pleasantness.

She gave Gary a withering look and marched back into the kitchen before Gary had a chance to introduce her to Sonny. Sonny watched Louise tramp into the kitchen. He felt sorry for Gary. *What an awful piece of work*, he thought.

Without a word, Gary reached for the roast beef and carved out slabs of the juicy red meat. Louise returned with a steaming bowl of vegetables. With a mild scraping sound, Morrie nudged his chair closer to the table. Tommy meanwhile tried to flip his spoon into his glass of milk.

"Tommy!" Louise admonished. She roughly yanked the spoon out of her son's hand. "I'm not going to tell you about spoon flipping again. And no hair at the dinner table." Sonny watched the kid pull at, what was now obvious to Sonny a wig, from the top of his head, revealing a close-cropped shock of yellow hair. He dropped the wig beside his utensils where it lay like a large squashed South American spider.

He had only been out of prison for a couple of hours and Sonny found things on the outside more than a little confusing. When he was a kid, Sonny would have never have acted the way Tommy did in front of his folks. What the hell was going on in the world, and what ten- year-old boy wore a wig, for chrissakes?

Louise sat at the opposite end of the table from Gary. Without a word, the five of them began to eat. Gary smiled at his wife, his gaze swinging from Sonny then back to her. "Honey, you haven't properly met Uncle Morrie's friend yet," he said. "Sonny, this is my wife Louise."

"Thank you for your hospitality, Mrs. Cooper," Sonny offered. "This roast beef is delicious."

Louise gave a curt nod and reached for the potatoes. They returned to dining in silence once again. Except for the sounds of the cutlery scraping across the china plates, all was quiet. To Sonny's embarrassment, he realized he was indulging in two habits he had picked up in prison. He was eating too fast and he was using a spoon. He switched to his fork and knife and with careful deliberation, settled into his meal.

The guys retired to the living room with their coffee after the awkward but delectable dinner. Gary took his place in the overstuffed chair while Sonny and Morrie settled in on the sofa. Morrie gulped his coffee and asked Gary how things were going at work.

Gary brightened. "Oh, it's shaping up beautifully. This show could turn out to be bigger than the one with Elvis."

"Elvis?" Sonny asked. "What's an Elvis?"

"What's an Elvis?" Gary chuckled. "Elvis Presley. You never heard of him?"

"Nope. That reminds me, though. I was in the can with a guy named Elvin Lafferty. He was a gooseberry lay artist in Poughkeepsie."

"Gooseberry lay artist?"

"Elvin liked to steal women's clothes from clotheslines."

"Well, your friend Elvin may have been an artist but Elvis Presley is a very popular entertainer."

"Oh, Elvin was a pretty popular entertainer too, but not for the reasons you think."

Gary grinned. "Elvis has been on the Ed Sullivan Show three times so far. We had sixty million people watching the first time he was on. Imagine that. It was the biggest single audience in television history."

"Ed Sullivan? I think I remember him. Wasn't he a sportswriter for the Graphic?" asked Sonny.

"The New York Evening Graphic? Wow, you have been away for a long time. Ed Sullivan hasn't been a newspaper writer in years. He's my boss and the host of the show. It's pretty much a Sunday night institution."

"It is a pretty big deal," said Morrie. "It's kinda like the Major Bowes Amateur Hour."

"Yes, kind of like that, only with upcoming talent and we have major stars on as well," said Gary.

"And now we've got the Beatles. And would you like to know the best part? These fellows fell right into our laps. Their manager — oh, what's his name? I'll have to check with my assistant. Anyway, he called us. He believes this is going to be their big break in the U.S."

Sonny shrugged. “I heard their music and I don’t get it. Whatever happened to Glenn Miller? Man, those were the days.”

“Trust me,” said Gary, “it’s going to be historic. The whole country will be watching.”

“I think I’ll pass,” said Sonny, and in an affected English accent he added, “Not my cup of tea.”

Gary smiled. “That’s all right Sonny. What’s one viewer compared to seventy million?”

CHAPTER THREE

Friday, January 31, 1964

Calvin Spencer checked his watch again in the dim foyer of the Jersey Social Club. He yawned. He couldn't remember the last time he had ever been up so early, but the man he was about to meet liked to do business as soon as the sun came up - and the man he was about to meet he was someone accustomed to doing things his way.

The thumping of heavy footsteps against the dark, scuffed up wooden floor startled him. He looked up to see Renzo Genna. He was ramrod shaped, dressed in a sharp, navy blue Italian suit, a bright, white shirt and lemon yellow tie. Renzo motioned to him. "Come on in Cal. He'll see you now."

Spencer stood up and followed Renzo down the hallway. He led Spencer to a door flanked by two muscle-bound bodyguards. As Renzo gestured to one of the bodyguards, the diamond in his oversized pinkie ring seemed to wink at Spencer. Spencer wondered how much the ring was worth. He always wondered about such things. After all, it was his job to wonder about such things.

The bodyguard ushered them both into an office. As he stepped into the room, the pungent odor of fried onions, garlic and grease slapped Spencer's senses. A gargantuan man with the biggest head Spencer had ever seen sat at a table in a chair that looked like it was better suited for a child. It was a comical scene. The hulk chomped on a soggy fried egg sandwich, studied a racing form and held a tiny cup of espresso in his fat fist. He could have slipped the handle of the cup over one of his sausage-sized fingers and worn it like a ring. Spencer swallowed the chuckle that bubbled at his lips.

Using his shirtsleeve to wipe the glistening grease from his mouth, the behemoth looked up from his racing form and nodded at Spencer.

"Come. Sit." His voice was low and raspy.

Spencer took a seat opposite him. "You wanted to see me, Mr. Provenzano?"

Bruno "The Butcher" Provenzano was one of the most powerful men in New York City. He was a man who instilled fear in everyone up and down the Eastern coast as a caporegime, a captain in the Ferenza crime family. However, unknown to most in the crime world, Provenzano had never actually killed anybody. He was no hitman. At three-hundred-and-twenty-four pounds, his physique kept him from doing anything that could be described as "physical." The fear he engendered was actually, due to the fact that he was Gaetano "Tony" Ferenza's cousin, the boss of the crime family that bore his name.

"It's an honor to meet you," Spencer said. "I've heard quite a lot about you." Provenzano sat back in his chair and patted his protruding gut.

"Lengthwise, I'm sure."

Spencer raised his eyebrows. Lengthwise? He shifted his gaze toward Renzo, who mouthed the word "likewise". It appeared that Provenzano earned his nickname "The Butcher" from his unique mangling of the English language.

"My fren' Renzo here says that youze can get stuff done." Provenzano yanked a purple handkerchief out of his pocket and rubbed it all over his fleshy, perspiring face. "I need me a guy who can do a lil' sumpin' for me."

"That's what I'm here for, Mr. Provenzano."

Provenzano smiled. Once, when he was snorkeling off the coast of Grand Bahama Island, Spencer had seen a tiger shark up close. He noticed how similar Provenzano's predatory leer was to the shark's toothy countenance.

"I unnerstan' that youze guys," Provenzano pointed to Renzo and then to Spencer, "go back a ways." He brought the cup to his meaty lips and slurped. "I want you to know dat I trust Renzo with all my heart. Implissintly, as some say."

Spencer marveled at the man's complete lack of command of the English language. Provenzano continued. "Renzo says youze got lots of — uh — money people? Is he right?"

Spencer nodded. "I have contacts in the financial community."

Provenzano leaned forward, clasping his hammy hands together in front of him. "Okay. I wanna propose to you. Ah shit, no I don't. What I mean is…" He squinted his eyes and his face reddened as if he was about to pass a brick between his butt cheeks. "Uh, fuck me —" He looked at Renzo. "What's that goddamn word again?"

Renzo turned to Spencer. "A proposition," Renzo gently offered.

Provenzano puffed out his cheeks, smacked his chest with his fist and burped. "Yeah. That's it."

Calvin Spencer knew what was coming next. He had many connections with many financial institutions all over New York, New Jersey and Philadelphia. At thirty-two years old, he was considered the man to know when it came to the practice of engaging in illegal financial transactions in order to conceal the source of ill-gotten cash. There was no real term for it, but in later years, it would be called "money laundering." Spencer's contacts were invaluable. And it paid well. His last transaction was for a cool million and it personally netted him ten grand.

"How much are we talking here?" Spencer asked.

Provenzano picked up a bottle of beer and downed the contents in one long swallow. He pointed the bottle toward Spencer and chuckled. "How do you like dis fuckin' guy, Renzo?" Provenzano's chuckle turned into a long string of burps, each one louder than the last. He leaned over to the side and lifted a massive thigh. A lengthy, high-pitched squeak escaped between his cheek and the chair. It was followed by an awful scent that mugged Spencer's nose. Spencer's face flushed as he held his breath.

"Ahhhh." Provenzano let out a contented sigh. "We are talkin' ten million. Maybe a little more."

Spencer expelled a large breath. He made sure to appear cool and unimpressed, but his heart danced the Watusi against his ribs.

Ten million dollars? Spencer had never handled that much before. Ever. He usually worked with small companies, not crime families, but a lot of them worked in the same way. Small companies often had hundreds, sometimes thousands of dollars that couldn't be deposited into bank accounts without drawing suspicion from authorities. Deposits that large had to be reported. Spencer provided a conduit from these companies to his contacts who were already taking in large amounts of cash into their own businesses. These contacts would then take the cash from the small companies and deposit it into their own accounts. They would turn it around and write a check to the small companies, after taking a cut. The small companies would then deposit that check into their accounts and no one was the wiser. Spencer hardly had to do a thing but he collected a huge fee for his services.

"That won't be a problem." Spencer hoped his forced confidence masked his barely contained excitement.

Provenzano shoved fried onions from the greasy plate on to a bread roll. "Ya need ta unnerstand dat da money. It ain't mine." He bit down on his sandwich, bread crumbs flew out of his mouth as he spoke. "It belongs to my cousin Gaetano, and he encrusted me with the job to which I encrust to you."

Spencer gasped, and then coughed to mask it. "Your cousin Gaetano? You mean Tony Ferenza the mob —?" He caught himself. "I mean, Tony Frenza of Ferenza Construction?"

"Yeah, dat's him. Dere's a lotta heat on him right now, so he — dat is, we need to move dis money around."

Spencer made some mental calculations and placed his sweaty palms on the table. Ten thousand dollars for doing this job wouldn't cut it. "Mr. Provenzano, with a transaction this large, the premium would be fairly large as well." He blinked and swallowed hard. "Say, two hundred and fifty thousand?"

Provenzano didn't respond right away. He seemed to ponder the amount when the sound of urgent, hushed tones behind him diverted his concentration. He turned his huge head around and saw Renzo speaking in a quiet but affected voice into the telephone. Renzo noticed his boss glaring at him and put the receiver to his chest.

"Sorry Bruno," he said. He pointed to the receiver. "Ex-wife."

Provenzano grunted. "Why you gotta do dat now? We're in da middle of business here."

Renzo offered a weak smile and held up a finger. He returned to his conversation on the telephone. "Okay. Fine. Fine, I said. I have to go," he hissed. He hung up the receiver and shrugged apologetically.

Provenzano turned his attention back to Spencer. "Two hunnerd and fifty grand, huh? That's a lot of scratch for sumpin' like this." He turned his billboard-sized face toward Renzo who then gestured to one of the bodyguards.

"Give us a moment, would you Cal?" Renzo said to Spencer.

The bodyguard led Spencer out of the room. As soon as he stepped into the hallway, a cascade of sweat dribbled down his arms inside his shirt. He rubbed his wet palms on his pant legs as he thought about what he had just pulled off.

Two hundred and fifty thousand? What balls. The most he had ever received was ten grand. This was big time. He would have asked for more if the money had actually belonged to the fat slob himself. However, it was Tony Ferenza's cash and Spencer was well aware of Ferenza's reputation.

Tony Ferenza started out as a soldier in Lucky Luciano's family. He was a brutal mob enforcer. Even made men were wary of the vicious hitman. The rumor was that he was responsible for at least thirty murders. All Bruno Provenzano was responsible for was committing grammer-cide with the English language.

Still, two hundred and fifty thousand...

After a few minutes, the door swung open and Renzo ushered Spencer back inside. Provenzano stood next to Renzo and gave Spencer a subtle nod. With Renzo's thin frame up against Provenzano's almost perfect circular shape, it occurred to Spencer that he was glimpsing a physical manifestation of the number ten.

Provenzano waddled over to Spencer and stuck out his hand. Spencer took it. With revulsion, he watched his fingers disappear into Provenzano's puffy, tepid flesh.

"How soon we do this?" asked Provenzano.

Spencer withdrew his moistened hand and shoved it into his pocket. "I'll have to check with my contact, but I'm fairly certain that we could have it all wrapped up by the tenth. I'll be in touch with Renzo."

"Great. Tony's gonna crap his shorts. I should have the dough for ya soon." He graced him with another omnivorous smile, but this time, there was no trace of humor. "You listen close. It's important this transfakshun goes off with no hinch, capiche? Dis could be a big payday for youze guys. So don't get any bright ideas, like fuckin' off to Switzerland with all them there Swedish banks with Tony's dough."

Spencer smiled. "Not to worry, Mr. Provenzano. The last thing I want to do is to make your cousin angry."

“Right.” Provenzano shook two sausage fingers at him. “It’s not a good idea to eat from the hand that bites ya.”

“Bite the hands that feeds you, boss.” Renzo said.

“Dat too.” Provenzano thumped his chest and lifted his leg again. *Jesus, not again*, Spencer thought.

“Could be very dentalmentral to youze guys health, ya know.”

So could your ass, thought Spencer.

“Guys who fuck with Tony’s dough — well, they don’t get no more fuckin’.” He squinted, spearing Spencer with warning daggers. “So to speak.”

So to speak, indeed.

CHAPTER FOUR

"Well, would you look at that?" Sonny stopped walking and pointed at the gothic building. In large, snow-dusted letters, above the doorway, were the words The Hudson National Bank and Trust Company.

"Place hasn't changed much." Morrie brushed the accumulation of snow from his coat.

"No, it hasn't."

"Hey, I'm really sorry about yesterday. The whole Eddie Bishop thing."

Sonny waved him off. "Water under the bridge."

Morrie pulled his coat closer together. "Come on, let's keep going. I'm freezing my keister off."

"In a minute," Sonny said. He yanked his own coat's collar up around his neck. As he stared at the bank's faded bricks, memories of that fateful day twenty-five years ago flooded his memory. "It would have worked," he muttered. The plan was simple. All they had to do was walk into the bank and take the cash. There were three guards on duty that day. One was out sick and another was running late, thanks to well-placed bribes. The third was two weeks away from retirement and didn't particularly care about doing a good job. Guns were unnecessary. Their ace in the hole was a bank teller — Eddie Bishop, their accomplice. All he had to do was hand them the cash without alerting the guard. They would have been in and out in a matter of minutes.

That is if Bishop hadn't screwed them over. He tipped off the cops and since the gang was unarmed, it was an easy arrest.

Morrie's rough cough and his exclamation of "oh no" snapped Sonny out of his daydream. He followed Morrie's gaze to an older man, exiting the bank with a young, attractive woman. Clad in an expensive overcoat and topped with a wool derby stood Eddie Bishop. He reeked pomposity and entitlement. In his left hand, he carried a leather briefcase and twirled a brass topped antique walking stick in his right.

"I don't believe it," Sonny muttered. When he was in jail, Sonny often imagined many different scenarios involving Eddie Bishop. Every single one of them ended, at the very least, with Sonny knocking him on his fat ass. However, not one of them involved his nemesis standing in front of the bank that he tried to knock over so many years ago. Sonny curled his hand into a fist. Morrie noticed and took hold of Sonny's arm. "Let's get out of here," said Morrie.

Sonny gave Morrie a grim smile. "Not until I say hello to our old friend," he said.

Bishop checked his watch and scanned the street. "This is ridiculous," he said to the woman. "Where are all the cabs?" He took off his hat and brushed the snow from the brim. "This city can be so frustrating."

Sonny sidled up to Bishop who gave him a cursory glance. "If you're looking for the soup kitchen," he said pointing, "it's about three blocks that way."

Sonny shook his head. "How's it going, Eddie?" he asked.

Bishop turned. In a tone dripping with disdain, he asked, "Do I know you?"

Sonny clenched his jaw. "You should. You owe me about thirty grand and twenty-five years of my life."

Bishop examined Sonny as if he were a bug under a microscope. "Well, well. If it isn't bank robber extraordinaire, Sonny Carter," he said. "Knocked off any banks lately?" The condescension in his voice was palpable. "Sarah," he said, turning to the woman standing next to him, "allow me to a introduce you to a couple of old acquaintances." She smiled at both Sonny and Morrie and held out her gloved hand.

"Nice to meet you, she said cheerfully. I'm Sarah Garrett."

Bishop made a face and pulled her hand away from them. "I was being facetious, dear."

"Facetious?" Sonny asked. "That means squealer, right?" Sonny would have loved nothing better than to grab Bishop's walking stick and rearrange his pale, priggish face with it. He turned to Morrie. "You'd think that with that cushy job that he got by fucking his buddies over, he woulda learned to be a little bit nicer."

"Please," Bishop said. "If you're referring to that incredibly boneheaded attempt to rob this place twenty-five years ago, then yes, my information to the police about that pathetic endeavor certainly helped my career advancement."

"How do you sleep at night?" Sonny asked.

"In very expensive silk pyjamas."

Sonny gave serious thought to grabbing the walking stick again. "You asshole. You knew how important that job was to me."

Bishop snorted. "Oh, for God's sake. Sonny Carter and his poor, frail mother. Cue the violins. I'm sure she was very proud of you and your pathetic stretch in the slammer. Tell me, did she ever get to see you decked out in your prison grays?"

Sonny fumed. Morrie noticed the crimson color in Sonny's face. He inched closer to him, ready to grab him if he decided to get physical. Bishop continued. "Did you really think that you feeble fuck-ups, pardon the language Sarah, had a hope in hell of pulling that off?"

"Do you really have any idea what a massive prick you are?" Sonny said, his jaw pulsing.

The warmth that spread under his collar and across his cheeks was now burning.

A malevolent smirk curled Bishop's lip. "Why yes. Yes, I do." He turned to Morrie. "From the criminal mastermind to the criminally stupid. Hello, Cooper."

Morrie shrugged. "Still as loquacious as ever, I see," said Bishop.

Morrie blinked. "What?" he asked.

"Yes, an excellent riposte, as usual." Bishop put his briefcase down and reached into the inside pocket of his coat. He extracted a leather wallet, removed some bills and held them out to Sonny, like a bone to a hungry dog. "Here's fifty dollars. Why don't we let bygones be bygones?"

A single throbbing vein emerged along Sonny's forehead. "Why don't you cram it?" he responded.

"Charming as always. Suit yourself."

Sarah took a moment from her cab hailing duties and said, "Hey, I've got an idea. Why don't you come to the bank on Monday and we'll set up an account for you?"

Bishop frowned. "Sarah, please—"

"Why not Edward?" Sarah asked. "I think two men starting over could use a little help and consideration."

"You're very kind Miss," said Sonny. He nudged Bishop with his elbow. "You could learn a lot from this girl, ya putz."

"Oh right," Bishop said to Sarah. "That's a fabulous idea. Imagine the irony - you putting money into the bank instead of trying to steal it."

Sonny leaned in close to Bishop. "How'd you like me to deposit five right now into your stupid looking face?"

Sarah placed herself between Sonny and Bishop. "I see a taxi, Edward."

"Thank God." Bishop twirled his walking stick. "It's been a real treat seeing you two again. Maybe we can do this again in another twenty-five years."

Sarah gave Sonny and Morrie a sweet smile. "Nice to meet you, fellows."

Sonny nodded. "Same to you too Miss," he said, returning the smile. "And to you - Edward - see ya and take care. And by 'see ya' I mean 'screw you' and by 'take care' I mean 'go fuck yourself.'"

Sarah put her gloved hand over her mouth to hide her laughter as she and a sneering Bishop got into the cab. As it pulled away from the curb, Sonny noticed Sarah giving him a little wave. Now that was interesting, he thought. Something stirred inside him, something he hadn't felt in decades.

He turned his attention to the snow covered letters of the Hudson National Bank and Trust Company. He remembered when the cops threw the four of them up against the wall and handcuffed them after their aborted heist attempt. He also remembered Bishop's smug face when one of the cops said to him, "Thanks for the tip," the cop said.

Bishop grinned at Sonny. "It's just business," he said with a smirk.

Sonny broke away from the cop that was holding him and charged at Bishop, who let out a high-pitched scream. Sonny, his fist raised, was only a few feet from Bishop when it all went black. When he awoke, he was in a jail cell with an egg-sized knot on the back of his head. That day was his introduction to his quarter-century stretch behind bars.

As the memory faded he looked up at the sign again and murmured, "I wonder—"

Morrie gave him a curious look. "You wonder what?" he asked.

Sonny shoved his hands deep into his pockets and eyed the bank. "Just thinkin'."

CHAPTER FIVE

Finn's Saloon was Sonny's favorite watering hole. A wave of nostalgia washed over him. Not much had changed with the place. Faded posters of The World's Fair, Gone with the Wind and Blondie Bringing up Baby adorned the walls. The bar was almost empty, so Sonny and Morrie were able to get a booth in the back. They ordered a couple of beers from a bored waitress while they waited for the others to arrive. Sonny spun the saltshaker, spilling grains of white crystal all over the table.

"That's bad luck, you know," Morrie admonished.

Sonny grunted. "You know I don't believe in that shit."

Morrie shrugged. "Look what happened to my uncle."

"Your uncle? The one who was hit by a streetcar?"

"Yep. He spilled salt before he got hit."

"I also recall that he stumbled out in front of the damn thing, shitfaced on Bushmills."

"Still," Morrie said. He shrugged again and took a sip of beer. "Sure was funny running into Eddie today," he said.

"Yeah. Real hilarious," Sonny muttered.

Morrie brightened. He reached into his inside pocket and pulled out a faded photo. One of the corners had worn away. "Look what I found the other day." He passed it over to Sonny. A huge smile broke out across his face. It was a picture of Sonny and Morrie, in their twenties looking like the epitome of youth.

"Holy shit! Look at your hair," said Sonny. "Jesus, look at my hair. Where was this taken?"

"Sixty-First Street between First and Third, if I remember. Near Billy Vincent's place."

"Billy Vincent! Jesus —"

Morrie chuckled. "His dad owned that candy store near the Battery. Our first heist."

"Yeah, I remember."

"Man, was your Dad mad," Morrie said.

"No shit. I had to sleep on my gut for a couple of days." He sucked in a deep breath. "You know, it was my Mom that I felt bad for."

"Yeah, I remember. She wouldn't let us play together for weeks."

Sonny stared off into the distance. "Things were never the same after that," he said in a quiet voice. "Sometimes I wish —" He lowered his head. After a few moments, he looked up. "Do you mind if I keep this?"

Morrie nodded. "Sure. I won't be needing it."

Sonny looked perplexed. "What do you mean?"

Just as Morrie was about to respond, Sonny's eye caught Al and Bernie coming their way.

Sonny hadn't seen Al since the aborted heist. He was shocked to see how fat Al had become. It looked like he put on about sixty pounds since thirty-nine and his hair was thinning at an alarming rate. The lenses on Al's glasses were as thick as moon pies. The magnifying effect of the lenses made his eyes look like faded green beach balls.

"Somebody call the cops," Al said. "I think we got a crime syndicate here."

Sonny stood up and slapped Al on the back. "If it ain't Al Capone's ugly cousin."

"Distant cousin. Capone was a loud mouth and dumb as shit."

Al slid into the booth. "At least I pay my taxes."

Sonny and Bernie sat down in the booth and ordered drinks. "So," Sonny said, "what are you doin' these days Al?"

Al hunched his shoulders and clasped his hands in front of him. "If you must know, I'm at the library."

Sonny chortled. "The library? Are you kidding me? Librarians are old ladies with gray hair and specs yellin' at everyone to shut the fuck up."

Al gave him an annoyed look. "Up yours. I'm the accountant."

"Oh. So you don't read the books, you cook 'em, huh? Good for you."

"Have you thought any more about coming to work at the garage?" asked Bernie.

Sonny tossed him a dismissive wave. "Changing the oil in some asshole's Packard don't sound like much of a career."

"They don't make Packards anymore Sonny."

Sonny sighed. A heavy silence hung over the table for a moment. "Yeah, I guess there's a lot of stuff they don't make anymore."

A few seconds passed. A sardonic expression crept across Sonny's face. "You'll never guess who we ran into today."

"Uh — Rita Hayworth?" asked Bernie.

Al chimed in. "Lana Turner?"

"Seriously," Sonny said.

"Doris Day?"

"Ish Kabible?"

Sonny smirked. "You guys done?"

Al shrugged. "All right. Who?"

Sonny paused for effect. "Eddie Bishop."

"Eddie Bishop? Bullshit," said Bernie.

Al made a fist and asked, "Did you punch him in the throat? I woulda punched him in the throat."

"Oh, believe me, I wanted to. He was with some pretty little knockout, otherwise, I woulda." Sonny took a long pull on his beer. "The asshole hasn't changed at all. Still a massive punk."

"Al's right," said Bernie. "You shoulda punched him."

Al nodded. "Definitely. Right in the throat."

Sonny leaned forward. "I gotta say, though, seeing that rat bastard today got me thinking. About the Hudson, actually."

"Lemme guess," said Al, "you wanna work in a bank now?" He chuckled.

"Oh yeah," Bernie said, jerking his thumb toward Sonny. "Can you imagine this guy as a teller?" He cleared his throat. "Thank you for your business, ma'am. Now go fuck yourself," he said.

"Is that supposed to be me?" said Sonny.

"I thought it was perfect," said Al. "I didn't know who to look at."

"Oooh my sides," said Sonny. "Anyway, it got me thinking."

"Thinking?" Al asked. "What are you talkin' about?"

"If it wasn't for that asshole Bishop, I mean." Sonny's eyes narrowed. "You know," he said in a low voice.

Al made a slow hissing sound through his teeth. "Are you serious?" he asked.

Bernie looked at Al. "Is he serious about what, Al?"

Al shook his head. "You're a fucking maniac, Carter."

"Why is he a fucking maniac, Al?"

Al sat back in the booth and placed both palms flat on the table. "He wants to try to knock over the Hudson — again."

Bernie's mouth fell open. He stared at Sonny.

"Are you kidding?"

"The more I think about it, the more I like it," said Sonny.

"Then stop thinking," said Al.

"You know, it's because of that prick that we wound up in jail," Sonny said, his voice raising. "Because of him—" He shook his head and with force, tapped two fingers on the table. "He owes us."

Al and Bernie exchanged awkward glances. "Are you drunk?" asked Bernie.

"You seriously want to knock over the Hudson because you want — what? Revenge?" Al folded his arms. "You're nuts."

Sonny's eyes glowed with defiance. "Yeah, maybe."

"No, not maybe. Absolutely." Al shook his head. "Same old Sonny. All mouth and no brains."

"Do you really want to wind up back in jail?" asked Bernie. "You just got out."

Sonny looked to Morrie for support but Morrie's response was just to stare at his hands. Sonny wasn't expecting this reaction at all. He looked at each of them. "So you don't wanna do this?"

"Let me make this perfectly clear," said Al. "I, in no fucking way, want anything to do it."

"Yeah. No way," Bernie said.

An uncomfortable silence permeated the booth. Sonny glared at both Al and Bernie then looked at Morrie who continued to stare down at his hands. Al huffed and slid himself out of the booth. He pulled a couple of bills out of his wallet and dropped them on the table. "I know I'm a boring old accountant. I'm okay with that," he said. "I'm fifty-nine years old, my wife's gone and I don't take care of myself too good. And I probably don't have a whole lot of time left." He pointed to his chest. "But it's my time." He paused. "I - I should say, we - we all did stupid things when we were young. I lost a whole chunk of my life that I can't get back, so I'm bein' careful with what I got left. So I'll just say good luck, and I hope you don't do anything stupid."

"Thanks," said Sonny. "Helluva speech."

"We had our chance twenty-five years ago." Al put his hands on the table and leaned forward. "You want some advice? Get a job, have a beer and forget this shit."

"Are you done?"

"No. Banks aren't the same as they used to be. They have alarm systems and vaults on timers. They're practically bust-proof. If you try to break one open, you'll find yourself behind bars again, and at your age, that's a death sentence. For chrissakes, Sonny, take the time to appreciate the second chance you've got." He stood up and gave a curt wave to the group. "I gotta go. My daughter'll be getting worried."

Sonny watched Al shamble toward the door. Unbelievable, Sonny thought. The Al Cardinelli he remembered was a spit-in-your-eye kind of guy. No bullshit. Maybe all those years in the can had taken their toll on him. Sonny was sure that there was still a spark somewhere inside the man. Maybe Sonny just wanted to believe that there was still a spark. In all of them.

He turned his attention back to Bernie and Morrie.

He observed their saggy jowls and then stared at his own reflection in the mirror over the bar. It saddened him to see the wasting effects of time. He didn't feel old, even if his reflection projected the weathered scowl of a man just past his prime. Maybe he was a step slower and he'd packed on a few pounds in the joint, but that stuff happens when you get older. It sure as hell didn't mean it was time to curl up into a little ball and give up.

"Think about the garage Sonny," Bernie finally said to break the silence. "It's a good job."

Sonny held up his hand. "Forget it. If I wind up under a car or behind a desk, I'm finished."

Bernie slid out of the booth. He offered Sonny a smile. "Take it easy, buddy," he said. He patted his shoulder on the way out.

Sonny and Morrie sat in silence. Sonny turned to Morrie and asked, "I suppose you're with 'em too, huh?" Before he could answer, Morrie began to cough. He grabbed a napkin from off of the table and held it to his mouth. A few moments later, he lowered it. Sonny noticed, to his horror, that it was specked with blood. "Jesus Christ Morrie!"

With a look of complete resignation, Morrie said, “Yeah, it’s not good.” His voice sounded weak.

“What the hell?”

“I’m sorry Sonny.” Morrie coughed again. “Even if I wanted to do this, I don’t think I’d be much use to you anyway.”

Sonny sat back and studied Morrie. His face was pale, almost gray. He didn’t just look old to Sonny, he looked beaten. A wave of anxiety flooded over Sonny. Morrie gave him a defeated look and in a small voice said, “I got cancer.”

Sonny felt like he was punched in the gut. It took him a moment to find his voice. “Cancer,” he said. “Are you sure?” Morrie didn’t respond. He wiped his mouth with the napkin. Sonny put his hand on Morrie’s arm. “How much —?”

“Time?” finished Morrie. He shrugged. “Who knows? The doc ain’t even sure, exactly.”

Sonny was reminded of the time when he found out his mother was sick. He was behind bars, powerless to do anything to help her. He felt utterly useless and hopeless at the same time. But nothing topped his feelings of rage. That exact feeling enveloped him now.

“Can’t they do anything?”

Morrie shook his head. “Let’s go home,” he said. “I’m pretty tired.”

Sonny helped Morrie on with his coat. As they turned to leave, they passed by a large, wildly colored Wurlitzer jukebox. Sonny recalled the last time he was at Finn’s, “If I Didn’t Care” by the Ink Spots had been playing on it. The vocal now blaring out of the speakers wasn’t Bill Kenny’s haunting tenor. It was the same cacophonous noise on the record player that mop- topped Tommy was bopping his head to the previous night. Sonny buttoned up his coat and they stepped into the crisp wintry air. As the icy wind bit into his unprotected ears, Sonny pondered the events of the last few days. Instead of jubilation at seeing his friends, he was downright melancholic. Sure, prison rips you up but Bernie and Al were tenacious and hard as nails. Now they were just a couple of old stiffs waiting to die.

And Morrie. Fuck. Sonny felt weak and disconsolate. The two of them walked in silence along the snowy sidewalk. Sonny couldn’t speak. What was there to say?

Why the hell couldn’t things just stay the same?

CHAPTER SIX

Saturday, February 1, 1964

The next day Sonny sat alone in a booth at a greasy spoon located down the street from the Hudson. He toyed with his runny scrambled eggs and dry sausage. Gary offered to make him breakfast, but Sonny declined. He knew that he wouldn't be able to stomach both pancakes and Tommy playing the same Beatles record for the twelfth time in a row. Besides, he needed to be alone.

He stabbed his fork into a piece of sausage and thought about the previous night's discussion. He knew Al and Bernie were right, yet the idea of knocking over the Hudson had him by the balls now. He ruminated on what Al said about alarm systems and bank vaults. He was probably right. It wouldn't be easy. But, he didn't say it would be impossible. Three things were certain - he wouldn't be able to do it during the day, he couldn't do it alone and he needed someone on the inside.

I'm gonna do this, he thought. The thought of the take made him warm all over, but it was nothing compared to the idea that it was that squealing prick Bishop's bank. That was the icing on the cake.

Revenge? So what? There was no turning back now.

As he chewed a mouthful of scrambled eggs, he saw a copy of the New York Times on the table next to his. The headline read "Beatlemania Hits America - Rock and Roll and the British Invasion." Is there nothing else happening in the world? he thought. He grabbed the newspaper anyway and began to read the article.

The basic gist of the story was that rock and roll (whatever that was) began in the mid- fifties and was seen as a fad. Five years later, it was still around but on its way out. All the seminal stars were gone from the scene and a void was ready to be filled - all thanks to a fifteen- year-old schoolgirl from Maryland. She happened to catch a performance of a British group called the Beatles singing, "She Loves You" on CBS. She wrote to her favorite local disc jockey and asked the magical question, "Why can't we have this music in America?" The disc jockey wondered the same thing. He arranged to have a copy of the latest Beatles single, "I Want to Hold Your Hand," delivered to him directly from England.

He played the song on the air and invited listeners to comment on the tune. The switchboard lit up like a veritable Fourth of July fireworks display. The disc jockey then sent a copy of the song to another disc jockey in Chicago. He also played it on the air and received the same response. The same thing happened in St. Louis. All three major markets had a song that wasn't supposed to be released until the New Year now in heavy rotation. Capitol Records, the Beatles American label, decided to capitalize on the situation. They moved the release date of the song ahead to December 26, 1963. As a result, the three New York Top radio stations jumped all over the song. Teenagers on Christmas vacation glued themselves to their transistor radios. Kids with grandma's Christmas money burning holes in their pockets flooded the record stores. They bought "I Want to Hold Your Hand" by the wheelbarrow. Within weeks, it was the number one song in New York. Many other cities followed suit. The song hit number one in the country the week before the Beatles were to arrive in the States for their appearance on Ed Sullivan.

Timing is everything and no one in the whole history of music proved to have better timing than four lads from Liverpool in the beginning of February in 1964.

The tinkling bell over the diner's door interrupted Sonny's reading. Two cackling teenage girls stepped inside, dragging the winter wind with them down the aisle. One of them clutched a small transistor radio to her chest. Sonny put the newspaper down and groaned. Much to his annoyance, the girls chose the booth across the aisle from him. Both girls ordered sodas with no ice. Sonny wasn't sure what was worse, the nonsense from the radio or the teenagers' constant giggling fits. He waved to the girl holding the radio and asked her to turn it down. She rolled her eyes, ignoring him.

"Ohmygod, Wendy," the radio-clutching girl squealed. "I don't think I can make it until Friday. I swear I think I'm gonna die. We have to find out where the Beatles are staying. We just have to, or I'm going to die. I swear I'm just going to die!"

The drivel was endless. The words Beatles, Friday and die were repeated ad nauseam for about ten minutes. Wendy waved her hands in front of her face as if she were drying her fingernails. "I just have to see Paul or I'll die. He's sooo beautiful. Do you think I'll get to see Paul? I have to see Paul or I'll die." All the color drained from her face. "Oh, God Carol — uh- oh. I feel dizzy."

"Geez, Wendy." Carol blew out a big, pink bubble with her gum and smacked it. "You look all white and everything. You're not gonna puke, are you? Are you gonna puke? Let's go to the bathroom before you puke."

Carol grabbed a hold of Wendy's arm, and the two of them rushed toward the bathroom.

They left the radio, blaring at maximum volume on the table. Sonny watched them leave and then looked at the radio. He sighed. He reached over and snatched the offending gadget. While he looked for a way to turn it down, he accidentally thumbed the tuner dial. He noticed that the music changed. He smiled. He fiddled with the dial until he found a station playing classical music. Satisfied, he jammed his thumb against the tuner dial until it disappeared inside the radio. He put it back on the girls' table. He signaled to the waitress. "Check please," he said.

He paid his bill and left the diner.

Blowing his breath into his hands, Sonny trudged along the snow-splattered sidewalk. As he wound his way through the crowd, he noticed the surfeit of Beatles posters on walls, in shop windows, even on telephone poles.

This whole town's gone loopy.

The February wind picked up dramatically. Snow mixed with ice pellets slapped Sonny's unprotected face. He was aware that his body wasn't the well-oiled machine it once was when he was twenty-nine. However, it still surprised the hell out of him how slow he had become over the years. He slogged through the winter slop for a few blocks until he was out of breath.

"This shit's wearin' me out," he huffed. He paused to catch his breath outside a record shop. A gaggle of wailing teenage girls and a couple of women old enough to be their mothers surrounded a cardboard cut-out of the group in front of the store. Sonny could not fathom how or why any woman would find these guys remotely attractive. And that hair. They had a name for guys like that in the joint.

The door of the record shop swung open. Two teen-aged girls and two teen-aged boys with mop-top hair ran out, grasping their purchases under their arms like footballs. Against his better judgment, he decided to duck into the shop to warm up. There must have been about a hundred teenagers, packed to the rafters in the store. They all clamored for the latest Beatle record. He felt thoroughly conspicuous as the only adult in sight. Every corner of the store had Beatles album covers stapled to the walls. Beatles posters covered the windows. Life size Beatles cut-outs stood next to the cash registers like security guards. Sonny recalled the crazed crowds when Benny Goodman played the Paramount but it was nothing like this. It was as if these guys were the second coming of Jesus Christ.

"This is nuts," he mumbled. Like a New York Giant linebacker, he muscled his way to an empty corner by the opera records. He surveyed the scene in stunned silence. When it came to choosing music, there was no dividing line between the boys and girls. Everyone wanted the goddamned Beatles.

"Can I help you, sir?"

Sonny turned and saw a young shop clerk of about twenty, dressed in a collarless gray jacket and a Beatles wig. The poor kid had the blank look of a shell-shocked soldier. Sonny shook his head. "No thanks, kid. Just looking."

The clerk nodded wearily, adjusted his wig and stumbled back into the crowd. The din of Beatles music and sonorous snatches of conversations about their appearance on the Ed Sullivan show fought for dominance.

"Sunday night on Ed Sullivan. I don't usually watch the show, but I'll be watching that night."

"It's about time there was something decent on the show instead of those stupid dancing bears and jugglers."

"What songs d'ya think they'll play?"

"Even my mom and dad are going to watch. Ya know, my dad thinks they're a Communist plot about to take over America."

"That's dumb."

"Yeah. But he also thinks Walter Cronkite's a Communist too."

It was all starting to make Sonny's head hurt. He figured that he had warmed up enough to get out of the store. Once again, he elbowed his way through the mob until he got to the door. It might be freezing outside but it was certainly preferable to the insanity inside.

The wind abated somewhat so he trudged toward the Hudson National Bank and Trust Company. Within minutes, he found himself in front of the building.

For the first time, he noticed the brass plate anchored to the left of the main doors. 'Edward V. Bishop, President.' The sight of it made him feel like he'd just swallowed a gallon of sour milk.

"Well, Mr. Bank President," Sonny said. "I may not know much, but I do know one thing - payback's gonna be a real bitch."

CHAPTER SEVEN

Monday, February 3, 1964

"Tommy! Wake up. Now!" Louise's banshee-like shriek roused the whole household. Her sharp heels clacked down the hallway toward Tommy's room to get him ready for school. Rather than being annoyed, Sonny was happy for the wake-up call. He had plans today. He sipped his coffee while he waited for Morrie to get dressed.

Louise leaned over the banister like a hog caller and cupped her hand to her mouth.

"Tommy! Get down here - NOW!" She clip-clopped into the kitchen while adjusting her hat. She noticed Sonny at the table and gave him an icy glare. "I suppose you'd like some breakfast?" she asked, her tone dripping with mild confrontation.

Sonny smiled. "No thanks, Mrs. Cooper. We—"

"Great. I have to get Tommy to school. TOMMY!"

A bedraggled Morrie, followed by bewigged Tommy made their appearances. Louise bared her teeth. With the reflexes of a lioness on the Serengeti, she ripped the wig off Tommy's head. She waved it front of his face. "What did I tell you about wearing this monstrosity to school?" She thrust a brown paper bag into his hand and bum-rushed him out the door.

Morrie shook his head and poured himself a coffee. "Poor kid," he mused. "One day she's going to take his head off with the wig."

Sonny chugged his coffee. "Personally, I think that kid could live without a head," he murmured. "C'mon, hurry up with that Joe. We gotta get a move on."

"We do? Where are we going?"

Sonny winked as he grabbed his coat. "You'll see," he said.

An hour later, the two of them hopped off a downtown bus and crossed the busy snow covered street toward the Hudson National Bank and Trust Company. "What are we doing here?" asked Morrie.

"Remember that filly that was with Bishop the other day?" asked Sonny.

"What about her?"

"She gave me a good idea. Actually, she gave me a great idea," said Sonny as he pushed Morrie through the main doors. Once inside the bank, Sonny took in the interior, noting how the design had changed over the years. A massive portrait of the bank president adorned the bank's main wall. Thoroughly annoyed by the sight, Sonny turned away from the asshole's image.

He noticed a long line of people. They wound themselves through a gold rope maze that exited near several teller windows. The teller cages of the past were gone. A low wall that made contact between bank employee and customer more personal replaced them.

Sonny counted the number of guards. His instincts were confirmed - the heist would have to be done at night. Yet that presented a different set of problems. He needed to investigate further and do more research.

Over by one of the teller cages, he spied the woman who had been with Bishop, speaking with one of the bank guards. She saw Sonny staring at her and with a look of warm recognition, gave him a wide smile. Sonny felt his face flush and smiled back. "Not hard on the eyes at all," he thought to himself. "I wonder if —"

"Casing the joint, Carter?"

Sonny turned to see Bishop standing between himself and Morrie. With his arms crossed in front of him, he resembled a haughty lord of the manor.

"As a matter of fact, I was," Sonny said with a sardonic tone to his voice. "I thought I'd knock it over just for old time's sake."

"Mmm, yes," Bishop said in a tone laced with sarcasm. " I'd say 'just like the last time' but that wouldn't be entirely accurate, now would it?"

"Yeah, but sayin' you don't take it in the ass wouldn't be entirely accurate either."

"Droll." Bishop narrowed his beady eyes. "What do you want?"

"Actually," Sonny responded. "I'm just taking your lovely assistant's advice."

Bishop raised an eyebrow. "Advice? What advice?"

Sonny smiled. "I wanna open up a bank account. In this bank. Right now, in fact."

"Um, no you're not," Bishop said.

Morrie pretended to be interested in the pattern on the ceiling. Sonny looked around and then jerked a thumb at Bishop's portrait. "You know, except for the shitty artwork, I like it here."

"Sarah was kidding you imbecile. Kidding. She wasn't at all serious."

"Well, I happen to think that it was a fantastic idea, so here I am."

"There are other banks in New York," said Bishop. "Quite frankly, we don't need you as a customer."

"Why, Edward, after all we've been through together?" Sonny said in mock surprise. "Hey, did you know that Morrie's nephew Gary works for — what is it again, Morrie?"

Morrie kept his eyes glued to the ceiling. "CBS Television."

"Yeah, CBS Television," Sonny said. "I'm sure Gary has a lot of pals in the news department. Maybe they'd like to hear how one of New York's finest and largest banks refused to let a poor ex-con get on with his life. It'd be a great human interest story." Sonny then leaned in and in a stage whisper said, "Or maybe they'd like to hear how you and I actually met?"

Bishop put his hands up and let out an exasperated sigh. "All right. Fine. Let's get this over with." He motioned to Sarah. She waved back and walked over to the group.

"Sarah, you remember Mr. Carter, don't you?" Bishop said. "Apparently he's here because of you."

Sarah nodded and turned to Sonny. "Really? I must say I'm flattered."

Bishop sighed. "He's here because of your suggestion the other day."

"Your fantastic suggestion, that is," said Sonny. "This boob is underselling it." He gave her a wide grin. "I'd like to open up an account right here at your lovely institution."

"Well, that's wonderful Mr. Carter," said Sarah. "We can do that right now."

Sonny grinned. "Hey, that's swell." Then cocking his head toward Bishop, he said, "Oh, and can we lose this stiff?"

Bishop grit his teeth. Sarah suppressed a smile and led Sonny and Morrie to her office. "Right this way, gentlemen." Sarah sat down and pulled forms out of one of the drawers, as Sonny and Morrie took chairs opposite her desk.

Sonny put out his hand. "Thank you for taking the time to help me out, Miss—"

"Garrett, but you can call me Sarah." She took Sonny's hand in her own.

Her skin was soft and her handshake was firmer than Sonny expected. He studied her as she sorted out the forms. He figured her to be in her mid-thirties, but then again she could have been a little bit older. Her long brown hair was stylish without being showy. Her expression held warmth and friendliness without a trace of reserve. Most prepossessing, however, were her large, dark brown eyes. They were expressive and playful and lit up in concert with her smile. He was surprised to find himself more than a little beguiled with her. Sonny decided that she was probably the most beautiful woman he had ever seen.

She scribbled on one of the forms. "How much would you like to deposit today?" Sonny continued to stare at her. Morrie nudged him out of his trance.

"What?" Sonny asked.

Sarah smiled at him again. "I asked you how much you'd like to deposit into your new account."

"Uh — geez, I don't know." He made a face and turned to Morrie. "How much money you got on you?" he whispered.

"What?"

"I need a couple of bucks."

Morrie sighed. "Geez Sonny. If you don't have any money then why—"

"Just loan me twenty bucks, wouldja?"

Morrie grumbled and reached into his wallet. He removed two ten dollar bills. Sonny took the two bills and placed them on the desk, side by side in front of Sarah. He beamed at her, hoping to get her to her smile again, but instead she took the bills and handed Sonny a blue form to fill out.

"Excuse me." Sarah stood. "I'll be right back."

Sonny watched as she disappeared around the corner. Nice ass. Very nice.

Once Sarah was out of earshot, Morrie leaned in toward Sonny. "Can you tell me something?"

Sonny shook the pen to get the ink moving. "Shoot," he said.

"Why are you doing this?" Morrie asked.

"Isn't it obvious?" Sonny responded. "I'm opening up a bank account."

"Seriously?"

Sonny stopped shaking the pen and cast a furtive glance behind him. "Jesus, relax. I just needed an excuse to take a gander at the place."

"Oh no," Morrie said. "I thought you were done with this."

"I was." Sonny turned his attention to the blue form. "But then I thought about it and now I'm not."

Morrie put his head into his hands. Sonny twirled the pen between his fingers like Buddy Rich at the Copa. "Besides, I gotta pay you back that twenty bucks, don't I?"

"Not funny," Morrie said.

Sonny put down the pen and leaned in. "I want you to call Bernie and Al and tell them to meet us at Finn's tonight."

"They won't come."

"Sure they will. All I need to do is—" Sonny trailed off. He noticed Sarah standing over by a teller's window talking on the telephone. As she spoke, Bishop wandered over and put his hand on her shoulder. Sarah put her hand over the mouthpiece and ducked away from his hand. He tried to touch her again. This time she held the receiver away from her and roughly shoved his hand back at him. When Bishop attempted to touch her a third time, Sarah grabbed his index finger and bent it backward. Bishop yelped like a wounded puppy and stalked away in a huff.

"Now how about that?" Sonny said with a smile. "She can't stand the worm either." At that moment, Sonny realized that he liked Sarah Garrett. In fact, he liked her a lot.

He finished filling out the form and, indicated for Morrie to follow him. "I've finished filling this out," Sonny said, holding out the form to Sarah. Bishop stood next to her rubbing his finger.

"That's fantastic," Sarah said.

"All in order. And please, call me Sonny."

"All right then. Sonny, it is."

She took the form from him. Their hands brushed against each other and their eyes locked. Sonny blinked as a warm feeling started from his toes and made its way to his face.

Sarah shook his hand, giving it a squeeze before she released it. "Welcome to the Hudson National Bank and Trust Company family, Sonny."

Bishop cleared his throat. "Yes, Carter. I hope we'll have a, uh — a long and profitable association." The sentiment dripped with oily condescension.

Outside Sonny gave Bishop a mirthless grin but inside he laughed. *It won't be a long one, you sonofabitch, but it sure is going to be a profitable one*, he thought.

CHAPTER EIGHT

Even though the temperature was just above freezing and the heater in the bus wasn't working, Morrie's forehead glistened with sweat. "You know that Al and Bernie won't show," he said. His voice was barely audible above the growl of the bus and the chorus of the riders.

"What's with the sweats?" Sonny said. "You look like you just got out of a Turkish bath."

Morrie rubbed his palms down the sides of his pant legs. "I don't feel so good."

"Geez buddy, I'm sorry I dragged you out today," Sonny said as he fished out a handkerchief. "I shoulda known better." Morrie took the handkerchief and swabbed his forehead. He cleared his throat. To Sonny, it sounded like he was gargling with gravel. He decided to change the subject. "What do you think of Sarah?" Sonny asked. "She was flirting with me, right? At least I think she was flirting."

"Sonny—"

"Maybe she wasn't flirting. Fuck, I've been away too long."

Morrie tried to cut in again. "Sonny, listen —"

"How old do you think she is?"

Morrie's face flushed scarlet. "Sonny. Listen to me for a minute."

Sonny stopped talking. Morrie handed the handkerchief back to Sonny and said, "I really don't think you should try to do this thing. At the Hudson, I mean." He rubbed his sweaty forehead again. "Al is right. You're gonna wind up back in jail."

"You wanna know somethin'?" Sonny asked. "I did forget about it. For twenty years, I didn't give it a second thought. I won't lie to ya. For the first five years, all I thought about was that bank and that stoolie fucker. I often thought how I'd twist his head off his neck and punt it through the uprights at the Polo Grounds." He winced then rubbed his stomach. "An ulcer can change that way of thinking pretty quick. I knew I was done with that shit and that was that."

"Then why change your mind now? I don't get it."

Sonny's eyes narrowed. "When we ran into Bishop the other day. He hasn't changed. He's the same smug turd that screwed us over and all that shit came flooding back. I thought about all those years he stole from us and I want payback."

Morrie coughed. "Well, I won't be part of it. I won't go back to jail."

Sonny nudged himself closer to Morrie. "Keep down that jail stuff, wouldja?"

Morrie put his fist to his mouth to quiet his coughing. "I mean it Sonny. I'm not going back to the can."

"You gotta lower your voice."

Morrie stood up and in a loud voice declared, "I'm not going back to the can!"

Every head within earshot turned toward the pair. Sonny held up his hands and offered everyone a reassuring smile. "Everything's fine, folks. Just a little tummy trouble, is all." He pulled Morrie back into the seat. "Jesus, what's the matter with you? You sounded like you said you were gonna shit yourself."

"I don't want to go back to jail," Morrie whispered, bending over and cupping his head in hands. "I can't."

"You won't," Sonny said. "I'm gonna make it work this time."

"Just like the last time."

"Okay, so I was wrong then. This time I'm not."

Morrie sat up straight and closed his eyes. He leaned his head back against the seat.

Sonny was about to speak again but decided not to. He decided to give him his space.

At the next stop, a kid of about sixteen with a transistor radio glued to his ear got on.

He took the seat across the aisle from Sonny. Much to Sonny's exasperation, the kid's radio was blaring. To take his mind off this new irritation, he began to read the ads on the bus walls. One soda advertisement grabbed his attention. It depicted a young couple, both dressed in red.

They held their bottles in front of them. Their foreheads were touching as they stared into each other's eyes. Straight away, the thought of Sarah Garrett popped into Sonny's head.

The willowy, brunette bank teller with the sultry voice invaded his thoughts. He recalled how glad he felt watching her brush Bishop off when he tried to touch her. He also recalled the feel of her silky skin and the way his insides tightened when she squeezed his hand.

He sighed and laid his head back against the seat of the bus. Was she flirting, he wondered.

Maybe...

CHAPTER NINE

Bishop watched the baby blue Cadillac Coupe de Ville's white wall tires splash through the slush. It slowed to a stop next to the curb in front of the bank. Behind the wheel of the caddy, Renzo Genna toyed with his large pinkie ring. Beside him sat Cal Spencer. In the back seat were half a dozen suitcases lined up like tin soldiers. Each suitcase was large enough to hold about a week's worth of vacation clothes.

It was after six o'clock. Bishop's customers and employees were emptying out of the bank for the night. One particular employee, a buxom blonde with an architecturally structured beehive caught Renzo's attention. She rolled her curvaceous hips as she glided through the slippery snow. Renzo lowered his window. "Hey there gorgeous," he said in a voice dripping with lasciviousness. "I got some very special mortadella for you." He laughed and playfully elbowed Spencer. "Mortadella, get it? I mean the sausage in my pants."

Spencer responded with a blasé smirk. Renzo chuckled. "Whatsa matter with you. You don't like women?"

Bishop called out to the two of them. "Move it!" He made circular motions in the air with his finger and walked around to the rear of the bank. Renzo put the car in drive and followed Bishop.

At the rear of the bank, Bishop opened the back door and waited for the Cadillac. Renzo put the caddy in park and they got out. They walked around the car to the trunk. Eight more of the large, leather suitcases were jammed inside. Spencer pointed to Bishop. "Renzo, this is Edward Bishop. Have you two met?"

Renzo nodded to Bishop. "Yeah, maybe once or twice before, I think. How're you doin'?"

"Yeah, yeah, nice to see you," Bishop said without much enthusiasm. His eyes were on the suitcases. "Come on, let's hurry it up."

Renzo sighed and grabbed at one of the suitcases. "Hey," he called out to Bishop. "How's about a little help? These things weigh a ton."

Bishop huffed. "Are you serious? I'm the president of the bank."

Renzo muttered a string of Italian oaths until he finally managed to get the suitcase out of the trunk. He dropped it to the wet pavement with a resounding splat. “Christ all mighty,” he said. “This thing is heavier than my old man’s cock.”

“Your father must be incredibly endowed,” Spencer drawled.

Renzo hefted the suitcase with a loud grunt and glared at Bishop as he passed by. Spencer followed with another suitcase. They continued in this fashion until all the suitcases were inside the bank by the back stairway. At the top of the stairway, Bishop unlocked the door and headed down a long hallway.

“Where are the guards?” Renzo asked Spencer.

“Eddie sends them out for dinner whenever there’s a delivery,” Spencer explained. “They’ll be gone for about an hour.”

“Jesus, it’s probably going to take an hour to move all these goddamned suitcases.” Spencer and Renzo each dragged a suitcase along the corridor until they got to an office at the end of the hall.

Bishop unlocked the door and flicked on the light. “Put them over there by the desk and go grab the rest,” he said.

With a large grunt, Renzo dropped his bag and left to get another. Bishop grabbed a bottle of Glen Mhor scotch from his well-stocked liquor cart and showed it to Spencer.

“This is a big one, Cal. We need to celebrate,” Bishop said.

Spencer declined the offer. “You don’t know what you’re missing, my friend. It’s single malt. Only the best.” Bishop poured himself a tall glass and took a long swallow. He sat down in his buttery soft, leather office chair and made a big show of putting his feet up on the desk.

“Is everything set?” Spencer asked.

Bishop and Spencer had done quite a few deals together in the past, but this one was by far the biggest. They both stood to make a killing. However, the more Bishop thought about Spencer’s cut, the more it set his blood boiling. He was the one that did all the work. He was the one that had to deal with distributing the cash. He was the one who arranged the financial transactions with the Zurich banks. He was the one that took the real risks and Bishop decided it was time for a change.

"Yeah, everything's set," Bishop said. "I'm not going to mess around with this one. I have a number of wire transfers set up with the Banca del Rivera in Zurich next week. The bank president is a close personal friend of mine. He can be persuaded to look the other way if the transactions are above the threshold, but his fee will have to be larger than usual."

The 'threshold transaction' wasn't complicated but it required a certain amount of finesse to pull it off. The threshold was the maximum amount of cash involved in the transaction.

Usually anything above or close to the threshold was reported to the authorities. Thresholds tended to be low so large amounts of hidden cash needed multiple transactions since the larger ones were usually a tip off to the authorities. Ten million dollars would require an unusually high number of transactions. Thanks to Bishop's contact (and some well-placed bribes), this wouldn't pose a problem. In fact, the process would be expedited with larger than normal threshold transactions. It ensured that it could all be done in a matter of days.

"How much larger?" Spencer asked.

Bishop took another sip of scotch. "Ten million is quite a bit of money to work with so his fee is two hundred and fifty thousand."

Spencer coughed. "Two hundred and fifty thousand? Are you kidding me? That's outrageous."

"Yes it is. Very outrageous. Unfortunately, that's his fee."

Spencer shook his head. "My client won't be happy. Two hundred and fifty thousand, plus your ten thousand —"

"Yeah, Cal, I've been meaning to talk to you about that. My fee's gone up as well."

Spencer glowered at Bishop. "Really? And what, pray tell, is your new fee?"

Bishop pressed a finger to his chin. "My usual fee for this kind of extraordinarily large transaction is not going to cut it this time." He paused. "I believe that seventy-five thousand would be acceptable."

Spencer sputtered. "What? You can't be serious."

"Oh, I'm very serious," Bishop said.

"That's ridiculous. I can't do it."

"Why not?"

"It will severely cut into my client's principle."

Bishop banged the glass on the desk. "Really? And how much are you getting? A hundred? A hundred and fifty? What exactly are you making on this little venture anyway?"

"That's none of your business."

Bishop took another sip of Glen Mhor. "I think it is. I'm taking all the risks. I'm the one who has to run the cash through so-called legitimate businesses and casinos. It's my bank and my ass on the line here."

Spencer shook his head. "Sorry. It's unreasonable and impossible."

Bishop leaned back in the chair. "Well, now that's too bad." He placed his hands behind his head. "If you want to use my bank and my Swiss banker, that's what it costs. It's a small price to pay."

"That's horseshit," Spencer said. "You're just being greedy."

Bishop chuckled. "I'm greedy? That's hilarious coming from a leech like you."

Spencer didn't speak. He only asked Provenzano for two hundred and fifty thousand because he figured that Bishop would only take his ten. This fucked everything up.

"Listen," Spencer finally said. "We both stand to make a lot of money here. If you're willing to cut back a bit, well then, maybe I can too. I'm telling you that my client won't stand for this cost."

Bishop poured himself another drink. "Your client is expecting me to move ten million dollars. Tell him that this is the cost of doing business."

Spencer's rage showed on his face. "All right then," he said in a curt voice as he reached for one of the suitcases. "Could you give me a hand then? I'll need to bring these back to my client."

Bishop choked on the scotch. "Now hold on a second — "

"I can't leave all this cash here if we don't have a deal. Mr. Provenzano would have my head."

Bishop blinked. "Provenzano? As in Bruno 'The Butcher' Provenzano?"

Spencer gave him a cold smile. "You mean Tony Ferenza's cousin, Bruno Provenzano. You've heard of Tony Ferenza, I presume? I'm pretty sure Mr. Provenzano is going to be very disappointed with these new developments. Shall I give him a call and tell him you're not interested in helping him?"

A cold sweat broke out on Bishop's forehead. "For Christ's sakes Cal, relax. No need to get all pissy here." The very last thing Bishop wanted was the mob coming after him.

"It's just business, right? Let me speak to my contact in Zurich and see if I can get him down a bit. I think if you and I make some adjustments, I'm sure everyone will be happy."

Spencer dropped the suitcase to the floor. "Are you sure the cash will be safe here?" Spencer asked.

"Of course. This is my office. It's locked up tighter than your asshole. Hell, it's even tighter than my asshole." Bishop checked his watch. "It's getting late. We need to get all these suitcases in here now. The guards will be back soon."

The sound of Renzo's grunting and shuffling outside the door caused them both to turn.

Renzo's face was crimson. He dropped the suitcase he was carrying to the floor. "All right you two bastards," he said. "Which one of you lazy fuckers wants to check me for a hernia? Cal, I'm looking at you."

CHAPTER TEN

Tuesday, February 4, 1964

Sonny checked his watch and realized he'd been standing on the corner for the better part of an hour. He didn't even notice the time. That's one thing about doing a long stretch in the pen - doing nothing for long periods of time was old hat. One time, he lay on his bunk and spent two hours counting how many times a cockroach skittered back and forth across his cell floor. For the record, it was eighty times before he squashed it.

Sonny flipped his collar up, covering most of his face and shoved his hand back into his coat pocket. When he looked up, he saw Sarah Garrett step out of the Hudson.

Good, he thought, *she's alone.*

Sarah slipped on a pair of gloves, looked across the street and started walking. Sonny followed, keeping a safe distance between the two of them. After walking a block and a half, he saw her go into Mike's Place - the same greasy spoon where Sonny had breakfast the other day. Sonny slowed his pace. As he neared the diner, he noted a hand painted sign in the window: 'Lunch Special - Soup and a Sandwich in Five Minutes or you EAT FREE.' He checked his watch, waited a few minutes, then went inside.

Sarah sat alone in a corner booth, digging into the soup and sandwich lunch special.

Sonny scanned the rest of the diner. He was surprised to see only one person, the cook, working the entire restaurant. He watched him behind the lunch counter dump a ladleful of soup into a bowl. He then slapped a slice of lettuce, ham and cheese between two pieces of white bread. He scooped the plate of food into his right hand. With his left, he flipped the latch on a small door that separated the kitchen from the rest of the diner. He burst through the opening like a thoroughbred at the starting gate. He bolted over to a table where a customer was concertedly looking at his watch. The plate and spoon clanked on the table, startling the customer. The cook/waiter pointed at the clock on the wall over the stove and crossed his arms in triumph.

The customer shook his head. "Another fifteen seconds, Mike—"

The cook gloated. "No freebies while Mike Berezniki's on the floor."

The customer sipped the soup and made a face. "This is cold."

"Christ, Richie." Berezniki snorted. "You expect fishy-sauce for seventy-five cents?"

"It's called vichyssoise, you troglodyte."

"Hey," Berezniki said. "Didja get the tickets?"

Richie shook his head. "Jesus Mike, I'm still trying. Those friggin' things are harder to get your hands on than Sandra Dee's tits."

"Some big shot you are," Berezniki huffed. "You said that you knew all the big wigs at CBS."

Richie gave the cook a dirty look. "I do. The problem is that the Sullivan show is the most popular goddamn thing on TV right now. Everybody and his goddamned mistress are looking for tickets. Jesus, these limeys. I tell ya, I've never seen anything like it."

Berezniki nodded. "My kid's driving me crazy. You gotta get me tickets for that show."

"I said I'm tryin'." Richie took a bite out of the sandwich and made a sour face. "Jesus Mike, didja make this outta the same pig turd as the soup?" Berezniki ignored the insult and whistled a Beatles tune as he headed back behind the counter.

Those bastards are everywhere, Sonny thought.

He waited for Berezniki to pass by before he sauntered down the aisle toward Sarah's booth. He stopped at her table and feigned surprise.

"Hey there! Miss Garrett, right?"

At the mention of her name, Sarah looked up. "Oh, hello Mr. Carter. How are you?"

"It's Sonny, remember? I couldn't be better. I just stopped in for some lunch. How's the special?"

Sarah grimaced. "Terrible, but filling. At least it's fast."

"Sounds good to me. Mind if I join you? I'm starved."

She grinned. "This should be interesting. Just how do you plan on paying for your lunch?"

"How's that?"

She took a small bite of the sandwich and swallowed. "Anyone who has to borrow money to open a bank account might have a little problem paying for lunch."

Sonny placed his hand over his heart in mock horror. "It's a good thing I have thick skin or else I might be insulted. Besides, I don't need money for lunch."

Sarah raised her manicured eyebrows. "Really?" She put her spoon down. "Now I'm intrigued."

She's so beautiful, he thought.

"So — are you going to order?"

Sonny turned his head toward Berezniki. "In a second," he said. He held out his hand. "Can I borrow a nickel?"

"I thought you said you didn't need money."

"I said that I didn't need any money to eat."

"Ah, a technicality," she said. She opened her purse and handed him a nickel. "Okay. I have to see this."

Sonny motioned to Berezniki. The cook scrambled over with a small, weather-beaten pad in one hand and a grubby pencil stub in the other.

"Whittier want?" he asked in a bored voice.

Sonny winked at Sarah and then turned his attention back to the cook. "Is the special good?" he asked.

Berezniki shrugged. "It's fast and it's cheap. Whattya expect?"

"Oh, you make it sound so yummy. That's what I'll have, Mr —?"

"Mike Berezniki. I own this joint."

"Ah, Berezniki. That's a beautiful name."

Berezniki nodded without humor and left. Sarah giggled, making Sonny's neck break out in goose bumps. He stood up.

She looked puzzled. "Where are you going?"

Sonny flipped the nickel into the air like George Raft. "I'll be right back."

He proceeded to the rear of the diner toward the pay phone near the bathrooms. He picked up the phonebook and thumbed through it until he found the diner's phone number.

When the phone rang, Berezniki put his knife down and picked up the receiver. "Yeah, Mike's Place."

"Is this Mike Berezniki?" Sonny asked in a deep voice.

"Yeah, this is Mike. Who's this?"

Sonny noticed two ads taped to the wall above the phone. One was for Campbell's soup and the other was for Tareyton cigarettes.

"My name is Campbell Tareyton," Sonny said. He paused for effect. "I'm with CBS television and your name has been entered into a draw to win a pair of tickets for Sunday night's Ed Sullivan show."

"Holy shit," Berezniki yelled and dropped the receiver into the pot of soup. "Goddamn it." He threw his hand into the pot and fished around for the receiver. "Wait. For the love of Christ, don't hang up."

"What the hell are you doin' Mike?" asked one of the customers at the counter. Mike shot him a dirty look.

"I haven't got time for this Roy. I'm talkin' to CBS."

"CBS?" asked Roy. "They doin' a news story about the health inspector closin' this place down?"

Mike found the receiver and pulled it out of the pot. "I'm tryin' to win Beatles tickets," he said as he shook the soup off the receiver.

Roy laughed. "I never figured you for a mop-top Mike. I always thought of you as more of a Johnny Ray kinda guy."

"Are you still there, Mr. Berezniki?" asked Sonny.

"Yep, I'm right here." Berezniki held the dripping receiver away from his ear. "I just dropped the phone in the soup."

Sonny stifled a laugh. "You didn't burn yourself, did you?"

"Naw, it's not even hot. You said something about tickets to the Ed Sullivan show?"

Sonny checked his watch. "Yes. As a matter of fact, your name was entered into a draw and it was chosen. Congratulations! You must be excited."

"I'm fartin' bubbles of joy here — oh, Jesus, sorry." He smacked his forehead with his hand. "This isn't on TV right now, is it?"

Roy guffawed. “Christ, are you ever stupid! They don’t do live TV over the phone!”

Berezniki’s face reddened and covered the receiver with his hand. “Shut up Roy, I know it.” Berezniki was leaning so far over the stove that Sonny was sure his face was going to catch fire. He checked his watch again.

“Before we can give you the tickets, you need to answer a skill-testing question.”

“A what?”

“A skill testing question, but don’t worry. It’s not that hard.”

“Oh — okay.” He rubbed his knuckles across his forehead. “I just hope it’s not math or something like that.” He let out a nervous laugh.

“Don’t worry, Mike.” Sonny checked his watch again. “Are you ready for the question?”

“Yeah. I guess.”

Sonny waited for two beats. “Name the Beatles.”

Berezniki’s eyes widened and his jaw dropped. “Oh, I know this, I know this. Kenny — that’s my boy — he listens to those bastards all the time. I know this.”

“There’s no rush. Take your time, Mr. Berezniki,” Sonny said, smiling as he looked at his watch. “We would really hate for you to get it wrong.”

“Oh, crap. I know this. Wait a sec.” A knowing look crept across his face. In halting fashion, he raised one finger. “Okay, okay. I got it. There’s John.”

“That’s right, Mr. Berezniki. Keep going.” He raised another finger.

“Uh, and Paul.”

“That’s two. Take your time. You’re doing fabulous.”

Berezniki paused, smacked his forehead and held up a third finger. “George.”

Sonny glanced at his watch. “One more Beatle and those tickets are yours.”

Sweat broke out across Berezniki face. “I gotta know this, goddamn it.” He looked up at the ceiling as if it had the answer. After about thirty seconds, he smiled and yelled, “Bingo! It’s John, Paul, George and Bingo. I got ‘em right, didn’t I?”

Sonny shrugged. He had no idea. "You sure did!" he said. "Congratulations! You've just won two tickets to the Ed Sullivan show for this Sunday."

Berezniki hopped up and down with excitement. "Holy shit. My kid's gonna go crazy. Hey, thanks a lot there, Mr. Tareyton. When do I get the tickets?"

"Um — just call CBS later today, around four o'clock. They'll make arrangements for you. Once again, congratulations and enjoy the show." Sonny hung up the phone and headed back to the table. He slid into the booth and winked at her. Sarah eyed him with suspicion.

Berezniki hung up the phone and whistled. He grinned at Roy. "My kid's going to flip. Kenny's been pesterin' the hell out of me to get these tickets." He pointed to his head. "Thanks to my smarts, I'm gonna get me some peace and quiet and my kid's gonna think I'm Superman."

Roy grinned. "More like Fatman."

"Up yours, dipsh —" His words trailed off when he saw Sonny waving at him and pointing to his watch. Berezniki spun around and gaped at the clock. He had about half a minute to get Sonny his lunch.

"God damn it," he yelped. Bererzniki groped for the ladle and slopped the soup into a bowl, spilling half of the liquid in the process. With his other hand, he fumbled with the bag of bread, trying to remove two slices. He fought with the bag until it ripped open sending bread into the air like a deck of cards. Catching two slices before they hit the floor, he shuffled them together with a piece of lettuce, a couple of slices of ham and a piece of cheese. He tossed the finished sandwich on a soup-splattered plate next to the dripping, noodle-covered bowl.

Mike scooped up the meal and rushed to the small door. He jiggled the latch back and forth. "Sonofabitch," he hissed. "Open up!" It popped open and Berezniki hurtled himself toward Sonny and Sarah like a Mercury rocket ship. The soup bowl bounced on the plate and splashed its contents everywhere, creating a wet sponge out of the sandwich. As he neared the booth, he leaped forward like an Olympic diver and managed to drop the food with a loud clatter onto the Formica table in front of Sonny. He crashed to the black and white tiled floor. Groaning, he lay on his stomach for a few seconds before he rolled over on his back. Sonny and Sarah peered over the table at him, and a smug Sonny pointed to his watch.

Berezniki scowled. “Ahhh, crap. Enjoy your lunch. On the house.” He heaved a sigh as he pulled himself to his feet and slunk away defeated.

Sonny waited until the cook disappeared then raised his hands in celebration. “Ta da.”

“That was pretty impressive.”

“It’s a gift. What can I say?” Sonny dug into the soggy sandwich.

“It must have served you well in prison.”

Sonny stopped chewing. “Wow. You sure are direct,” he said.

“I’m sorry,” she said. “Did I embarrass you? I didn’t think someone like you could be embarrassed.”

“Someone like me?”

She stared into his eyes and smiled. “Sure. You know — tough, self-assured.” She winked. “Kinda cute.”

Sonny cleared his throat. “Jesus, c’mon,” he said.

Sarah giggled. “I haven’t seen a face that red since I threatened to crush Edward’s genitals with my knee at the Christmas party last year.”

“Lemme ask you something,” Sonny said, leaning forward. “How the hell can you work for — ‘scuse my French — a shit stain like that guy?”

“Aw, and I thought you were old buddies.”

Sonny leaned back in the booth. “He’s a worthless wad of crap. Did he bother to tell you that he was involved in that heist back in thirty-nine?”

“As a matter of fact, Edward did tell me,” she said. “The way he says it, he was some kind of a hero for foiling your plans.” Sonny rolled his eyes and wiped his mouth with a napkin. Sarah pushed her plate away and crossed her arms. She seemed to be studying him. “He said he was working undercover for the police at the time.”

Sonny laughed. “Undercover? What an asshole. I’m not surprised he’d try to feed you that load of bullshit, though.”

“Neither am I. Everything that comes out of his mouth is garbage.” Sonny brightened. “Not a big fan of Eddie, are you?”

“He’s okay if you like perverted neanderthals. It’s just that perverted neanderthals aren’t my type.”

“I have no idea what a neanderthal is but I’m sure ol’ Eddie is one.”

He leaned across the table. "So, how about ex-cons?" he asked with caution. "Do they do anything for you?"

Sarah gave him a wary look. To Sonny's surprise, he actually found himself holding his breath in anticipation. It was as if he was sixteen years old again, asking a beautiful girl out on a date.

She gave him a coy smile. "I have to get to know them first."

"Okay, then," Sonny said. "How about getting to know one over dinner tonight?"

"Sounds wonderful," she said. "But it'll be my treat. I don't think that phone trick is going to work at a real restaurant."

CHAPTER ELEVEN

The pretty young receptionist at the Hillsdale Retirement home offered Bernie her warmest greeting. "Hello, Mr. Miller. We haven't seen you for a couple of days. How are you today?"

Bernie removed his hat. "Hi, Angela. I'm okay, I suppose. Sorry I haven't been by lately but the garage is hoppin'. How's he doing?"

A look of concern replaced her sunny countenance. "I'm afraid he had a bad night. He had another episode. We found him in the downstairs bathroom. Dr. Westin was in to see him this morning." Her voice softened. "We're not sure how long he was in there."

"Jesus," he mumbled. He thanked her and started down the hallway toward his father's room.

The "episodes" were starting to happen more frequently. At first, Bernie thought his father's little incidents were due to his advanced age. That all changed when he stopped by his father's house one night. He found the elder Miller trying to open a can of soup with a large kitchen knife. His father bled profusely from the cuts all over his hands and arms. Worse yet, was the fact that Bernard Miller Sr. didn't recognize his own son.

He seemed to be getting worse every day.

He was about to go into his father's room when he saw a tall, balding man in a rumpled white lab coat coming around the corner. Dr. William Westin nodded toward Bernie and motioned him over.

"Mr. Miller," he said in a deep voice as he shook Bernie's hand.

"Hello, Doc."

Dr. Westin directed Bernie into a large empty sitting room. The tastefully decorated room had comfortable chairs and muted colored prints. It had an ambience of calm serenity. Bernie took a seat by a large picture window that overlooked a pristine, snow-covered lawn. Marring the lovely view, however, were dull black metal bars in front of the window. Dr. Westin took a chair opposite Bernie.

"Why do they have these on the windows, Doc?" Bernie rubbed his index finger lightly up and down one of the bars. "It's a retirement home, right? Not a jail."

The doctor glanced up at the barred window. "It's for our guest's protection. Some of them suffer from the same disorder that your father has. You might recall that we had an incident last year that made it rather necessary for the precaution."

Bernie continued to peer through the bars at the lawn outside. He remembered the headlines. He wondered if his father would ever reach the point where he would jump out of a window too.

"Ever since my mom died, I've been worried about dad," said Bernie. "He and my mom were married for fifty-eight years. I thought that maybe his — I don't know — his odd behavior was because she wasn't around anymore."

The doctor shook his head. "Your father is suffering from dementia. His cognitive faculties are deteriorating and it seems that he has aphasia and disinhibition."

"I don't know what that is."

"Your father is having trouble recognizing people and places. When the orderlies found him in the bathroom last night, he had no idea where he was. He actually urinated on himself in spite of the fact he was standing next to a urinal. He's exhibiting signs of aphasia. That means that he's having trouble comprehending what people tell him. In your father's case, he's starting to have trouble making himself understood as well."

A cold chill gripped Bernie's spine. "What was that other thing you said he had?"

"Disinhibition," Dr. Westin replied. "It means that he's apt to react to his feelings as if he's losing his self-control. For instance, if he feels threatened, he could lash out at whatever or whoever he feels is threatening him."

"My father? Are you kidding me?" Bernie scoffed. "He's harmless. I mean, he never even punished me when I was a kid. When he was a school principal, he never even strapped anybody. Even the pricks who deserved it. He hates violence."

"When the orderlies tried to get your father back to his room, he took a swing at one of them. When he missed, he tried to bite him."

Bernie was shocked. "I don't believe it," he said.

"Unfortunately it's true, Mr. Miller. It happens sometimes with dementia. There's still much about this disease that we don't know, and it may take many years to fully understand it." The doctor removed his glasses and cleaned them with a handkerchief. "A German psychiatrist named Alois Alzheimer identified the first case almost sixty years ago. Not much has changed since then."

"Just how sick is my father?"

Dr. Westin put his glasses back on and reviewed his notes. "There are usually three stages to this disease. The first stage is barely noticeable. When exactly did you first sense a change in your father's behavior?"

Bernie thought for a minute. "I guess it wasn't long after my mother died. Like I told you, I thought it was his reaction to her death."

Dr. Westin nodded. "The second stage is more noticeable. When did you notice your father having problems with relatively simple tasks?"

"Well, that would have been just before I brought him here. When he was trying to open a can of soup with a knife and he cut himself."

Dr. Westin once again reviewed his notes. "I'm going to be blunt, Mr. Miller. I'm afraid your father has entered the last stage. He requires constant supervision because there's a good chance he could hurt himself or someone else." He looked up from his notes. "As I said before, he's having some difficulty speaking. As the disease progresses, he will lose the ability to swallow foods and fluids."

"Jesus Christ," Bernie said. "How much time does he have left?"

"It's hard to say. I've seen some patients live for years, but others pass on within months of the last stage. I'd say it all depends on your father."

"Dad's tough." Bernie sucked in his breath. He turned his attention toward the window, fighting to stay in control. "What do I do now?"

Dr. Westin stood up, clutching the clipboard to his side. "I'm afraid you'll have to get him into a facility that can better help him. We're just a retirement home here. We're not equipped to help someone with your father's advanced dementia. I can give you the name of a good place if you'd like."

Bernie contemplated everything the doctor told him for a few minutes. A "good" place? "Good" places were expensive.

Dr. Westin expressed his sympathies and left to start his rounds. Bernie continued to look out the window at the serene scene below. For the first time since his mother died, he felt like he was about to lose it. He started to hyperventilate. Jesus, I better relax, or else they'll lock me up too.

Bernie stared out the window at the blanket of snow. He recalled one Christmas many years ago.

He was ten years old and Christmas was around the corner. He wanted a sled. It was beautiful cherry red with silver lightning bolts emblazoned on each side. He had pestered his father daily about it leading up to Christmas. His dad had scoured the city and upstate New York until he finally located a store in Maine that sold them. On Christmas Eve, his dad made the long trip to buy it for his son.

Bernie was beside himself on Christmas morning when he unwrapped it. He wanted to try it out right away but because of the busy road, it was too dangerous to play with it in front of the house. His father said he'd have to wait until the next day to take him to the park. Bernie begged his father, promising to take the sled for just a couple of runs on the sidewalk. His father finally relented.

Bernie made a couple of slides. On the last run, he veered too far off course and found himself sliding straight into the path of an oncoming car. The car swerved at the last second but clipped the back of the sled. Bernie went tumbling into a concrete stairwell. The sled was destroyed. He flew down the stairs, shattering his right collarbone and arm. His horrified father watched the scene unfold from the front window and was out the door in a flash. Within seconds he held Bernie's battered body in his arms.

"Don't worry, son," he said. "I'll take care of you." He kept saying it over and over again. At the hospital, his dad slept in a chair beside Bernie's bed for the duration of Bernie's stay. When Bernie returned home, he slept for two straight days. When he awoke, he found a new sled waiting for him in the corner of his bedroom.

Bernie loved his father with all his heart and soul.

He crossed the hall and opened the door to his father's room. The only light that illuminated the darkness was the sinking sunset, streaming through the small window on the far wall. Bernie was saddened to see that the window had bars like the one in the sitting room.

In the corner, his father sat quietly in a weathered chair. The criss-cross of the light from the barred window splashed across his face and chest.

It looked like his father was in prison. “Hey, Dad,” Bernie said.

There was no acknowledgment from his father. Instead, he stared blankly out the window. When Bernie spoke again, his father turned his head. Bernie was utterly dismayed when he saw his father’s face. It was cadaverous and the skin hung from his jaw. His mouth was slightly open and Bernie could hear his labored breathing in the still of the room. The change in his father was dramatic and horrific. Bernie looked into his eyes, hoping for some sort of recognition. Instead, the watery, pale blue orbs stared back uncomprehendingly.

“Dad. It’s me.”

His father made a noise like he was clearing his throat to speak, but it was more of a gurgle than anything else. Bernie sat on the bed near his father. On a small table beside the bed was a framed photo of his parents that was taken about forty years ago. He looked at his mother and then studied his dad’s image. Bernard Miller must have been in his forties at the time of the photograph, but he appeared much younger. He had a lot of life in him back then. Bernie shifted his gaze to his father. His bony hunched shoulders and white, withered hands clutched the arms of his chair. It was as if he was afraid he was going to fall out of it.

It was more than Bernie could take. He decided that he was going to get his father the help he needed, no matter what the cost. He went over to his father and kissed him on the forehead. “Goodbye, Dad. I love you,” he whispered. He brushed the hair out of his father’s eyes and headed toward the door. “Don’t worry Dad. I’ll take care of you. I’ll take care of you.”

As the pale glow of the moon lit up his face, Mr. Miller sat quietly in his chair and blinked, trying to moisten his dry eyes. He didn’t recognize the man who had visited him earlier in the day, or was it yesterday? He shrugged and gazed at the snow falling outside his window. Somewhere, in the back of his dying mind, a hazy image came to him. It was an image of a sled and a boy whose face he saw in his dreams. Sighing, he closed his eyes. It all seemed so familiar.

He wished he could remember what it all meant.

CHAPTER TWELVE

Wednesday, February 5, 1964

Renzo sat at the small table at the Jersey Social Club. He watched in mild revulsion as Bruno Provenzano shoved another almond biscotti into his fat face. Most of it seemed to be on his shirt. The rest of it sat conglomerated in a congealed lump around his massive lips until his swollen tongue snaked out and pulled it into his mouth. Renzo swallowed uneasily.

"How are tings wit Tony's cash?" Provenzano finally asked Renzo as he slurped the rest of his espresso. Marco, one of Provenzano's bodyguards saw the empty cup and dutifully went over to fill it up again.

"Not a problem." Renzo knocked on the table for emphasis. "All taken care of. As promised."

"Good. Glad ta hear it." Provenzano shoved another biscotti into his mouth. Crumbs flew down his front like a heavy snowfall. "Now, here's da ting." He swallowed and wiped his mouth with his hand. "I need you ta get it back."

Renzo coughed. "What?"

Marco returned with the espresso. Provenzano took the cup from Marco and put it on the table in front of him. He clasped his hammy hands together around the cup. "Ya got a hearin' problem?" he asked. "I want you ta get Tony's cash back for me."

"But why?" Renzo nervously twirled his pinkie ring.

"I don't get it."

"Ya don't need ta get it. Just get it. Da money, I mean."

Renzo was perplexed. "We dropped it off at the bank on Monday. Are you calling it off now?"

"You misunnerstand me. I don't wanna call it off. I jus' need you ta get the cash back."

Provenzano sat back, thumped his chest and belched.

Renzo shrugged. "Uh. Okay then. Let me call Spencer and I—"

Provenzano shook his head making his jowls flap noisily. "No, no, no. Just you, Renzo. You get it back. On da QT, capiche?"

At first, Renzo was confused but now a little light bulb went on inside his head. "So let me get this straight," Renzo said. "You set up the transaction for Tony — but then you take the money back, making Cal Spencer and the banker the fall guys for it, right?"

Provenzano touched the side of his nose with his chubby forefinger. "A far as anyone knows, da money was dropped off at da bank and den it disappeared." He bared his pointy, biscotti covered teeth. "As far as anyone knows, dat's the story, right?"

"Right. You're the boss, Boss."

"Good," Provenzano said. He leaned back in the chair and burped. 'Awright," he said. "Me an' Marco's got some stuff ta discuss. Lemme know when you got dis job done for me." Renzo nodded and stood up. He turned to leave and as he shut the door behind him he heard the "Butcher's" parting words.

"Remember — dis is on da QT — capiche?"

At his apartment on the lower East side, Renzo was speaking excitedly into his telephone. "That's right," he said. "It's all changed. I know what I said before, but this is the way it is now. If you want it, we do it my way." He paused, listening. "Right. You'll get it as soon as we're done. I swear to Christ, hand to God. As soon as it's over."

He hung up the phone and let out a big breath. He flopped on his bed and smiled. After all this time, everything was finally coming together.

Renzo believed in destiny and he always believed his destiny was to be rich - even if the path to it involved crime.

His criminal career began with local gangs. Mere punks, but he hit the big time when he met Jimmy "The Weasel" Calderone. Calderone was a rising star in the Ferenza crime family. Jimmy took Renzo under his wing and schooled him in the finer points of organized crime.

When Renzo turned nineteen he was already a seasoned pro in the up and coming drug trade. It was such an easy gig. Jimmy would set up "drug deals" with low level-punks. Renzo and a fellow wise guy, Carmine Ciccio, would dress as cops and bust in to nail the buyers. Renzo and Ciccio would handcuff the punks then grab the cash and the drugs.

It was quick and dirty and it taught him a valuable lesson - when you steal from crooks, you never got caught because crooks don't call the police. It was the perfect scam, unless the crooks got pissed and whacked you. But Renzo was too smart to get whacked. He was a good soldier and rose up through the ranks of the Ferenza family quickly. It wasn't long before Bruno Provenzano picked him up on his radar.

Renzo never thought much of the morbidly obese gangster, but the fat man was well connected. And that's what it was all about - connections. He figured that through Provenzano, he would make that big score one day.

Finally, on Sunday night, after four years of waiting, Renzo was going to fulfill his destiny.

CHAPTER THIRTEEN

Gargiulo's was filled to near capacity. Luckily, Sonny had made a reservation. He arrived early and sat at the bar. He was spruced up in a new suit jacket he had picked up on clearance at Macy's with cash he had borrowed from Morrie - who had in turn borrowed it from Gary, who had no intention of letting Louise know about the transaction.

Sonny took another sip of his bourbon. It was the first hard drink he'd had since he got out, not counting the beer he had at Finn's. He was never much of a drinker in the past. He could feel the alcohol going to his head. He gave in to the drink, considering this was his first date in decades. He also felt the need for some Dutch courage.

He took another sip of the drink and then headed to the bathroom. At the furthest sink, he turned the cold water tap on. His hand shook as he spun the faucet handle. Damn nerves, he thought. He splashed the cool liquid onto his face, letting the water run down his cheeks, careful not get his jacket or shirt wet. He looked up and scrutinized his reflection in the mirror.

Jesus, am I really that old? he thought. He wasn't sure how old Sarah was, but he figured she was probably fifteen years his junior. He wondered if the difference in their ages mattered.

Hell, he wondered if she was even going to show up at all.

His hands continued to shake. He was as nervous as a sixteen-year-old boy on his first date. He shook his head "What the hell am I doing?" He reminded himself that he needed information about the bank, not a relationship. "Stop thinking with your dick, stupid. You got a job to do here."

Still — He checked his watch. She would be arriving soon. He dried his hands and went back to the bar. To his surprise, he saw that she had already arrived. When he saw her at the bank in her business clothes, he thought she looked good. Tonight, however, in a muted red dress with a pair of smart, black shoes and her hair done up with a little flip that hung seductively over her eye, she was absolutely stunning. In his day, they used to say dressed to kill. Maybe they still said it. No matter what they said, she was the most beautiful woman he had ever seen.

Sonny walked up to her. "Wow. You're quite a dish." As soon as the words left his lips, he frowned.

Sarah checked her watch. "Really? I didn't realize that it was nineteen forty in here."

"Yeah, I knew it the second I said it. Maybe we should get our table." He held out his arm for her and they made their way to see the maître d'. "Reservation for Carter," Sonny said.

The maitre d' went down the list and then crooked a finger at one of the waiters nearby. They followed the waiter to a small table in the back. He took their drink orders and told them he would be back in a few minutes.

"So," Sonny said once the waiter departed, "this is a swell place, huh?"

Sarah chuckled. "You haven't done this in quite a while have you?"

"Yeah, well I've been away." Sonny shrugged. "The last time I was on a date was in nineteen thirty-two. Wasn't the best decision I ever made."

"Didn't work out?"

"You could say that," he said. "We got married."

"You're married?"

"Used to be. Gloria — my ex-wife — left me. She said I was too hard to live with. I think she was right." Sonny shook his head. "After the Hudson job I wound up at Elmira and she got remarried to a stock broker."

"I suppose being in jail can be tough on a marriage," Sarah said.

"Not for me. Worked out great."

"As long as you're happy," she said. She leaned back in her seat and folded her arms. "So, can I ask you a question?"

"Shoot."

"What were you really doing at the bank?"

A look of surprise crossed Sonny's face. "I was opening a bank account."

"No, you weren't. You were clearly casing the place."

"Listen to you. Casing the place. You sound like—"

Sarah leaned in and leveled her gaze at him. "One of your gang? Sonny, please. Who comes to a bank to open an account with no money?"

"Prove's nothing," Sonny scoffed. "So I forgot to bring some cash. I was—"

Sarah reached over and touched his arm. "Relax. I'm not going to tell anyone. Least of all Edward Bishop."

Sonny studied her face. It was as placid as one of the Virgin Mary statues he used to see in church when he was a kid. What's she up to? The woman must be a helluva poker player.

"I think you should know that Edward thinks you're going to try to rob the bank."

Sonny showed surprise at the allegation. "Well, Edward's an idiot and an asshole."

"Okay, but for what it's worth, I also think you're planning to rob the bank. And I do have to tell you that you'll never get away with it."

"I don't know where you're getting this from. Honestly, I wasn't casing the place."

Sarah gave him a scornful look.

"Seriously, I wasn't," he said. His protestations, even to his own ears, were becoming hollower by the minute.

"So why don't I believe you?" she asked.

"Well, if my marriage was any indication, it seems women are naturally suspicious of everything I do." He shoved his hands in his pant pockets and rocked back and forth in his chair. "You know, if women were a little more trusting, men wouldn't have to lie so much."

"Now there's a quote for Bartlett's," she said. She shook her head good-naturedly. "You're a very interesting man, Sonny Carter."

The waiter reappeared with their drinks. As soon as he left, Sonny scraped his chair closer to the table and leaned in. "Okay. Just for the hell of it. If I was actually going to do this - I mean - to try and do this, why exactly wouldn't I get away with it?"

"Well, for one thing," she said. "It's not nineteen thirty-nine anymore. You can't just walk into a bank and say 'Reach for the sky.' The Hudson has some of the toughest security implements in the business."

Sonny put up his hands in a defensive mode. "For the record, I would never say 'Reach for the sky.' I was more of a 'Stick 'em up' kinda guy." Sonny smiled. "If I had a gun, that is."

Sarah straightened her back and looked away for a moment. When she looked back, she caught Sonny's eyes on her chest. Embarrassed, he coughed. "Anyway, I heard all this stuff already," he said. "It's modern and sophisticated. The vaults are on timers, blah, blah, blah…"

"You'd be in handcuffs before you got two steps inside the building," said Sarah. "You simply wouldn't have a chance and you'd just wind up back in a prison cell."

"Yeah, I've been hearing that a lot lately," Sonny muttered.

"Well, it's true."

"Why are you telling me this?" He leaned in. "Why would you care if I went back to jail anyways?"

Sarah leaned in. He could almost taste her perfume. "Oh, I have my reasons," she said with a seductive smile.

CHAPTER FOURTEEN

Sonny and Sarah stood outside her apartment for a few moments while she fished around in her purse for her keys. Finding them at last, she pulled them out and dangled them in front of him. Her eyes sparkled as bright as the silver key she held up. "Here we are."

As she turned to the door, her keys slipped out of her hand, landing next to Sonny's right foot. Sonny reached down and picked them up. He noticed that his hand was shaking.

Jesus, what the hell is wrong with me? he thought. *I feel like a goddamn teenager.*

"You poor thing," said Sarah as she took the keys. "Are you still cold? That's funny. I find it really hot in this building."

Sonny shoved his hands deep into his pockets. "Just a little chill. I'll be fine in a minute," he said, hoping that he actually would.

Sarah stepped into the apartment and flicked on the light. Sonny peeked over her shoulder. Against the Easter egg green wall was a blood red sofa, so bright it seemed to vibrate. It sat next to an overstuffed gray armchair obscured by two massive frilly throw pillows. A strong, but pleasing vanilla scent permeated the room.

Well, this sure ain't Elmira, he thought.

"Are you coming in?" She tossed her coat on the armchair. "I can't carry you over the threshold, you know."

Sonny blinked twice and with a little trepidation, followed her inside. Sarah flicked off her shoes and headed towards the kitchen.

"It's been a long time since I've been in a woman's apartment," Sonny said. He removed his wet rubbers and then his shoes, letting his stocking feet sink into a plush yellow area rug. "Feels kinda strange."

While Sarah engaged herself in the tiny orange and walnut brown kitchen, Sonny sat down on the sofa. He sat at the far end, wedging himself into a tight ball in the corner, practically sitting on the sofa's arm. Running his fingers along the fabric, he surveyed the rest of the room. He was surprised to notice that there were only a few pictures on the wall and none on the end tables. He always figured gals were more sentimental than guys and they'd have a crap load of pictures all over the place.

He turned his attention to Sarah as she rummaged through the faux wood paneled cupboards. As she stood on her toes reaching for something on the top shelf, he zeroed in on her tight calf muscles. The way her back arched and curved caused her sexy ass to pull provocatively against her blue dress. Sucking in a quick breath, he loosened the top button of his shirt. He felt like he was burning up. Sonny figured the thermostat in her apartment must be broken. He could feel the heat at the back of his neck start to snake its way down south into his pants.

Had to be the temperature in the apartment. Had to be.

Shit, I need to calm down in a hurry.

"Would you like some wine?" Sarah asked.

He raised his eyes to meet hers. His face flushed. Her playful grin let Sonny know that she caught him ogling her behind.

"Sure," he said. To his own ears, his voice sounded as if he was about a hundred years old.

"It's red." She walked toward the sofa with a bottle and two wine glasses. "Just like your face."

"Jesus, is my face red?" he asked, feigning surprise.

"Like a cherry tomato. And sweaty too. You just felt chilly a few minutes ago. Are you feeling all right?"

"Oh sure," he croaked. "Man, it's hot in here? Aren't you hot?"

Sarah placed the bottle and glasses on the table and sat next to him, her knee lightly brushed up against his thigh. Sonny shifted, but Sarah moved in closer. Languidly, she reached over Sonny's lap for the wine. Her lips brushed his earlobe as she asked in a soft whisper, "Do you want some?"

Sonny opened his mouth to speak but all he could muster was a low grunt. He felt a river of perspiration cascade down his back.

She's so goddamn sexy, he thought.

"Wine, I mean," Sarah said and poured the wine.

He sighed. "Yes — wine," he said in a barely audible whisper.

She handed him the glass. "You need to relax, sweetie. I'm not going to bite." She lifted the glass, took a small sip and then ran her tongue along her top lip. "At least not hard."

Sonny hefted his glass and drained it in one shot.

"Man, that was good." He reached for the bottle. She took the bottle from him and filled his glass halfway.

"I said relax, not drink yourself into a coma."

He took another long gulp. The tightness in his throat seemed to loosen up. A warmth traveled throughout his arms and legs. He smiled.

Sarah eyed Sonny. "Something funny?" she asked.

"I don't know why, but I was just thinking about my first time," Sonny said. He quickly corrected his posture and added, "My first heist, I mean. With Morrie, that is. When we were kids."

She inched closer to him. "Really? How old were you?"

Sonny grinned.

"Nine. It's funny. Morrie and I were just talking about this. We knew this other kid named Billy Vincent. A real pain in the ass. He was the kind of guy kids would chase down in the park. When they caught him, they'd hold his head down and fart on them." He caught himself. "Uh, I mean, some other kids might do something terrible like that."

Sarah looked amused. "Yes, that is pretty terrible."

"Yeah, terrible. Anyways, his dad owned a candy store, so we thought we'd knock it over."

Sarah's eyes widened. "A candy store?"

Sonny shrugged. "Yeah. You gotta start somewhere, right? Anyhow, while Morrie distracted Billy's dad, I emptied the till."

Sarah took a sip of wine. "And so began the career of criminal mastermind Sonny Carter."

"Scored fourteen bucks. That was a lot of scratch back then, you know."

"Did you get caught?"

Sonny reached for his wine. "Oh sure. After we left the store, we split up and then met later in the train yard. The funny thing is, when I showed him the take, Morrie cried."

"He cried? Why?"

"He thought we were gonna steal candy. I felt so goddamned bad about it that I spent the whole fourteen bucks on peppermint sticks, Heath Bars and Goldenberg Chews for him."

Sarah chuckled. "You spent it all on candy? The money you stole from a candy store?"

Sonny shook his head. "I know. Stupid, right? That's how we got caught. The owner was suspicious of two kids flush with that much cash so he called the cops. Jesus, was my dad pissed. He couldn't care less about me robbin' the store, though."

"Why not?"

"He was sore that I'd spent our take on candy and worse, that I got caught." Sonny leaned back and rubbed the back of his neck. "I never really got along with my old man too good before that and after? Well…"

"But you spent it all on Morrie. That was sweet. I've noticed you have a real soft spot for him."

"Morrie's aces. He's probably my closest friend." His voice trailed off. "He's had a tough ride."

She squeezed his knee. "Sounds to me like you may have had a bit of a rough ride too."

Her hand felt comforting. That, mixed with the wine made Sonny's flesh start to tingle.

He finished his wine and refilled his glass. "Oh sure. But it was really tough on my mom, though. She was a beautiful lady. I know a lot of guys say that their mothers are angels, but mine really was. She saved my ass from my dad hundreds of times." He pressed his lips together tightly. "Not that I didn't deserve it, though. If I were in my dad's shoes, I woulda torn a strip off my ass too. I was quite a piece of work in those days." He smiled. "Not much has changed, I guess."

"Where are your parents now?"

"My dad died when I was nineteen. I was the man of the house after that. I was all my Mom had left."

She squeezed his knee again. "I'm so sorry, Sonny."

Her touch was electric. He wished she would never let go. "That heist at the Hudson was supposed to be the big one. And the last one. My cut was all gonna go to her, for the medical bills…" His voice trailed off. He started to reach for his glass but instead sat back into the corner of the sofa. "She counted on me. And I let her down."

Sarah laced her fingers into his. He felt blood rush to his fingertips.

"I wrote her a bunch of times to explain how it all happened when I was in the joint, but she never wrote back." He grit his teeth. "I never blamed her, though. She died a few years later."

They both sat in silence for a few moments.

"Such a sensitive soul, you are," said Sarah. She slid her hand from his knee up to his thigh. Another wave of heat swept across the back of his neck. She then leaned back into the sofa, crossed her legs towards him and trailed her toes along the top of his foot. "I find that attractive in a man."

"Oh yeah?" he asked. He reached for his wine and gulped it down. The alcohol washed away the rest of his tension. The sight of her delicate ankle, however, was provocative.

Sarah inched closer to him. "I do. I also like them a little older, with a little snow on the roof. Very sexy." Smiling, she ran her fingers through his hair. The spark from her playful gesture almost made him jump out of his skin. He poured himself another glass of wine.

"If you're talking about what I think you're talking about, I should warn you – the last time I came close to anything like this was in the showers at Elmira."

Sarah laughed. "You poor thing. How did you handle that?"

Sonny winked. "I took a lot of baths. The wolves can't do anything to you when you're sitting down."

Sarah raised her eyebrows. "Baths in prison? You expect me to believe that?" Sonny drained his glass and looked pleased with himself.

"Just tryin' to be cute. Is it working?"

Sarah stood up. Sonny closed his eyes and let the scent of her perfume wash over him.

"Well," she said. "Maybe just a little bit. Speaking of bathing, I think I'd like to take a shower myself. Would you mind? It won't take long."

He coughed. "Oh sure, sure. Take your time."

She spun around. "Could you unzip me please?"

A quick intake of breath and he stood up. With shaky fingers, he reached for the zipper. *Be cool, stupid*, he said to himself. *What the hell is wrong with you?* He reached for the zipper but his trembling fingers prevented him from completing the simple task. He let go.

"Is it stuck?" she asked.

Sonny tried to answer her but the only response he could make was a small, strangulated gasp.

"It's not that complicated. Just give it a yank."

Sonny took hold of the zipper again and began to pull it. His hands shook all the way to his elbows as if he was having a seizure. He made it past the clasp of Sarah's bra all the way down to the top of her white panties. It took all his concentration to finish unzipping her.

"Got it," he rasped.

Sarah turned around and gave him a peck on the cheek.

"Won't be long, I promise."

Sonny's eyes locked on her shapely rear end as it gyrated its way to the bathroom. "Fuck me," he muttered. Man, what a walk! It was more like a sashay, actually.

A provocative, rhythmic, boner - inducing stripper strut that did exactly what it intended. He couldn't wait until she shut the door of the bathroom.

He needed to do something about the painful bulge straining against his left thigh. It threatened to blow the teeth of his zipper across the room like buckshot. He collapsed on the couch. He heard the sound of the water splashing against the shower curtain. He reached inside his pants to adjust himself and was shocked to feel how hard he was. It felt like he could poke a hole in a concrete wall.

Holy crap!

I'm going to explode any minute, he thought.

A wave of panic swept over him. After all those years behind bars, the prospect of having sex with a gorgeous woman made him feel he like he was about to go off like a roman candle.

What if they do wind up in bed and he finishes before he even gets his clothes off? Sweet Jesus Christ on a pogo stick, he couldn't let that happen.

He stood up and hurried over to the refrigerator. He wrenched open the door and vainly thrust his crotch inside, knocking over a jar of mustard. He hoped that the cool air would help his predicament. After about a minute it was clear that it wasn't going to work. He limped back to the couch. He tried to fill his head with un-sexy thoughts in the vague hope that it would make his errant erection go down. He concentrated on multiplication tables he learned in school. He pulled out memories of his work details in prison. When that didn't do the job, he thought about sermons he sat through in church. He even gave his ex-wife's nagging insults a quick thought.

Nothing worked.

He then recalled Bernie's "Old Faithful" story about his date with the Rockette. He looked down at his crotch and then at the sock on his right foot. Sonofabitch.

Now was not the time to start whacking off like a horny teenager but what choice did he have? He made a desperate scan of the apartment. There was only one bathroom and Sarah was showering in it. Christ. The image of her naked body, slick with soap and water didn't help the situation one bit.

Sarah began to sing in the shower. He could hear her voice, soft and gentle and too damn sexy.

Shit, she's making this impossible.

But he had to do something. It was throbbing now.

Fuck it! Sonny whipped off his sock with one hand. With the other, he unzipped his fly and pulled out his offending hard on. With all the blood gathered in his nether regions and the wine rushing to his other head, he found himself getting woozy. He jammed the sock over his hardened member and started to stroke it. His hand was a blur, like a hummingbird's wing.

"C'mon," he whispered in a hoarse voice. With all his attention concentrated on his wayward hard-on, he didn't notice that the singing and water had stopped.

"Can I help?"

Sarah's voice caused Sonny's eyes to bulge out of his head. For a moment, it was as if time had stopped. Sarah stood at the entrance to the hallway and stared at him. She was draped in a bubble gum pink towel that barely covered the top of her thighs. Her damp hair fell in tendrils and clung to her shoulders. It snaked across the top of her breasts in wet strands that accentuated their arousing curves.

So seductive and sexy as hell.

Perfect legs with silky smooth skin disappeared into the towel that covered her impressive contours. Her crossed arms lifted and pushed her breasts together, tempting Sonny to stare long and hard at the extraordinary and inviting cleavage it created. His gaze traveled to her face where his carnal trance was shattered by her quizzical expression.

Mortified, he realized what it must look like to her as he held his sock-covered penis in a death-like grip. In a panic, he flipped himself away from her and landed face down on the couch. A tiny strangled whimper emerged from the cushion.

"Christ!" He sounded like a newborn kitten crying for milk. Sarah hurried over to him.

"Are you all right?" The concern in her voice was tinged with a note of absurdity.

"I think I bent it," Sonny said in a brittle voice.

Sarah shook her head. "I thought when men reached a certain age they stopped doing that sort of thing."

Could this possibly get any worse?

"It's not what it looks like," he said.

"Really? It looks to me like you were playing what my dad used to call 'a little one- handed pinochle'."

Sonny buried his face in one of the sofa cushions. "Okay, it does look like what you think it is, but I can explain."

"This should be good."

In slow motion, he turned around. He pulled himself up into a sitting position, covering the sock covered bulge with his one of his hands. "I couldn't help myself," he said in a small voice.

"Oh. So you had to masturbate on my sofa?"

He raised one hand in a defensive posture, the other protected his crotch. "No, Jesus, no, that's not it." He sighed. "I was — I mean you're just, you're so — you know, beautiful, that it just — got hard. It was killing me so at first I tried to move it. I swear I thought it was gonna shoot out the other side of my thigh. But the sonofabitch wouldn't go down so — uh, I had to do something." He repositioned his leg. The swelling in his dick subsided with each embarrassing revelation. It appeared that confession was not only good for the soul but it did wonders on a stubbornly stiffened rod.

"I'm flattered, I think," said Sarah. "And the sock, I assume, is for…"

Chagrined, Sonny said, "Yeah. I was afraid that if we — I mean, you know." He jerked his head toward the bedroom. "I mean, it's been a long, long, long time since I…"

"Had relations?" offered Sarah, hiding a smile.

"Yeah. Exactly. And I thought I might — uh, finish — too quickly, and I just wanted to — please you, that's all." He cringed. "So I put it in the sock to — you know. So when I was with you I wouldn't — uh, go Old Faithful all over the place."

Of all the admissions of guilt Sonny made over the years, this was his most embarrassingly awful confession ever.

Sarah rolled her eyes. "Go Old Faithful?"

Eyes downcast, Sonny mumbled, "I was just — I just wanted it to be special."

Sarah giggled. "Well, nothing says 'special' like a sock covered penis. You know, a bow would have been sweeter."

"Okay, I feel like a complete idiot."

Sarah took his hand and helped him up so that they were facing each other. "You know what? You're cute when you're an idiot."

Her eyes met his and he saw that her pupils were dilated. She leaned in to him, kissing him full on the lips. His hand touched her face, softly stroking it. Their mouths parted and their tongues met. Sonny felt the warmth again, this time the heat gave him pleasure, not nerves or distress. Electric tingles ran down the back of his neck and along his spine. His heart thudded like a tympani against his chest. His knees weakened, an intense desire gripped him tight.

Sarah dropped the towel to the floor and Sonny felt her breasts rub against his chest, the imprint of her hard nipples making water circles on the fabric of his shirt. He was nervous as all hell, but at the same time, his incredible desire for her overcame his anxiousness.

He wrapped his arms around her slim waist and kissed her passionately. She responded by gently sucking his bottom lip between her own. Her tongue darted inside his mouth again. The subtle, yet enticing aroma of talcum powder and soap was sweet. He moved toward her neck and nibbled the soft skin just under her jaw, feeling her pulse bubble against his lips. Sarah moaned. She pulled his shirt out of his pants and ran her hands up his back. Her damp fingers scraped his skin, sending shivers along his backbone. His passion rose even higher.

He tried to remember the last time he had ever felt so good.

As he kissed her once more, he froze the moment in his memory. She pulled back and gazed deeply into his eyes. He felt her stare burn straight into his soul.

He wanted her.

He wanted all of her.

Sarah smiled and reached down between Sonny's legs just before Sonny lifted her into his arms. Her mouth curled into a mischievous grin as she held the sock in front of his face, then tossed it over his shoulder. "We won't be needing this," she purred.

CHAPTER FIFTEEN

Thursday, February 6, 1964

The next morning at the diner, Sonny dug into his bacon and eggs like he hadn't eaten in days. He couldn't remember the last time he was so hungry. Then again, it had been a while since he had worked up an appetite from the kind of exercise he got the previous night.

Sarah reached out and put her hand on his. "Slow down," she said. "I need you to really listen to what I'm going to tell you." She leaned in and spoke to him in a low voice. When she finished, Sonny almost choked on his breakfast. He wasn't sure if he heard her right.

"Say that again," he said in a booming voice, causing every head in the diner to turn toward them.

Sarah put her finger to her mouth. "For God's sake, not so loud," she admonished. "Do you want everybody in on this? You need to lower your voice."

Sonny coughed and then swallowed. "You wanna do this on Sunday because, why?" he asked.

"Because that's when the Beatles will be on Ed Sullivan." Sonny's face went blank.

He blinked twice. "What?" he asked.

Heads turned again. Sarah rolled her eyes and shook her head. "Does your voice have to be so damned loud?" she asked. "Do me a favor and lean in so I can tell you without the rest of New York finding out."

The garage was empty except for two tiny feet sticking out from under a 1957 Buick Caballero. Sonny chuckled. Bernie Miller had to have, without a doubt, the smallest feet he had ever seen on a man. He couldn't figure out how someone with such little feet was able to drive like a Grand Prix driver. Sonny figured his tiny dogs would slip off the pedals and yet, no one could handle a car like Bernie. Sonny stepped up to the automobile and nudged one of Bernie's minuscule feet with his own booted toe.

"Who's that?" Bernie called out from under the car.

"It's me. Sonny."

Bernie wheeled himself out and hopped up. Grease streaked his face from his forehead to his chin. "Hey, Sonny boy. How's it goin'?" He whipped a dirty rag out of his back pocket and wiped his hands before he extended one to Sonny. "So, you finally thinkin' of becoming a grease monkey, huh?"

Sonny rocked back and forth on the balls of his feet. "My friend," he said. "I'm about to make you a rich man."

Bernie's face fell and he raised his oil, blackened hands. "I already told you. No friggin' way." He dropped back down to his knees, flipped onto his back and slid back under the Buick. Sonny bent down, grabbed Bernie's ankles and pulled him back out.

"Listen, Bern. All I want is for you to come to Finn's tonight and give me two minutes of your time. If you don't like what I have to say, then I swear I'll never bug you with this again."

"Jesus — "

Sonny put his hand over his heart. "I swear to you on your sister's grave, I won't."

"My sister ain't dead, man."

"All right, my sister's grave then."

"You don't have a sister, Sonny."

"All right. Anybody's sister's grave, goddamn it."

Bernie wiped a wrench with his rag and eyed Sonny with suspicion. "What did Al say?"

"What do you think?"

Bernie chuckled. "I think he told you to go fuck yourself."

"Well, I can assure you with all my heart that he didn't."

Bernie scoffed. "Then that means that you haven't talked to him yet."

"Actually, he's next on the list."

The library was as solemn as a church during a funeral, except for the occasionally suppressed cough and the sound of pages turning. Sonny recalled the last time he was in a public library. He was about ten years old when he tried to steal a book from one of the shelves. Hell, nobody told him that you could borrow them for free.

At the main desk, a young woman with huge, round eyes chewed on her lower lip as she reached for the top book from a pile of fifteen high. She stuck the tip of her tongue out as her fingers brushed the cover of the top book.

Why doesn't she just stand up? thought Sonny. Inevitably the pile shifted. The librarian's eyes opened wider as the leaning tower of literature began to pitch forward.

"Oh no, no. NO! Darn," she yelped.

Sonny raced over and caught most of the books before they hit the floor. One of the heavy tomes smacked him square in the forehead. He swore under his breath. The librarian sat frozen with her hands against her mouth, her eyes bugged out like ping pong balls. Sonny placed the books he had managed to catch on the desk in front of her. He straightened the books and divided them into two smaller piles. When he was satisfied that they were stable, he retrieved the remaining books from the floor. It was then he noticed that the librarian had a white cast on her right leg. It started at her foot and disappeared under her dress.

"Here you go, Miss."

"Oh, thank you so much," she said in a nervous voice. "I'm such a klutz. Can I help you?"

"Yeah. I'm looking for Al Cardinelli. I hear he works here."

The librarian smiled sweetly. "Yes, he does. He's in the back." She picked up the telephone's receiver. "Who shall I say is looking for him?"

"Sonny Carter."

Her mouth dropped. "Sonny Carter? Uncle Sonny?" She pushed down on the desk and managed to bring herself to an awkward standing position. "Don't you remember me? It's me, Carrie. Carrie Cardinelli. See?" She grabbed the metal nameplate off the desk and thrust it at him. The nameplate caught him square in the chin. "Omigod!" she gasped. "Uncle Sonny. I'm so sorry. Are you okay?" Sonny backed away from her and rubbed his chin. If he didn't remember her before, he sure remembered her now.

The last time he saw Carrie, she was nine years old. She was the clumsiest kid that he had ever met. She was always falling down or running into walls. It seemed that she always had a scrape, a cut or a bandage somewhere on her body. The week before they had tried to pull the Hudson job, Carrie was learning to roller skate. The problem was that she hadn't yet learned the skillful, yet necessary art of stopping. After making an unsteady circuit around the street, she plowed head first into Sonny's lower midsection. She hit him so hard, one of his testicles swelled up. They had to wait a few days until the swelling went down before they could pull the job.

Sonny rubbed his chin. "I'm fine Carrie," Sonny said. "Please sit down." He winced. "I see you haven't changed much since you were a little girl." He leaned in slightly and pointed to his injured chin. "Is there a mark here?"

Carrie reached over and brushed her fingers across the affected area as if she were dusting a table. "Oh, just a teeny, tiny one. You can hardly see it," she assured him. Her trembling upper lip told Sonny otherwise. "So, how have you been?" she asked. "It's so great to see you. You know, my dad works here now."

"Yes, I know. I just asked you if he was in."

Carrie blushed. "Yes. Right. Why don't I go tell him that you're here?" She shakily stood up again. Her cast thudded against the marble floor, sending a reverberating crack throughout the somber atmosphere of the library.

Sonny placed his hands on her shoulders and eased her back down into her chair. "It's okay. Don't trouble yourself. Just tell me where he is and I'll go to him."

Carrie gave Sonny an awkward smile and pointed toward a hallway in the back. "It's the last door on the left."

He winked. "Thanks. Great seein' ya kiddo," he said, rubbing his chin.

Carrie waved. "You too, Uncle Sonny." She swung around in her chair, smacking her cast into the desk leg with another loud thud.

Sonny sauntered down the hallway until he found Al's office. He knocked on the door and waited until he heard Al's voice telling him to come in.

Al's thick glasses were perched on top of his head and his nose was almost glued to the adding machine. Without looking up, he said, "Who's that and what do you want?"

"Put on your damn specs, woudja?" said Sonny.

The glasses slid from Al's forehead to the bridge of his nose. "Oh. It's you. What happened to your chin?"

"It's nothing. I was just talking to Carrie and—"

Al sighed. "Yeah, of course you were." He returned to working the lever of the machine like a middle-aged woman with a cup full of nickels at a one-armed bandit in Vegas.

Sonny dragged a chair over and sat down opposite Al. He leaned the chair back on two legs, placed his feet on the edge of the desk and began to whistle. Al grit his teeth and tried to ignore the annoying distraction. Sonny was the world's worst whistler. He was tuneless, dissonant and drove anyone within earshot crazy.

Sonny saw Al's jaw clench tight as he worked the adding machine. Sonny upped the ante by raising the whistling a few decibels, but Al refused to give in. He got up and rummaged around in a filing cabinet behind his chair. He loudly opened and closed drawers to drown out the horrendous noise. He sank into his chair and dropped some files on his desk with a heavy thump. Sonny continued his energetic dissonant and even louder whistling. Huffing and puffing, Al rifled through the papers in the files until he finally let out a defeated groan.

"All right, all right. Enough. Please, just stop!"

Sonny lowered his feet to the floor and said with mock indignation, "So, still not a music lover, huh?"

"I love music. That's the problem. Whattya want?"

"Just wanted to come by and see what you're doing." Sonny gazed at the adding machine. "Addin' up numbers, huh? My oh my, you lead such an interesting life."

"Cut the shit."

Sonny shrugged. "What happened to Carrie's leg?"

Looking up from the adding machine, Al said. "You know what she's like. I saw her trip and fall but I swear to God, there was nothing in her way. Turned out it was her goddamn shadow moving around and she tried to jump over it."

"Her shadow?"

"Yep. She landed on a throw rug, slipped, and went ass over teakettle down a flight of stairs. She's lucky she didn't break her neck."

"She's always been pretty klutzy."

Al peered over his glasses. "Klutzy? She's a menace. I need to keep an eye on her all the time."

"You were always a little overprotective," said Sonny.

Al turned his attention back to the adding machine. "Someone's gotta be. A few weeks ago she went out dancing with her boyfriend and somehow she knocked the poor bastard out. Dancing, for chrissakes. She has some kind of strange talent for destruction."

Sonny chuckled. "Remember that time when she was little and was roller skating—"

"And she crushed your nuts?" Al chuckled. "Yeah, that was pretty funny."

"The hell it was. We had to call off the Hudson job 'til the swelling went down." Al grunted. "Yeah, well, we shoulda called that whole thing off anyways."

Sonny's expression soured. "Jesus, you're a real pill, you know that?"

Al snickered. "I'm a pill? What are you, one of the Dead End Kids? Nobody says 'pill' anymore."

Sonny put his hands behind his head and glanced up at the ceiling. "Okay, shitstick then. Do you have to be so goddamned negative all the time?"

Al stopped working the machine and gave Sonny a focused stare. "I'm not negative," he said. "I'm actually very positive. In fact, I'm pretty positive that you're here to talk about that stupid idea of yours about hittin' the Hudson again, right? I'm also pretty positive I want nothing to do with that."

"Such a shitstick, you are."

Al went back to his work. For a minute or two, the whirr-click of the adding machine was the only sound in the room. Al looked up and saw Sonny eyeing him. "Okay, you're giving me the creeps now," he said.

Sonny leaned in. "I got someone on the inside."

"I told you, I don't want to talk about that crap," Al sighed.

Sonny persisted. "Did you hear me? I said I got someone on the inside."

Al let out a mirthless laugh. "Ha! Like the last time."

"Look, would ya just hear me out?"

Al slammed his fist down hard on the desk. "No Sonny. I'm not getting caught up in your batshit lunacy anymore. I told you that the other night." He took off his glasses and rubbed his eyes. "If you're so hell-bent on going back to jail, I can't stop ya, but you're not takin' me with you."

"Bernie and Morrie are in."

Al put his glasses back on. "Bullshit," he said.

"Well trust me, they will be," said Sonny.

Al shook his head. '"Bullshit," he repeated.

Sonny sighed. "Listen, just think about it. That's all I'm asking. If you change you change your mind, we'll be at Finn's tonight."

Sonny waited for a response but it didn't come. Instead, Al turned back to his columns of numbers. Sonny waited for a few more moments and finally stood up. As he walked down the hall, all he could hear was the whirr-click of the adding machine.

CHAPTER SIXTEEN

"Hello boys." Sonny said as he and Morrie entered Finn's Saloon. He was somewhat surprised to see Al sitting beside Bernie, but his countenance betrayed nothing. He winked at him. "Couldn't stay away, huh?"

Al nudged Bernie. He took his thick glasses off and cleaned them with a napkin. "Jesus, I think you might need the table cloth for those," Sonny said.

"I'm only here because Bernie wanted me to come," Al said. "I was perfectly happy to stay clear of this place tonight."

"Well, trust me. You'll be glad you came," said Sonny.

"All right Sonny," said Bernie. "Say what you gotta say."

Sonny held up his hand. "I will. I'm waiting for one more person."

"Oh right," said Al. "Your mysterious 'inside man.' Hey Morrie, have you met this guy yet?"

Before Morrie could answer, he spotted Sarah entering the saloon. Clad in a tight-fitting blue dress that was both elegant and drop dead sexy at the same time, she gave them all a little wave as she sauntered to the table. Al and Bernie exchanged confused looks.

Sarah sat down in the chair next to Sonny and introduced herself. "Hello, everyone. I'm Sarah Garrett."

"Pleased to meetcha," said Bernie. "I'm Bernie."

"Hi, Bernie. Sonny tells me you're the 'wheels man,' if that's the correct term."

Bernie smiled. "Actually, it's 'wheelman' Miss." He then smacked his head with the palm of his hand. "What the hell am I saying? I'm a garage mechanic. I don't do that stuff anymore."

Al shot Sonny a look of skepticism. "So after all the bullshit the other night about banks being impossible to knock over, I — that is, Sarah here — has come up with a pretty foolproof plan," Sonny said.

"With all due respect Miss," said Bernie. "Sonny knows that we're not interested in this."

“Fuckin’ A,” said Al.

“We only came here tonight to humor him. No one wants to go back to jail.”

“Fuckin’ A,” Al repeated.

“Look you shitheads,” Sonny said, raising his voice. “Just listen to what she has to say. I’m telling you it’s a pretty sweet deal.”

“That’s exactly what you said twenty-five years ago, as I recall,” Al said. “I also remember goin’ to prison because of that ‘sweet deal.’” He waved his hand dismissively. “I’ll pass, thanks.”

“That’s it?” Sonny asked. “You’re just gonna reject it without hearing it?”

“Fuckin’ A.”

“Jesus Al. Just take five minutes to hear her out. If you don’t want in, then fine. I won’t push you.”

“Bullshit,” said Al.

“I swear to Christ I won’t,” Sonny said. “I promise. You can walk away and it’ll all be good.”

Al looked at him through shuttered eyes. “Five minutes,” he finally said, crossing his arms. “Five. Then I’m outta here.”

“That’s all we ask,” said Sonny. He nodded at Sarah.

“All right,” she began. “You fellows all know who Edward Bishop is, right?” Sarah asked.

A chorus of prick, asshole and cocksucker filled the air.

Sarah smiled. “Well, our good friend Edward has an additional source of income that’s derived from an extracurricular business that is not exactly legal.”

“What do you mean, not exactly legal?” asked Bernie.

“Edward has friends in the business world who occasionally need to hide excess revenues from the government. For a fee, Edward uses his financial contacts to help them hide the excess amounts of cash.”

“How you know this?”

“I’ve been at the Hudson National Bank and Trust Company for close to nine years,” Sarah said. “There’s not much that goes on in that place that I don’t know about.”

"Does Bishop know how much you know?"

A strained look took hold of her face. "Are you kidding?" she asked. "He hasn't a clue. You see, I'm a woman. To Edward, that means I'm just window dressing. The truth is I do my job very well. Extremely well. But to Edward, I'll never be good enough to do what a man can do." As she spoke, she picked up a paper napkin and began to twist it in her hands. "You know, I could run that bank. For one thing, I'm a whole lot smarter than Edward Bishop. If there was any justice in the world, it would be me sitting in that office and not that worthless son of a bitch."

Sonny saw her hands, shaking and blood engorged as she held the napkin in a virtual death grip. He wondered if Sarah imagined that the napkin was Bishop's neck. He reached over and put his hand over hers. "Hey," he said gently as he removed the roughly coiled napkin from her grasp, "take it easy."

Sarah blinked. "Sorry," she murmured.

Bernie leaned in close to Sonny. "She's wound up a little tight, huh?" he whispered.

Sarah smiled weakly. "I'm really sorry about that. It's just that Edward—"

Bernie gave her a reassuring smile. "Yeah. We know. He's a prick," he said.

"Go on," Sonny said to Sarah.

She cleared her throat. "Anyway, I always know when Edward is about to do one of these deals and there's one going down very soon. I saw Calvin Spencer there before I left. Calvin Spencer is Edward's go-between. Normally Calvin doesn't come to the bank, but this time he was there. Because of this, I believe that this is an especially big deal."

Sonny smiled. "Tell 'em how big."

Sarah looked at each of them before she spoke. "I can't say for sure but maybe a million dollars," Sarah said. "Maybe two."

They all looked at each other in stunned silence. An incredulous Bernie slapped the table, making a few of the bar patrons look over at them. "Are you shittin' me?" he said. In a lower voice, he added, "A million bucks?"

"Maybe two," said Sonny. He smiled at his gang.

"Sweet Jesus Christ! Is all that cash at the bank now?" asked Bernie.

Sarah nodded. Bernie let out a low whistle. "Jesus Al, a million bucks." He slapped him on the back. "Or two."

Al continued to sit quietly with his arms crossed. Sonny quietly scrutinized him. Al was never one to give much away. "So," Sonny said to Al. "Whatya think?"

Al looked at his watch and said, "Ya got two more minutes." Sonny glanced at Sarah. He felt his ire rising.

Sarah continued. "Okay, guys. There is a catch," she said.

"A catch?" asked Bernie. He moaned. "Why is there always a catch?"

"We need to do it this Sunday night between eight and nine o'clock."

"Sunday? Why Sunday?" asked Bernie.

Sarah's lips curled into a large grin. "Because that's when the Beatles will be on the Ed Sullivan Show."

Bernie's eyes went wide. Al rolled his eyes and snorted.

"It has to be on Sunday between eight and nine o'clock because that's when the guard's attention will be diverted from the bank."

"Diverted?"

"They'll be watching Ed Sullivan," said Sarah. "For that whole hour, they won't be watching the bank."

Al glowered at Sonny. "You've finally lost your marbles, Carter," he said, his voice tinged with distaste. "Every last one of 'em. Right now they're rollin' down Broadway."

Bernie touched Al's arm. "Just a second Al," he said. He turned to Sarah. "How do you know for sure that the guards are going to be watching that show?"

"I overheard them talking about it," Sarah said. "And I'm going to make sure that they do get to watch it."

"But how? Do you have TVs in the bank?"

Sarah nodded. "We do. When President Kennedy was assassinated, we bought two portable television sets so that the employees could watch the funeral. I'll make sure the guards have access to them."

Sonny could see Bernie's piqued interest but Al remained impassive.

He was determined to stay resolute in his stand against the idea. His jaw was thrust out like the bow of the Titanic and his brow was as furrowed as a farmer's field in April. When he finally spoke, he said, "This is one of the looniest things I've ever heard. All those millions in the vault and the guards will be watching TV? I call bullshit—"

"Jesus Christ Al," Sonny said.

"The guards don't even know about the money," Sarah interjected. "The only ones who know are Edward and Calvin Spencer. And me of course. Second, the money's not in the vault. It's always kept in Edward's office and I have that covered." She reached into her purse and held up a shiny key for everyone to see. "I had an extra made for his office when he changed the lock last year. Edward doesn't even know I have it."

A wide grin broke out over Bernie's face. "You know, I'm really startin' to like the sound of this."

Sonny rubbed his hands together. "You see? All we gotta do is walk in and take it. No guards, no vaults, no nothing. It's perfect."

Al grunted. "Yeah, just like the last time."

Sonny aggressively leaned across the table. "What is the matter with you? Don't you get it?" Sonny made a fist and was about to slam it on the table. Instead, Sarah reached over and put her hand on his, slowly lowering it. Sonny took a deep breath and continued. "I'm telling you, the guards are gonna be watchin' that show. And you wanna know why? 'Cause everybody in New York is gonna be watchin' that fuckin' show."

Sonny leaned back in his chair and rubbed the back of his neck. "For the last few days, I've been watching this town roll over, lay down and spread their legs for these guys. It's insane. It's like — it's like nothing else is happening in the world except for this." He jerked his thumb at Morrie. "I was talking with Morrie's nephew about it. He told me that there's gonna be over seventy million goddamned people watching that goddamned show on Sunday night. And I fuckin' believe it too."

Al stared at Sonny, stone-faced and unyielding and stood up. "Time's up," he said. "Good luck to you. Carrie's waiting for me."

"Are you serious?" Sonny asked. "I swear this is the closest thing to perfect as we're ever gonna get."

Without a word, Al put on his coat and headed for the door. Sarah looked like she was about to say something but Sonny shook his head. He silently watched Al leave and then turned to Sarah. "You know, I really thought he'd go for it. I really did," he said. He then turned to Bernie. "What do you think?"

Bernie appeared deep in thought. After a few moments he said "You know, it sounds like it could work. I mean, it really does."

"I don't want to push you into this if you don't want to do it," Sonny said.

"I know. I haven't told you but my dad — he's real sick."

"Sick? What's wrong with him?" Sonny asked.

"He's got dementia and he's getting worse. He needs to go to a proper hospital so they can care for him better. You know how expensive those places are. I just can't afford that."

Sonny remembered Bernie's father as a big, tough son of a bitch. He couldn't imagine him so sick that he needed to be in a hospital.

"Oh, I'm so sorry to hear that Bernie," offered Sarah.

Bernie nodded. "I need to do this for him. Two million bucks is a lot of dough. With that kinda dough, I can put him up in a nice place." He grinned. "I'm in."

"All right then," said Sonny. "Can you heist a bucket from the garage?"

"No cars there now. The only thing in the shop at this moment is a bakery truck. It needs a brake job but I can have that fixed by tomorrow."

"Jesus. A bakery truck?"

"Yeah, that's it."

Sonny sighed. "Well, beggars can't be choosers, I guess. We won't need it until Sunday."

"Not a problem. I told 'em it wouldn't be ready for a couple of weeks."

"A couple of weeks for a brake job?"

"Sure," Bernie said. "They have no idea. I also told 'em it needed transmission work, a new front axle and a bunch of other shit too."

Sonny laughed. "What a crook, you are."

Bernie smirked. Sarah checked her watch and stood up. "It's getting late," she said. "Just give me a minute and I'll meet you outside. I just need to make a quick phone call."

"Sure thing," said Sonny. As Sarah went to make her call, Sonny looked at Morrie nursing his beer. He started to cough and immediately put his hand up to his mouth.

"Are you okay Morrie?" Sonny asked with concern.

Morrie wiped his mouth with his sleeve. "Yeah, I'm all right. Just a little tired."

"Look buddy. I don't wanna push you into this if you don't wanna do it."

A small smile crossed Morrie's face. "Actually I've been doin' a lot of thinkin' Sonny. I figger I could spend the time I got left sittin' around just waitin' for — well, you know. I don't wanna do that."

"What about prison? You were pretty serious about not going back."

"Well, I figger if we pull this off, then that's great. If we don't — I figger by the time we get sent to prison, I'll probably be dead." He shrugged and offered a small smile. "It's a win-win situation. Sort of."

Sonny looked at Morrie's ashen face and wondered how much time he actually had left. The thought of his best friend dying was taking a toll on Sonny. Sadness gripped his heart. He clamped a hand on Morrie's shoulder and they walked toward the door.

Sonny hailed a taxi just as Sarah came out of the saloon. He opened the door of the taxi for Morrie and Sarah. As Morrie got into the back, he turned to Sonny. "Hey, could you do me a favor?"

"Absolutely," Sonny replied.

"The Beatles are flying in tomorrow morning and Gary has to go to meet with them and their manager. Tommy's driving him crazy to tag along."

"So?"

"So, Gary wants me to come along to keep an eye on Tommy, but Tommy — he doesn't exactly listen to me. I thought maybe you could go with me and give me a hand."

"Geez Morrie, I'll do anything for you, but that kid—"

"I wouldn't ask, but this is real important to Gary. It's only for a couple of hours."

Sonny sighed. "Okay," he said.

Sarah touched Sonny's arm. "My apartment is only a few blocks from here," she said. "Do you mind walking with me? I was thinking that maybe you could come up for a nightcap or maybe a coffee."

"Coffee? I would, but now I gotta get up early tomorrow and help Morrie. Coffee would just—"

Sarah shook her head. "Sonny. I don't have any coffee." Sonny's face turned crimson.

"Oh. Right."

Morrie leaned out of the cab. "Hey, Sonny. Are you two coming?"

"No, you go ahead. I'll see you in the morning. I'm gonna walk Sarah home and have a coffee with her."

"Yeah, but she just said that she doesn't have any coff—"

Sonny shut the cab's door, cutting Morrie off in mid-sentence. He tossed Morrie a goodnight salute as the cab pulled away.

It started to snow again. Sarah took his hand in hers. "Wow," he said. "This is real nice."

"Nice?" she said with mock indignation. "Just nice?"

"What I meant to say was—"

Sarah placed her finger against his lips. "Tell you what. Let's go back to my place and I'll help you work on your vocabulary."

Sonny grinned. "I always liked learning new things," he said.

CHAPTER SEVENTEEN

Al found his apartment door unlocked when he got home. After letting out a frustrated sigh, he eased it open and stepped into the living room. The soft glow from the television, bathing his daughter in a pale colored light welcomed him home.

Carrie was fast asleep, sprawled out on the sofa with her cast teetering on the sofa's arm. He removed his shoes so he wouldn't wake her and tiptoed across the carpet. He noticed an unusual stain on her cast. What the hell happened now? He moved closer to get a better look and stepped into a squishy, sticky mess.

"Goddamn it."

He glanced down at his foot stuck in the middle of an irregular circle of purple goop next to an empty bottle of NuGrape Soda. He grunted and went into the kitchen to get a cloth to clean up the stain. He dampened a dishcloth with warm water and returned to the living room. As he began to wipe up the soda mess, Carrie stirred. She stretched and swung her cast off the arm of the sofa at the exact moment that Al lifted his head. Out of the corner of his eye, and too late to react, he saw the blurred white movement heading for his skull. It was a direct hit. Al went down on his belly as if he were pole axed.

After what must have been a few minutes, he opened his eyes.

"What happened?" he asked.

Once he was able to focus, he looked up at a mortified Carrie hovering over him. "Never mind. I remember," he said. He pulled himself into a sitting position, his head pounding like he had a helluva hangover.

Carrie helped him on to the sofa and thrust a glass toward him. "Here, Pop. Drink this." She turned her attention to the spill on the floor and let go of the glass. It dropped into his lap like a cold, wet rock.

Icy water flooded his lap. "Christ."

Carrie spun around. In one outstanding sweeping motion, she knocked the lamp off the table to the floor with her forearm. She groaned in dismay. Al pushed himself away from her, spilling the rest of the water onto the sofa. When she moved closer to him, he put his hands up. "It's fine, honey." He smiled. "I'm okay. Really."

Carrie mopped up the water with the damp dishtowel. "I'm such a stupid loser," she mumbled.

Al heard what she said and took hold of her hand. “Hey, knock that off.” He lifted her chin. “You’re not stupid and you’re not a loser. Don’t talk about yourself like that.”

Carrie stared up at him—her twinkling eyes, large and round, resembled her mother’s.

“I’m such a klutz.”

Al kissed her forehead and helped her up off the floor. He moved her away from the wet sofa to the green easy chair in the corner and sat next to her on the chair’s wide arm. “How’s the leg?”

“It’s fine, but you must be hungry. I’ll get you something to eat.” She braced herself and pushed forward as if she were about to get up.

Al gently eased her back in the chair. “I’m not hungry. You just sit.” He got up, turned the volume down on the television and leaned against it, facing his daughter. “I had something while I was out visiting with Bernie, Morrie and Sonny tonight.”

Carrie brightened. “It was nice to see Uncle Sonny at the library.”

Al nodded. “Yeah, sure. He hasn’t changed much in all these years.”

“Speaking of change,” Carrie said tugging on an errant thread on the couch, “I kind of have some news.”

“Now what’s happened to you?” Al quickly surveyed his daughter for any new bruising, casts or cuts.

“After the day I’ve had, I could use some good news. What is it?”

Carrie averted her eyes. “Robby proposed. We’re getting married.”

Al caught his breath. “You’re getting married?”

“Yes,” Carrie said, her eyes on the floor, the errant thread from the couch slowly growing longer with each passing second.

“Well sorry honey, but you don’t look like you’re very excited. Am I missing something?”

Carrie raised her eyes, big blue pools of water brimming at the edge. “I know you don’t have a lot of money, Pop. I don’t want you to worry about it. We can pay for some of it. I don’t want anything fancy. Honest!” As drops of tears began to slide down Carrie’s face, Al had only one thought on his mind. She looks so much like her mother.

"Carrie, honey, I'm happy for you. Robby is a good guy. I want you to have the wedding you want. Don't worry about money. I have some saved for something just like this."

Carrie yanked her hands up in joy, the thread on her finger pulled away from the sofa leaving behind a bald patch in the fabric.

"Really? You do? Honest, Pop?"

In a flash, Al could see his beautiful daughter draped in white silk, her arm perched over his as he walked her down the aisle to a new life. She would look as beautiful as her mother and she deserved the best wedding money could buy.

"Yes, Carrie. I do. You're going to have the wedding of your dreams, I promise. I don't want you to worry about a thing."

As Carrie flung her arms around her father's neck he nestled his nose into her hair the way he used to do when she was a child.

"I knew I could count on you, Pop! You never let me down. You never have!"

And I never will, he thought.

As his mind calculated the sum total of his assets, he realized he didn't have enough money to pay for a decent hall, let alone the endless other things he'd have to pay for with a wedding.

Carrie scuttled off to call her fiancée Robby. Al could hear her gushing to him over the phone, "Pop is going to pay for the wedding, Robby! He says he's got the money to cover it!"

Well he didn't have it yet. But he was fairly certain he knew someone who could help him get it.

"Oh yeah, and I meant to ask you," Carrie said with the phone still attached to her ear. "Robby wants to come over to watch the Beatles on Sunday. Is that okay?"

Al smiled. "The Beatles, huh? Man, that's all I've been hearing about lately."

"We really wanna see them. Is it okay?"

"You know, as a matter of fact, Sonny asked me to help him out on Sunday night. I wasn't gonna do it at first but I think — I think I might help him out now."

"Aw, that's sweet. Old buddies hanging out together again. Just like old times, huh?"

"Yeah," he said as he grinned at his daughter. "Just like old times."

CHAPTER EIGHTEEN

Friday, February 7, 1964

"This is unbelievable," muttered Sonny. In bewildered fascination, he surveyed the teeming throng of five thousand, mostly female teenagers outside Kennedy International Airport.

"Wouldya look at this shit, Morrie?" He pointed to the swelling crowd, jostling for position. Morrie stuck his fingers in his ears and nodded. The crowd never seemed to stop growing. It looked as if it would reach unruly mob proportions at any second. The cacophony of the rabble even drowned out the thunderous engines of the Pan Am Boeing 707 jetliner, taxiing across the tarmac.

The powerful din was interrupted by a male voice that boomed from a loudspeaker somewhere in the airport.

"Ladies and gentleman," it said, "let's give these English boys a big American welcome!"

Minutes later, the aircraft's doors opened. The howling from the crowd instantly exploded into a deafening roar as the four lads from Liverpool made their way down the portable stairway.

"Oh my God!" a teenage girl standing next to Sonny screamed. "It's George Harrison! George! George!"

Sonny's fingers went instinctively into his ears.

"OMIGOD LOOK!" shouted another teenager. "It's John Lennon. JOHN!"

"PAUL," another girl yelled. "I see Paul! There he is!" She waved her hand in front of her flushed face and jumped up and down.

As soon as Paul McCartney came into view, the screaming got even louder. Sonny shook his head as he witnessed hordes of teenage girls dissolving into tears. Two women — not teens — women for chrissakes, spun their eyes to the back of their heads and collapsed to the ground. Two uniformed men rushed over and dragged them out of the way.

"Look! It's Ringo Starr! He's even cuter in person!"

The Beatles, dressed in black suits, white shirts and black ties ran across the tarmac toward the customs area. They looked both thrilled and utterly bewildered at the hullabaloo.

As Sonny took in the sheer craziness of it all, he felt Morrie's elbow in his side. Sonny turned towards where Morrie was pointing and saw a frantic Gary waving at them. "I think Gary wants us to follow him," Morrie said. He showed Sonny the laminated card hanging around his neck. "Better put your pass on." Sonny took the CBS press pass out of his pocket and looped it over his head. They squeezed their way through the pack of journalists assembled inside the International Arrivals building. One journalist, in a gray, seen-better-days hat, with a press pass stuck on the front like he just walked out of a revival of The Front Page, took a pencil out of his breast pocket and scribbled some notes on a pad. He turned to a photographer standing next to him.

"Oh man Benny, this is gonna be a slaughter," he said.

The photographer grinned. He pressed his eye into the viewfinder of his Graflex Speed Graphic press camera and adjusted the lens. "I give these clowns two weeks, tops. Mark my words, Chuck. Then this'll all be over."

Chuck smirked. "It's amazing what passes for talent these days."

"Look at those fuckin' mops," Benny laughed. "Captain Kangaroo on a bad hair day."

Chuck closed his notepad, stuck the pencil in his ear and gestured for Benny to follow him. "Let's get this over with so we can send 'em back to England. Payback for the Boston Massacre."

"This is not gonna be pretty," Sonny said.

The mocking reporters didn't notice the dapper gentleman standing to the left of the microphone array. Brian Epstein, the Beatle's manager watched the reporters with the wary eye of a bear protecting its cubs.

It was more than just a fairy tale. He had taken four scruffy boys from a sweaty warehouse cellar in Liverpool called the Cavern Club and turned them into the sharply dressed performing unit that had recently taken England by storm. "Beatlemania," was the term for the frenzied fan behavior that had Britain in its grip. The time had now come to unleash this phenomenon in the United States.

For several months, Epstein worked hard planning the trip to the United States. Nothing was left to chance. The tour was going to be the one that would turn them into household names worldwide. However, as he eyed the crowd, nausea roiled in his gut. He nervously chewed on one of his nails. In England, the British press adored the Beatles, but on this side of the Atlantic, it looked to be a completely different story. And it didn't look like their fairy tale would have a happy ending. It seemed that the fruits of his labors were about to be destroyed by a ravenous American press.

The majority of the U.S. press didn't take the Beatles' music seriously at all. They referred to them as mop-top interlopers with little to no talent. What was especially egregious was that these Limey bastards supplanted homegrown American acts on the charts.

Epstein closed his eyes and clasped his sweaty hands together. Enveloped in trepidation, he waited for the press conference to start. "Let the feasting begin," he heard one reporter intone to the rest. Brian massaged his throbbing temples. What had he gotten his boys into?

Decked out in their own CBS credentials—Gary, Tommy, and Gary's twenty-five year old personal assistant, Genevieve Doupierre waited in anticipation for their own close-up view of the Beatles. Gary turned to Genevieve. "This is exciting, isn't it, Guinevere?"

"Mon p'tit tabarnac d'estie d'enfant de chienne calisse," she mumbled under her breath. Genevieve, a pert brunette with expressive green eyes and pouty lips that always seemed to be curled in a permanently pinched expression of annoyance, had been working for Gary for the last year and a half. In all that time, he believed her name to be Guinevere, like King Arthur's wife in Camelot. He also labored under the faulty impression that she was from France instead of a small French Canadian town in Canada. Although Gary had no malicious bones in his body, he unintentionally exasperated the poor thing on an almost daily basis. Her usual response to this was a slew of French Canadian oaths that blissfully went over his head. She did, in spite of all this, harbor a soft spot for her clueless boss.

Tommy's Beatle-wigged head bobbed up and down as he strained to see above the ocean of reporters and television technicians.

"Where are they?"

"Dey 'haff to go troo custom first." Genevieve's accent was as thick as a Québécois style pea soup.

Gary rubbed the top of his son's head, sending the wig sliding down his face. "Just relax. It won't be long, son." Tommy grunted and hummed a Beatles tune as he continued to scan the crowd for his idols.

The customs office door opened. The Beatles walked toward the forest of microphones.

When the relentless noise of the press refused to abate, John Lennon stepped up to one of the microphones. He thrust his hand up at the pack of two hundred reporters and photographers assembled in front of them. "Sharrruuup," he commanded, in a loud Liverpudlian scouse.

A surprised and quiet hush gripped the room. A sea of hands began to wave for attention. One reporter flourished his notebook in the air. "How do you boys like the welcome to America you just received?" he asked.

Ringo Starr surveyed the room. "So this is America? They all seem out of their minds."

The sound of hundreds of cameras clicking filled the air. "Are you going to get a haircut while you're here?" another reporter shouted.

"I had one yesterday," George Harrison responded without missing a beat.

More hands went up. "What do you think of Beethoven?"

"He's great," Ringo Starr said. "Especially his poems."

"There's some doubt that you can sing."

John smirked. "We can, but we need money first."

"Would you please sing something?"

"NO," they replied in unison.

"Sorry," Ringo grinned, "next question."

The crowd buzzed with astonished murmurings followed by surprised laughter.

Something altogether unexpected was happening. The previously hostile American press, who had hoped to carve up the British invaders like Christmas turkeys, were defused by the Beatles' charm. The captivated reporters changed tactics and decided to have some fun with the boys instead. Brian Epstein started to breathe a little easier.

"What about the campaign in Detroit to stamp out the Beatles?"

Paul McCartney flashed brilliant white teeth. “We’ve got a campaign of our own to stamp out Detroit.”

“What do you do when you’re cooped up in your hotel room between shows?”

George beamed. “We ice skate.”

“Do you guys hope to take anything home with you?”

“Rockefeller Center.”

“Were your families in show business?”

John leaned into the microphone with a mischievous grin. “Well, me dad used to say me mum was a great performer.”

The press erupted in laughter. They had just fallen head over heels in love with the Beatles.

Sonny watched the performance and nodded in admiration. For a bunch of longhaired kids, he had to admit, albeit grudgingly, that the Beatles handled themselves like real pros.

A commotion to his left caught his attention. He turned to see Morrie spinning around in circles as if he were searching for a lost puppy. “Where’s Tommy?” he asked.

Sonny shrugged. “I thought he was with you.”

Morrie froze and his eyes widened. “Ah, crap,” he pointed in front of him. “Look.”

Tommy, resplendent in his Beatle’s wig and collarless jacket, slowly shuffled toward the Beatles.

“Shit,” said Sonny. They both took off running after Tommy. They were about twenty feet from tackling Tommy when without warning, two of New York’s finest stepped in front of them.

“Okay, fellas, that’s far enough,” one of the cops ordered.

Morrie pointed at Tommy and the Beatles. He pleaded with the officers. “Please, I have to go over there. It won’t take me long. Just let me through for thirty seconds.”

The two cops exchanged sneering glances. “Aren’t you guys a little old to be Beatles fans?”

Sonny smirked. “Aren’t you guys a little young to be adults?”

One of the cops took a step toward Sonny. “Hey, Arnie,” he said to his partner. “We got us a regular Joey Bishop here.”

Gary managed to elbow his way through the crowd and was now conversing with Brian Epstein. Unbeknownst to Gary, Tommy had also evaded the pack. He was now standing motionless in front of his idols.

"Well, who do we have here?" Ringo knelt down until he was eye to eye with Tommy. "What's yer name, son?"

Tommy's face remained as immobile as a piece of granite. The Beatles exchanged bemused glances. "A gabby sort, isn't he?" said Paul.

George reached out and tousled his hair. "I like yer haircut." Tommy's hair cascaded down to his chin causing him to sputter.

"Ah-ha." John chuckled. "That's his problem, George. He's flipped his wig."

Tommy pulled the wig back on his head and found his voice at last. "You're the Beatles."

"Only on the weekends, my little friend," John said. "The rest of the week we're 'Randy Fellows and the Winchester Wankers.'"

Paul nudged him with an elbow. "Jesus, John."

John clamped a hand on Paul's shoulder. "Sorry, Randy."

Genevieve, standing next to Gary noticed Tommy surrounded by the Beatles. "Tabernac!" she said. She tugged on Gary's arm. "Uh, Gary – "

"Please, Guinevere. I'm speaking with Mr. Epstein."

"H'okay, den. But I tink your son want to join da Beatle."

"How's that?" Gary turned toward Genevieve and followed her arm to where it was pointing. "Oh, Jesus! Please excuse me, Mr. Epstein," he called out over his shoulder as he made a mad rush toward Tommy and the Beatles.

George Harrison tapped Tommy on the shoulder. "I'm not sure son, but I think this gentleman wants to see ya." Tommy turned. Gary tried to stop on the slippery floor and started to slide. He snagged Tommy's arm as he slid by.

"Did anyone get the number of that bus?" asked Ringo.

Gary caught his breath and limped back to the Beatles. "I'm really sorry fellas," he gasped as he dragged Tommy across the floor. The boy hung like a half-filled scarecrow in his father's clenched hand. "My son's a big fan."

Tommy struggled in his father's grasp. "Hey! What gives?" he yelped.

Gary didn't respond. His attention was diverted by the sight of Sonny wagging his finger perilously close to a policeman's nose. Brian Epstein, who had rejoined the group said to Gary, "Would you like to meet at the hotel to discuss the arrangements? I can see you're needed elsewhere."

"I think that would be a good idea," Gary responded as he hurried over to diffuse the growing conflict between Sonny and the cop.

John struck a heroic pose and held an imaginary sword aloft. "To the hotel! Lead on, MacDuff," he said in a loud stage voice. He turned to Ringo. "Shakespeare, you know."

"Oh, yeah," Ringo said with a wink. "He's a great singer."

Sonny was about a minute from being hauled off to the police station. Morrie grabbed Sonny's arm and pulled at it. The burly ex-bank robber was resolute. Gary, with Genevieve and a somewhat subdued Tommy in tow, tried to insert himself in between Sonny and the policeman.

"Excuse me, officer, my name is Gary Cooper. Is there a problem here?"

The cop named Arnie guffawed and nudged his partner. "Hey Ansel, look at this. It's Gary Cooper."

The other cop, Ansel, chuckled loudly. "You were great in *High Noon*."

Gary resisted the urge to roll his eyes. "Yeah, I've never heard that one before," he mumbled. Genevieve stepped between Gary and the two cops. The top of her head only reached Ansel's chest. She planted her hands on her hips and lit into the two of them with scorching Gallic fury.

"Tabarnac d'estie. Why don' you guys give h'out some maudit parking ticket to h'old lady? You enfant de chienne."

Ansel glared at the invective, sputtering French Canadian. "What the hell?"

"You 'erd me. Mange le merde."

"What did you say?"

Arnie shrugged. "I think she asked if you're married."

"No, I din't. I tol' you to eat sh —"

Gary clutched Genevieve's wrist and pulled her away before she finished her sentence. In a calmer voice he said, "Say, fellas, I'm from CBS. I work for the Ed Sullivan Show and these men are my associates." He gestured to Sonny and Morrie.

"Come on, you guys. I have to meet Mr. Epstein at the hotel and you two, — um — are needed in editing, right? Let's go!" Gary offered his best disarming smile to the cops and motioned to the others to follow.

Sonny shot the cops one last black look. "Goddamned punks," he said.

Ansel chortled at the remark. "Fuckin' old geezer," he said.

Sonny caught the remark and stopped in his tracks. Gary bumped into him and dropped Tommy to the floor like a sack of spuds. "Owww!" Tommy whined. "What the — "

Sonny spun around and glowered at the cops. His fingers curved into a tight fist. Morrie stepped into his path. "Sonny," he said in a low voice. He put his hand on Sonny's forearm and leaned in close. "Sarah," he whispered. "Think of Sarah."

Sonny blinked twice. Morrie nudged Sonny away from the cops. "Let it go. It ain't worth it." Sonny grimaced, but he knew Morrie was right. He unclenched his fist. Ignoring the rude remarks from the cops, they joined Gary, Genevieve and a whining Tommy.

"Aww, geez, Dad," Tommy moaned. "I didn't get any autographs."

Gary was at his wit's end and Tommy was dancing on his last nerve. "I'm seeing Mr.Epstein this afternoon," Gary said. "I'll get you an autograph then."

Tommy's wig slipped down below his forehead. If it fell any lower, he could have been mistaken for Cousin Itt. He held up four fingers. "But I want four autographs. I want one from each of them."

Gary froze. He crouched down and leaned in so that his nose was almost touching Tommy's. He slid Tommy's wig up past his forehead until his eyes were parallel to his own. "If you don't stop talking right now, I'm going to autograph your ass with my shoe."

Sonny chuckled and wrapped his hand around the back of Gary's neck in a friendly squeeze. "Remind me to never piss you off, Cooper," he said.

CHAPTER NINETEEN

"I don't think this was such a good idea," Sonny said between deep breaths. "Why don't we just go for lunch?" The February air, less bitter right after a snowfall, invited the lunchtime crowd to take advantage of a bright afternoon for an ice skate at Rockefeller Center. Sarah giggled as she watched Sonny, legs stiff and unsteady on rented skates, shudder and shake across the ice. With his arms outstretched in front of him for balance, he looked like Frankenstein's monster.

"Hang on," said Sarah. She sped toward Sonny, confidently weaving in and out between the good skaters and the wobbly ones.

Sonny, with arms askew, spewed salty adjectives into the air as he teetered back and forth in a crooked line. "For chrissakes," he said. Sarah grabbed his wrist and helped him regain his balance, saving him from certain disaster. His head jerked backward from the sudden surge forward.

"Don't be such a baby," Sarah chuckled. She shouldered him on the arm. "Behave and I'll buy you a hot chocolate."

"Now there's a great idea." He bent over and rested his hands on his knees. "Let's get one now." Sarah scrunched up her nose and led Sonny off the ice. As soon as he was close to the bench, he fell on it with a long groan. "So you do this all the time, huh?" he asked when he finally caught his breath.

"Every Friday during my lunch hour and in the summer I jog."

"Jog? You mean you run? On purpose?"

Sarah giggled. "It's great exercise. How do you think I keep this girlish figure?"

Sonny winked. "I thought maybe you were just in shape from dodging sweaty old men like me."

"That too," Sarah said and smiled.

Sonny removed his gloves and bent over to untie his skates. "Aren't you going to take your skates off?"

"In a minute," she said. "I just want to watch the others for a bit."

"You were good out there," Sonny said as he pulled at one of his laces. "Did you skate as a kid?"

"I did," she said. A wistful look crossed her face. "You know, I used to dream of becoming a figure skater when I was young."

Sonny glanced up at her. "No shit? A figure skater, huh?"

She continued to watch the skaters. "I met Sonja Henie when I was fifteen. Do you know who Sonja Henie is?"

"Nope."

Sarah laughed. "She's an Olympic figure skating champion from Norway. I was on a team and one day she came to New York for a figure skating demonstration. I was one of the skaters picked to perform a routine for her. After my performance, she came over to me and told me I was Olympic caliber."

"Did you ever make it?"

Sarah's wistful expression clouded. "I didn't think I was ready so I decided to wait. Then the war happened. By the time the Olympics came around again, I had missed my chance." She sighed. "I guess what they say is true."

Sonny pulled off a skate. "What's that?"

"That when opportunity knocks you better answer it."

Sonny dropped the skate with a loud plonk between his feet. "Aw, I don't believe that crap." Grunting, he yanked at the other skate's lace. "Life's full of opportunities. Look at me. Twenty-five years ago, I went to jail. It didn't mean I was done. I got out and now I got another chance and this time, I'm gonna run with it. Al told me the other day to appreciate the time I have left, and believe me, I do. I think you can do whatever the hell you want to do when you want to do it. Sometimes, you have to make your own opportunities."

"What about fate?" asked Sarah. "Don't you believe things happen for a reason? Maybe my missing out on the Olympics was meant to be."

Sonny shook his head. "How boring would life be if it was all charted out for us ahead of time? Don't you think it would be better if we made our own choices and lived with the results? If I screw up, it's because I made the mistakes. It's not because of fate or some stupid plan laid out for me by God or anyone else."

Sarah regarded him for a moment. “You’re not particularly religious, are you?”

“Nope,” he responded with pride in his voice. “Think about it. If spending all those years in prison was already planned for me, then the way I see it, somebody owes me twenty-five years. That’s only fair. But, I made the choice to commit a crime, and I got caught. It was my decision.”

“But aren’t you mad at yourself for making that choice?”

“Nah. I didn’t see any other way out to help my mother. Shit happens, I got through it. If I regret anything, it’s who I trusted. That was the bad decision.” He continued to wrestle with the skate, grimacing. “This is pissing me off.” He lifted his foot into the air and smirked. “I got a fuckin’ knot here. Must be fate, huh?”

“More like bad luck.” Sarah stood. “Would you mind if I took another couple of laps while you try to get that off?”

He grunted and gave the stubborn knot another pull. “Go ahead. This might take a while.” Sarah stepped on to the ice and glided around the rink’s perimeter, building momentum.

She shot toward center ice, spun around and leaped into the air, executing a near perfect axel.

A murmur rose in the crowd as she landed the jump with grace, her arms out flat and parallel with the ice. She made two circuits and performed two more jumps in the same manner.

“Hey, Sonny!” She waved at him. “Watch this.”

Taking another circle around the rink, she picked up speed and shot out toward the middle of the rink. She leaped high into the air and spun, executing a perfect triple jump. She landed on her right foot and swept past the crowd, her face beaming with happiness. The onlookers broke out into spontaneous applause as she returned to the bench.

Sonny was on his feet applauding with the rest of them. “That was great!”

“I don’t think anyone has ever done that before,” she said as she sat down on the bench. “I feel like I’m fifteen years old again.”

“Looks like you haven’t lost a thing,” Sonny said.

She slapped her hands on her thighs and caught her breath. “That was a hoot.”

Sonny turned his attention back to his unyielding knot. With a mighty tug, Sonny yanked at the lace and the knot finally came free. "A-ha," he said. He dropped the skate like a shitty diaper next to the other with a smug air of satisfaction. He reached under the seat and then looked up, confused. "What the hell?" He leaned over and looked under the bench.

Sarah untied her skates. "What is it?"

"Some asshole stole my boots." He kicked at the skates and crossed his arms sullenly. "This city is full of fuckin' crooks."

Sarah fished out her own boots from under her seat and put them on. "Wait here. There's a haberdashery across the street."

"A what?"

"A men's shop. I'll go there and buy you another pair." She gave his upper arm a light pinch. "Stop pouting. Monday morning, you'll be able to buy all the boots you want."

She turned in her skates, crossed East 50th and headed toward the haberdashery. As she was about to enter the shop, she abruptly found herself face to face with Edward Bishop.

A sneer rippled across his upper lip. "Late lunch, Miss Garrett?"

Annoyed, Sarah bit back a snide remark. "As a matter of fact I'm on my way back to the bank," she said.

Bishop pointed his walking stick behind her. "The bank is that way."

"I'm aware of that." She moved closer to the shop's door. "I need to make a quick stop in here to pick up a pair of boots."

Bishop pointed at the sign over the door with his walking stick. "This is a men's haberdashery. They don't carry women's boots."

"Who said I'm buying women's boots?"

Bishop sniffed. "I see. Well then, perhaps you would like my assistance in picking out a nice pair."

His oily tone grated on her nerves. "Thank you, no. I'd like to pick them out myself," she said. "I want something with a little style," she added.

Bishop glared at her, narrowing his eyes. "I won't take that as an insult," he said in a taut voice. "I'm sure you didn't mean it that way." He checked his watch. "I'll see you back at the bank in, say fifteen minutes?"

"More like twenty-five, I should think." Cool and poised, she entered the store.

Edward watched her through the window for a minute. He saw her speaking to a salesman and pointing to a pair of boots behind him. As the salesman went to get the boots, she noticed Bishop watching her through the window. Embarrassed at being caught, he pretended to check his watch again. When he saw that she was still looking at him, he decided to leave. He stalked off in the direction of the bank. However as he stepped around the corner, he spun on his heels and flattened himself against the side of the building. He peeked around the brickwork.

"Boots my ass," he said under his breath. "Let's see what you're really up to here."

Sonny rubbed his feet with vigorous strokes in a vain attempt to keep them warm. He stood and arched his back, listening to every joint pop. The cold wreaked havoc with his muscles. He was conscious of every minute of his age yet the thought of the imminent heist made the pain melt away. Thoughts of Sarah filled him with a wonderful sense of life. The idea of screwing Bishop over was pretty sweet too. After watching the skaters for a while he looked across the street toward the haberdashery where Sarah went to buy the boots. It was then he noticed someone suspiciously peeking around the corner of the building.

What the hell? He squinted in the afternoon sun, trying to get a better look at the figure who was hiding by the wall of the shop. Sonny put his hands up to his forehead. He swore when he recognized who it was.

"Fuck! It's the worm."

He saw Sarah leave the haberdashery with a large box under her arm. She glanced up and down the street and then when it was clear, started to cross. Bishop stepped out from behind the building and followed.

"Shit!" Sonny muttered loudly. "What the hell is he doing here?" He slammed his hand against the rink's boards. In desperation, Sonny looked around. He couldn't let Bishop see him, especially with Sarah. He needed to disappear. Fast. He scanned the area as a large group of skaters glided by. He then eyed his skates.

Sarah kept a tight hold on Sonny's new boots as she crossed the street. She hoped the boots were the right size. She glanced at her watch. If she was going to get back to the bank before her hour was up, she had to hurry. Once she was across the street, she saw that one of her laces had become loose. She crouched down to tie it. Out of the corner of her eye, she saw Edward slinking toward her. She quickly turned her attention to the rink. Sonny had disappeared from where he had been standing. She blinked hard as she looked at the skaters on the ice.

"Oh, my God," she said under her breath. "What the hell is he thinking?"

Sonny was back out on the ice. He had presumably hoped to blend in with the crowd but somehow, he had become the caboose of a large crack the whip chain. As the skaters in the chain picked up speed, the joyous shouts of the participants muffled Sonny's shocked howl of panic.

"Hang on, buddy," yelled the skater that held Sonny's hand. "This is gonna get crazy." What the skater couldn't see was the expression of abject terror plastered all over the caboose's face.

Bishop was halfway across the street when he saw that Sarah noticed him. He froze. "Goddamn it," he said under his breath. Stuck in the middle of the street, he spun around to hide his face. The sound of an approaching vehicle caught his attention. Bishop watched in terror as a blue Chevrolet Impala hurtled toward him. The driver of the vehicle, shocked to see someone standing in the middle of the street, spun the wheel. The Impala swerved then fishtailed. It began to slide sideways, skidding closer to Bishop.

Sonny's feet weren't on the ice any longer. His feet were about an inch and a half from the surface. He was going so fast that when the whip finally cracked, he flew through the air like a Mercury rocket. He hurtled toward a large pile of snow. To Sonny's blurred perception, it looked more like an iceberg than a soft spot to break a fall. He closed his eyes and crashed with a tremendous thud against the frozen bank of ice. A sharp piercing pain stabbed his lower back. He moaned in agony through clenched teeth.

The blue Impala slowed but the impact of car and banker sent Bishop sprawling. He slid across the street into a fire hydrant, cracking his ankle.

"Hey pal, are you all right?" Bishop eased his eyes open. A chubby hot dog vendor in a condiment-covered apron hovered over him. "Man, did you ever fly. When I saw that car comin' at ya, I thought for sure you was a goner." Bishop groaned. The vendor rubbed his head. "Hey, what was ya doin' standin' in the middle of the street like an idiot for anyways?" he asked.

Bishop tried, without success, to lift himself up. A bolt of lightning ripped through his right ankle sending him back down. At first, he thought he had landed in a pile of dog feces. With a frustrated grunt, he realized that he'd shat himself. He turned to the vendor and pointed at his walking stick by the curb. "Would you mind fetching that for me, please?" he asked.

"Sure, no problem buddy." The vendor went over to pick it up. When he handed it to Bishop, he became aware of an unpleasant odor. His lip curled. "Hey buddy, do you smell dog shit?" he asked.

Bishop ignored the query and looked where Sarah had been standing. To his disappointment and frustration, he saw that she had disappeared.

When Sonny opened his eyes he saw that he was surrounded by a large crowd. He heard many suggestions as to what should be done to help him. However, no one moved to implement any of them.

"Somebody, get him to a bench."

"No, Jesus, don't move him."

"I think he must have flown a hundred feet."

"Has anyone called a doctor?"

"Milton, you're a doctor," a woman said to the man standing next to her. "Do something."

"Shut up Grace," the man hissed. "I can't afford another malpractice suit." Sonny grunted and started to roll over, but the sharp pain in his back prevented him from doing so. He scanned the crowd. "Hey, everybody, don't nobody move or nothin'," he grumbled.

A familiar voice calling his name grabbed his attention. He craned his neck in the direction of the voice and saw Sarah's worried face looking back at him.

"Sonny! Over here."

She waved at Sonny and pointed at a waiting taxi. As he started to stagger to his feet, two men stepped forward to give him a hand. They each took an arm and led him toward the taxi, his feet still in the skates scraping along the concrete. When they got him to the cab, he saw Sarah sitting in the back, holding out a pair of boots. He sluggishly slid in beside her.

"Forget the boots," he said. "I need traction."

The cab pulled away from Rockefeller Center and Sarah glared at him. "What the hell were you thinking? You could have been seriously hurt."

"I saw Bishop. I tried to hide in the crowd so he wouldn't see me, but someone grabbed my hand and I got caught up in that stupid chain." He winced. "My back is on fire."

She huffed. "If your back is out, it could jeopardize everything."

"I just need a little rest tonight. I'll be fine." He forced a smile but she continued to look daggers at him. "Honest. I swear I'll be fine," he assured her.

Sarah ordered the cabbie to take her to the Hudson. She shoved the boots and boot box onto his lap. She fished out some cash and a key from her purse.

"Here," she said. She made no attempt to hide her annoyance. "After the cabbie drops me off at the bank, go to my apartment and heal. I'll be home by five-thirty. Do you think you can stay out of trouble for the rest of the day?"

Bishop lay on a gurney in the back of an ambulance, a bundle of paranoia in shit-stained pants. Sarah's actions raised his suspicions. What' going on? he wondered. What was that crap about buying men's boots? He wasn't aware of any boyfriends. Who were they for?

She was pretty chummy with Sonny Carter the other day. Were the boots for him? And Carter, that prick. What was he really doing at the bank anyway? What's he up to? And what the hell is Sarah up to?

Paranoia is a ravenous beast and it was feeding time at the zoo in Bishop's head. Another disturbing thought crossed his mind.

Did Sarah know about the suitcases in his office?

Dammit. If she did…

An attendant at the front of the gurney sat reading a newspaper. "Hey, pal," barked Bishop, "any idea how long it'll take to fix up my ankle?"

The attendant lowered his newspaper. "How should I know? I'm not a doctor."

"Well, what good are you then?" Bishop muttered.

The attendant raised his eyebrows. "Well, at least I know how not to shit myself like an infant."

Bishop ignored the response and revisited his mounting paranoia. "Something is up," he said. "And I'm going to find out what it is."

CHAPTER TWENTY

A few hours later, a scowling Eddie Bishop hobbled through the main doors of the bank on a pair of crutches. He garnered a few stares from the employees as well as a few smirks.

Sarah hung up her phone when she saw him. "What happened to you?" Sarah asked.

Bishop ignored the question and continued on to his office.

A few minutes later, her phone rang. Sarah picked it up and heard Bishop's surly grumble on the other end.

"I need you. Now." Sarah uttered an oath and went to see Bishop.

Inside Bishop's office, she noted that his pants didn't match his jacket. "Are those new pants?" Sarah asked.

He motioned to his leg and grunted. "Never mind that. Could you help me, please?"

She reached down and took hold of his foot. With gentle care, she lifted it and placed it on the desk blotter near his telephone. With a deep breath, he leaned back in his leather chair. "Much better," he said. He reached inside his jacket and pulled out a package of cigarettes.

He extended the pack to Sarah who declined the offer. He shook one out for himself and lit it with a flourish. He exhaled, blowing a large irregular smoke ring. Sarah fanned her hand in front of her face to get rid of the smoke.

"Is that all you wanted, Edward?" she asked.

He took another pull on the cigarette and exhaled upwards, creating a small cloud above his head. "As you can see, I've had an accident so I'll be taking some time off. I just came in to straighten out a few things before I go."

Sarah gestured to his leg. "Does it hurt much?"

"I'm fine." He took another drag off the cigarette. "I was wondering if I could count on you to keep an eye on things while I'm away."

"Of course. How long — ?" Her voice trailed off. She spotted the suitcases behind Bishop's chair and quickly counted them in her head. Fourteen? Aware that Bishop was watching her, she averted her gaze. "How long will you be away?" she asked.

Bishop took another puff and stubbed out the cigarette. "About a week. I'll be back next Thursday or Friday. Since there's no pressing business coming up, I'm sure you can handle it." He gave her one his condescending grins. "Nothing to worry your pretty little head about."

Jerk.

"Thanks for the vote of confidence," she said. "Is there anything else? I've got a lot of things I need to finish before five o'clock."

"No, that should be all. Oh, could you tell Flynn that I want to see him, please?" Sarah sucked her teeth and shuddered. *Not that jackass*, she said to herself.

"Of course," she responded. She turned and left Bishop's office and walked as slowly as she could to Seamus Flynn's office.

Outside Flynn's door, Sarah fought the revulsion that rose in her throat. In truth, revulsion wasn't a strong enough word for how she felt about the security chief. She loathed him. He was a first-rate sleaze who hit on her with the tenacity of a hungry mosquito. Because Bishop never wanted to deal with the man, that duty usually fell on Sarah's shoulders. She often thought about what it would be like to crush his testicles with a well-placed upright thrust of her knee.

She sucked in a breath and knocked on the door.

"Who's that?" asked a voice in a thick Irish brogue. Sarah didn't reply. Instead, she stepped into the office. Flynn sat at his desk going through papers. He looked up and gave her a big toothy leer sending a rivulet of disgust down Sarah's spine.

"G'day, Sarah, me sweet," he said. "Yer lookin' luvlier than tall glass of whiskey on Christmas Day."

Seamus Flynn looked like your stereotypical New York Irishman. He was tall and broad- shouldered with flaming red hair. He had enough freckles to make it look like he had a suntan and an immense amber mustache that covered his top lip. Underneath thick ginger eyebrows were moss-green eyes that just screamed Emerald Isles. He certainly looked the part, except that it was just that — a part. He wasn't from Ireland at all. Instead, he was a third generation New Yorker from Brooklyn. For reasons that were known only to him, he spoke in a ludicrously affected Irish accent. He believed it made him more interesting and authentic. To Sarah and especially Bishop, he sounded utterly ridiculous.

His father Donal Flynn had been a beat cop who had been on the force for thirty-five years. Although it was rumored that he had ties to the mob, it was never proven. If he did have ties, he was smart enough to never get caught. Seamus wasn't as smart as his father, much to Donal's chagrin. After becoming a cop, Flynn was drummed out of the force for shaking down store owners. Thanks to a friend of his father's who was an acquaintance of Eddie Bishop, Flynn was hired as the head of security for the Hudson a year ago. Against Bishop's better judgment, he hired the feckless Flynn.

Sarah stood in front of Flynn's desk with her hands on her hips. "Edward wants to see you immediately," she told him in a curt tone.

Flynn sipped his coffee, admiring her from the tips of her black pumps to the top of her forehead. He was like a five year old drooling over a cake in a pastry shop window. Smacking his lips, he extended a meaty hand toward the chair in front of his desk.

"Why don't you have a seat, darlin'?" he said in his bogus Éire accent. "We rarely have a chance to socialize."

"Did you hear what I said?"

"Oh, lass. Still playin' hard to get, eh? Ain't you gettin' tired of this game?"

"Flynn —"

"Call me Seamus, me love."

"I haven't got time for your foolishness today, Seamus. Edward wants to see you — now."

Flynn flared his nostrils. He looked like a warthog reveling in its own musk. "Oooh, lassie, Yer gettin' me Irish up."

You perverted son-of-a-bitch, she thought.

He ogled her with a lecherous gleam in his eyes while patting his thigh. "Would ya like ta see how up it is?"

"Would you like me to throw up?" she said.

"Why do ya fight it so, my dear?" he asked. "I know yer dyin' for a little Flynn within."

So that's the game, is it? Sarah thought. Her eyes narrowed and her lips curled into a sly grin. If Flynn knew her better, he would have recognized that look. He would have known that she was about to screw him over.

"All right Seamus," she whispered in a breathy tone. "You know, I'm starting to feel a little warm right now." With one hand, she unbuttoned the top of her blouse and fanned herself. Seductively, she leaned across the desk offering him a perfect view down the front of her dress. Flynn's eyes widened as he took in her inviting cleavage. His breathing became more labored.

"As a matter of fact, I'm feelin' a bit warm me self," he said, his breath heavy with anticipation. "Excuse me if I don't get up right now."

Sarah's flirtatious smile widened and she moistened her lips. "Is it me or is it now getting hot in here?"

Flynn's forehead was drenched in perspiration. He rubbed his mouth with his sleeve. "I'm a bubblin' volcano, sweetie."

Sarah's lips were an inch from his cheek. She looked down and could see just how excited he was. "Would you like me to make things — " she purred, close enough so that her breath tickled the inside of his ear, "— even hotter for you?"

Flynn looked as if he was about to explode. "Sarah, honey," he said, his voice hoarse. "I want you to make me burn."

Smiling, she licked her lips in slow, sensuous strokes. She leisurely moved her hand closer to the edge of his desk. "As you wish, me laddie." Keeping her eyes locked on his, she put two fingers against his coffee cup and tipped it straight into his crotch.

"Ahhhh! Sweet Jesus Christ!" Flynn leaped out of the chair, screaming in pain. His Irish accent vanished, replaced with a flat Brooklyn dialect. "You rotten little bitch!"

"Now, are you ready to go see Edward?" she demanded. Stepping into the hallway, she turned and winked. "And fer God's sakes, laddie, you'll be wantin' ta change yer pants," she said in a perfect Irish brogue. "You look like you've gone and pissed yerself, darlin'."

"Rotten bitch," Flynn muttered. He pulled the wet crotch of his pants away from his testicles as he opened Bishop's office door. The liquid had cooled off, making it even more uncomfortable than it had been when Sarah scalded him.

"What took you so long?" Bishop rested his leg on the desk and a pair of crutches leaned against the wall. He pointed at Flynn's pants. "Seriously?"

Flynn's eyes narrowed. "I spilled me coffee. What happened to you?"

"I got hit by a car."

Flynn sniffed. "I suppose I should be lucky I only got some wet gonads. Are ya in any pain?"

"I just said that I got hit by a fuckin' car, dimwit. Of course, I'm in pain."

Bishop delicately pulled his leg off the desk. It slipped through his fingers and fell with a heavy thump into his wastepaper basket. A loud child-like squeal escaped his throat. He clutched at his injured ankle. Flynn rushed over and grabbed Bishop's foot. In his zeal to help, he twisted Bishop's leg. Bishop's eyes bulged like a fish out of water. His body flipped in the direction of the twist and he flew out of his chair, landing face first on the floor.

"Oaf!" Bishop gasped. "Just leave me alone. I'm fine."

Flynn lowered Bishop's leg and backed away as Bishop pulled himself into his chair. The wounded bank president's face was bright crimson. His always immaculately coiffed hair was now starting to resemble a small rat king. He steadied himself in the leather chair and opened one of the desk drawers. He took out a bottle of aspirin and popped the cap open with his thumb.

"Would you like some water?" Flynn asked.

Bishop grunted. He tossed three pills into his mouth. Seconds later he clutched his throat.

Flynn watched him flail for a few moments. "Are you all right?" he asked.

The aspirin stuck hard in Bishop's throat. "Gagh!" he gasped. He threw the bottle of aspirin at Flynn, bouncing it off his forehead. Bishop continued to gag and pointed at the water jug. Flynn rubbed his head and went over to get the jug.

"I asked ya if you wanted some water," he mumbled. He filled a tumbler with water and handed it to Bishop.

The bank president gulped it down like someone who had been lost in the Sahara for a week. He drained it and handed the glass back to Flynn who refilled it. Bishop coughed twice and wiped his mouth with the sleeve of his jacket. He cleared his throat and pointed at the suitcases on the floor. "I'm going to need you to help me with these suitcases tomorrow," he said when he finally regained his voice.

"Plannin' a trip, are ya?"

"No, I want you to move them to the vault."

"You want to move suitcases to the vault?" Flynn was surprised. "What's in 'em? The Crown Jewels?"

"None of your business what's in them."

"Do ya want me to get the guards — "

"Goddamn it Flynn. I want you to come in tomorrow — at ten — to move these fucking suitcases."

"What about moving them right now?"

Bishop rubbed his forehead. "Oh my God. You're really stepping on my last nerve, Flynn."

Flynn looked at the suitcases and shrugged. "Okay boss. Whatever you say. I'll meet you here at ten then."

As Flynn turned to leave, Bishop spoke again. "That's ten in the morning, right?" Flynn flashed him a toothy grin. "You betcha boss. See you at ten."

"And Flynn," added Bishop. "Knock off that Emerald Isle crap. You're from Flatbush, for Christ's sakes."

CHAPTER TWENTY-ONE

Outside of the Beatles' suite at the Plaza hotel, Genevieve Doupierre looked at the time while Gary impatiently brushed his suit. "That crowd outside was crazy," he said as he flicked away at his jacket. "I've never seen so many teenagers in my life."

"Dere were a lot of kids, sure," Genevieve said. "I dunno how dey get anyone in or out of dis 'otel."

"Look what they did to this jacket," he muttered.

"Why don't you knock on de door again?" Genevieve asked. "I 'av a million teengs I need to do back at de h'office."

"O-ffice." Gary continued to preen and brush the lint from his coat. "There's no 'h'."

"Maudit Saint-Sacrament!"

"Do I look all right?" he asked.

"Tabernac, I do h'it myselfs," Genevieve said. She raised her hand to knock on the door when, without warning, it swung open. A young man in his twenties grinned at them.

"Scared ya, did I?" the young man said in a thick Liverpudlian accent. "I saw yer both through the peephole. You're here to see Brian, then?"

Gary nodded and extended his hand. "My name is Gary Cooper. I'm from the Ed Sullivan show." Genevieve jabbed him in the side with her elbow. "Sorry. This is my personal assistant, Guinevere."

The young man shook Gary's hand and smiled. "Gary Cooper, eh? Yer my favorite actor." He turned to Genevieve. "What a beautiful name. Like King Arthur's wife, eh?"

"Mais, non," she said glowering at Gary. "It's Genevieve, calisse."

The young man stuck out his hand to the assistant. "Pleased to meet you Miss Calisse." Genevieve shook her head. "Non, it's not 'Calisse.' It's —" She sighed.

"Never mind." The young man continued. "The name's Aspinall. You can call me Neil. Come on in." They followed him inside. The room was overflowing with a collection of friends, acquaintances and general hangers-on. Genevieve nudged Gary and pointed. He looked over and saw Brian Epstein speaking with two important looking men in dark suits. A grateful smile broke out on Brian's face when he spotted Gary. He left the two men and came over. "Hello, Mr.Cooper. Thank you for saving me."

"Lawyers?" Gary asked.

"It's that obvious, eh?" Brian ushered Gary and Genevieve to a pair of chairs at a small table. "So, is everything arranged for my boys?"

"Absolutely," Gary said. "We'll send the cars on Sunday afternoon for a run through of the material. We can bring them back here for a rest and then, later on, we'll send the cars again at five-thirty for the show."

"I have a concern," Brian said. "I wonder if there's another way to get to the studio."

"Another way?"

"You saw the pandemonium at the airport today, and you must've seen the crowds downstairs when you came in."

Gary nodded. Brian glanced over at George Harrison who was leaning back in a chair with his feet on a small coffee table watching television. "George," Brian called out, "could you please do that window thing for Mr. Cooper?"

"Sure thing Brian," he said. He went over to the window. He opened it and stuck his head out into the cool winter air. A few seconds later, Gary heard a low rumble that was almost immediately transformed into high-pitched shouting.

"What in God's name is that?"

Brian smiled. "That would be the sound of a thousand screaming teenage girls. Every time one of the boys sticks his head out the window, the girls below lose their minds." He gave George a small nod. "Thank you, George."

Without warning, John jumped out of his chair. "You haven't seen this yet, Brian."

He began backing up toward the window as he fumbled with his belt buckle. Brian's face registered horror as John bent over and looked like he was about to drop his pants.

"That's quite enough, John." Brian shook his head. "Please don't tell me that you've done that before."

John shrugged. “All right then, I won’t tell ya.” He winked at Genevieve, making her blush.

“Do you see what I mean, Mr. Cooper? As soon as those girls see the limousines it will be chaos.” He nodded toward John and Paul, who were softly strumming their guitars. “Getting around is always a problem. One time we had to escape into a nearby fire station. The boys had to slide down the pole. We made our getaway in a police car while one of the fire engines created a diversion, I kid you not. Another time we used a laundry lorry.”

“Lorry?”

“Oh, I’m sorry. I guess you Yanks call it a ‘truck’.” He chuckled. “The odor of dirty nappies was a little overpowering, for our taste.”

“Laundry truck, huh?” Gary murmured.

His thoughts were interrupted by the appearance of Ringo Starr. His distinctive hair was disheveled and his sad eyes were cast at half-mast. He took the chair beside Brian.

The Beatles manager put his hand paternally on the drummer’s shoulder. “Did you have a good rest?”

Ringo nodded and yawned. “I needed that,” he said, punctuating ‘needed’ with an exaggerated stretch. “It was a hard day’s night last night.”

John stopped in mid-strum. He turned to Paul. “Have yer got a pencil?”

“Do you think it will be possible to arrange an alternate mode of transportation, Mr. Cooper?” Brian asked.

Gary thought about it for a moment. “Let me look into it and I’ll see what I can do.” Brian smiled. “I appreciate that, as do the boys. I would like to thank you and Mr. Sullivan for everything you’ve done. This is a very big moment for us.”

Gary grinned. “Oh, it’s a big moment for us too. Mr. Sullivan is very excited about the show. Ever since he saw the crowds going wild for your boys a few months ago at Heathrow, he’s been looking forward to this.” He leaned in. “We think this’ll be bigger than Elvis.”

Brian leaned back in his chair, with his hands locked behind his neck. “I am not one who is prone to hyperbole, but I think you may be right.”

CHAPTER TWENTY-TWO

Sonny lay on the sofa, partly watching, mostly ignoring, the TV in the corner. He turned the thing on more for the light and ambiance. He tried watching it but found it beyond boring. It was crazy to think that everyone would be glued to these things Sunday night. The sound of the door opening caught his attention. Sarah, arms laden with paper grocery bags, struggled to get the key out of the lock. Sonny started to get up to help her but a spasm of pain ripped through his back.

"Don't worry, I've got it," she said tossing the keys on the counter. "And don't move. I need you to get better in a hurry, knucklehead." She carried the bags into the kitchen and dropped them on the table. "Here," she said as she threw him a bottle of Aspirin.

He caught it with his left hand and tapped out two pills into his right. Sarah brought him a glass of water. Sonny propped himself up and swallowed the pills.

Sarah gave him a sardonic smirk. "So, Donald Jackson, how's the back?"

"Donald Jackson?"

"Figure skater. You both have the same moves on the ice. That is if he fell on his ass all the time."

"I told you skating wasn't a good idea."

"Not the way you do it." She went back into the kitchen and unpacked the bags. "You'll like this. Your best friend, Edward Bishop, got hit by a car."

Sonny smiled. "No shit? Please tell me he's in traction."

"No. But he busted up his ankle pretty good."

"Yeah?" Sonny said without a trace of compassion. "How 'bout some coffee?"

"You should have seen him," Sarah said. "It looked so good on him, limping around the bank." She took a mug out of the cupboard and poured Sonny a cup of coffee. "And that's not all. I think we're dealing with more cash than I thought."

"Really?" Sonny asked.

Sarah gave him a coy glance. "I'm not sure, but a conservative estimate might be around four million. Maybe even five or six, I don't know."

Sonny choked. "Are you serious?"

"Could be."

"How do you know?"

"I was in his office today and saw the suitcases. Normally there are only about four or five. Today I counted fourteen. Fourteen."

Sonny straightened up on the sofa, ignoring the sharp, stabbing pain that hugged his spine. "Holy crap. I think I just wet myself."

Sarah turned down the volume on the TV and flopped into a chair opposite Sonny.

"Whew! What a day today," she said breathlessly.

"Rough day at work?"

Sarah frowned with a mirthless smirk. "Anytime I have to deal with Seamus Flynn, it's a rough day."

"Who's Seamus Flynn?"

"He's the head of security for the bank. Edward went home early because of his ankle, but before he left he asked me to go and get Seamus Flynn." She sighed. "That man really tries my patience."

Sonny made a fist and mimed punching it into his open hand. "Did this guy bother you or something? I could have a little talk with him if you want."

Sarah smiled.

"It's nothing I couldn't take care of. A nice cup of hot coffee to the testicles did the trick. I tell you, I would have loved to have been a fly on the wall in Edward's office just to watch Seamus explaining how he his wet pants." She giggled. Sonny loved her laugh. It was girlish and sweet and filled with genuine humor. At that moment, he realized just how much he had missed the sound of a woman's laugh.

"You have a great laugh, you know," Sonny said.

"It's very cute." Sarah winked at him.

"No, you're cute."

Embarrassed, Sonny felt his face flush. He looked away. When he turned back Sarah had a curious look on her face.

"What is it?" he asked. "Something wrong?" She wrinkled her nose and knit her brow.

Sonny saw that she was deep in thought. "Are you okay?" he asked.

His question broke her concentration. "Sorry," she said.

"What is it?" Sonny asked.

Sarah shook her head dismissively. "Ah — it's probably nothing."

"It must be something. You were kinda gone there for a minute."

Sarah clasped her hands together and leaned forward in the chair. "Edward asked me to send Seamus to his office," she said, almost to herself.

"Yeah, you said that."

"It's just that he normally calls him on the phone because he hates dealing with him in person."

"How come?"

"Because the man is a dolt," she said matter-of-factly. "Edward has no patience for him at all. That's why he has me do all the face-to-faces with him." She gently bit her lip. Sonny noticed that whenever Sarah was deep in thought, she bit her lip. Another endearing trait Sonny loved about her.

He shrugged. "Okay then," he said. "So the worm had to deal with an idiot today. Good. He deserves it. Nice to know that — "

Something just occurred to him. His eyes bugged out and he promptly shot up straight on the sofa. He groaned loudly and winced. "Oh shit," he moaned.

"You can't jump around like that," Sarah warned. "You need to get better before Sunday."

Sonny put his hands to his head. "Fuck me," he muttered. "The suitcases."

"Yes, that's what came to my mind too."

"Sarah, this fucks up everything."

"No, it doesn't."

"Then why the hell would he bring this Seamus guy into his office?"

"Seamus is the head of security. And Edward is going to be away for a few days. It makes sense that Edward would want to see him."

"But if he was in Bishop's office, he woulda seen the suitcases."

Sarah stood up and eased Sonny back into the cushions of the sofa. "Please relax," she said and gave him a reassuring smile. "Even if he saw the suitcases, he doesn't know what's in them. And believe me, there's no way Edward would tell him."

"Are you sure?" Sonny asked.

"Absolutely. He never brings in that Irish potato head when he's doing a transaction." Sonny clutched the edge of the sofa. "Are you all right?" Sarah asked.

"My back is really messed up," he said through gritted teeth.

Sarah sat down next to Sonny and put her arm around his shoulders. "Baby, you have to relax."

Sonny's mouth fell open. "Oh Jesus — what if that asshole wants to move the suitcases to the vault?" he asked.

"Now you're being paranoid," Sarah said.

"But maybe that's why Bishop wanted to talk to that Seamus fuck. His ankle is busted and he needs help to move them." His mounting anxiety wreaked havoc on his back.

Sarah smiled again. "You're getting all worked up over nothing," she said in her most comforting tone. "The more I think about it the more I'm convinced that it's nothing. It's just protocol because Edward is going to be away."

"Okay. But what if — "

Sarah interrupted him. "Look, if you want, I can check it out. I'll go down to the bank tomorrow morning. The vault's on a timer that won't open until after eleven o'clock. I'll get there before then and keep an eye on things."

"What if someone sees you?"

"Nobody will see me. If I run into any of the guards I can tell them that I'm there to run an errand for Edward because of his injury."

"I really don't like this."

"I'm telling you, it will be fine."

She rubbed the back of his neck. "I'll take care of everything."

"Yeah, but — "

"Just shut your trap and pucker up." She brushed her lips against his, nibbling on his bottom lip as her hand traveled along the inside of his thigh.

Without warning, he jolted forward off the sofa. His head shot out and struck Sarah in the forehead, knocking her to the floor.

"Jeee-sus Kee-rist!" he gasped. He tried to straighten up but his back was bent over in a ninety-degree angle. Pacing wildly around the room, he looked like Groucho Marx.

"Are you happy now? You're all stressed out for nothing and now your back has seized up." She rubbed her head. "My turn for the aspirin," she groaned.

As she reached for the bottle on the table, she knocked over a magazine. A shiny circular object underneath it fell to the floor with a loud metal ping.

"Hey," Sarah said. "What is this?"

"What's what?" Sony asked. "I can't see anything but the goddamn floor."

"This." She held out a silver dollar with a ribbon taped to it in front of his face. "It fell off the coffee table."

"Oh." He rubbed his lower back. "That."

"Is this supposed to be some kind of a medal?"

He tried to turn his head around to see her but he couldn't do it without sending a sharp sting through his spine. "Could you please help me to the sofa?" he pleaded.

Sarah took his arm and helped him on to the spongy cushions. "Ah, that's good," he said. He saw Sarah holding the faux medal and he gave her a sheepish grin. "Yeah, kinda stupid, right? I just thought about you skating today and how you said you missed your chance at the Olympics and everything. You were so good out there that I thought that you — well, you deserved a medal. So — I made you one." He looked into her deep brown eyes. They were brimming with tears. "Oh God. You're not going to cry, are you?"

She wiped the tears away from the corner of her eyes. "This is the sweetest thing anyone's ever done for me." She leaned over with her arms outstretched and embraced him.

"My back!" he cried.

Sarah stopped and instead placed one arm gently around his shoulder while she studied the silver dollar medal. "Where did you get the ribbon?"

He eased his back into the sofa's cushions. "Found it in a drawer."

"Uh-huh. And where did you get the silver dollar?" She ran her thumb over the coin and eyed him with mock suspicion. "You don't have any money."

With all the self-consciousness of a kid caught in the bathroom with a nudie magazine, he shifted uncomfortably in his seat. "Yeah. I found it on your dresser. Sorry."

"Once a crook, I suppose," she said with mock seriousness. Sonny shifted again on the sofa. "What's wrong with you?" she asked. "Why do you keep moving around? You'll really mess up your back if you keep doing that."

Sonny angled his body again.

She eyed him with suspicion. "Something on your mind?" she asked.

"Yeah, actually there is," he responded. He looked down at his hands.

Sarah reached over and lifted up his chin like a mother with a recalcitrant child. She looked into his eyes. "Are you going to tell me or are you just going to keep fidgeting like a five- year-old in church?"

"All right. Can I ask you something?"

"Of course," she said. "Anything."

Sonny took a deep breath and asked, "Are you married?"

Sarah blinked. "What?"

Sonny took another deep breath. "Are you married?" he asked again.

Her eyes flashed. "Why are you asking me that?" she asked, her voice tinged with irritation.

Sonny reached into his pocket and fished out a shiny, gold wedding band. "I found this on your dresser when I was looking for the silver dollar." He placed the ring on the table and watched her as she got up and moved toward the window.

She traced her finger along the frost-covered glass. "No, I'm not married." Defensiveness replaced the annoyance in her voice.

"But you used to be?"

"I was."

"For how long?"

She sighed. "I'm divorced. For about a year now." She sat in the chair opposite him and reached for the ring. She placed it over the end of her index finger and ran her thumb along its smoothness. "I'm not comfortable talking about it."

Sonny scratched his head. "I'm sorry Sarah. It's just when I saw the ring, I thought, well — you know."

Her eyes flashed again. "I said I'm not married. Now, can we just drop it?"

The anger in her voice cut Sonny deeply. "I'm sorry," he said again. He felt like a heel. "I shouldn't pry. I just—"

Without a word, she dashed into the bedroom, slamming the door behind her. Sonny cringed as spasms raced down his back. The pain was nothing compared to how miserable he felt.

I'm such an asshole, he told himself. It was none of his business. All that his stupid question and his lack of tact managed to do was to get her pissed off at him. He contemplated going into her room to see if he could soothe her feelings but he thought it would just make the situation worse. Plus, the idea of getting up off the sofa felt like it might be impossible. He shifted slightly and tried to watch the television again. The news had started. The volume was low but he easily recognized the four now-familiar faces beaming at him.

"Hello, boys." He gave the TV a tiny wave. Although he could barely hear the music accompanying the film, he recognized the song as one Tommy played repeatedly on his phonograph player. It was something about knowing that she loves you and that you should be glad.

"Nice try fellas," he murmured as he closed his eyes and lay back on the couch.

CHAPTER TWENTY-THREE

Saturday, February 8, 1964

Sonny opened his eyes. As the sun streaked through the window and danced across his face, he felt much more invigorated. When he moved to sit up, a dull twinge near his ass jolted him, making him realize that he'd fallen asleep on the sofa. Not that he'd had any choice in the matter anyway. Sarah made it clear the night before that sleeping in her bed was out of the question.

The television was still on. His gaze drifted up to the window and the now brightened doodle that Sarah had drawn. The oil from her finger left the design, which appeared to be a figure eight. It reminded Sonny of Sarah's figure skating performance yesterday. He thought about how good she was and how happy he had been watching her. For the first time in a very long time, he really knew what it meant to be happy and now he'd possibly blown it.

So what if she didn't tell him that she had been married? It was over so what was the problem?

Sarah made him happy and that's all that mattered. It was time to make things right.

He slowly got up from the sofa. He pleasantly noted that in spite of the odd stitch and twinge, his body wasn't the aching mess it had been the night before. He gingerly walked towards the bedroom and tapped on the door.

"Sarah? Can we talk?"

There was no response. He knocked again.

"Can you please open the door?"

Still no response. Maybe she was still asleep. Either that or she was still mad as hell at him. Deciding to chance it, he nudged the door open and peeked inside.

The room was empty except for a note on her pillow.

Sarah sat in a booth by the window at Mike's diner. She sipped her coffee and thought about Sonny and their conversation the previous night. Her wedding ring lay on the grimy table next to a coffee stained saucer. She nudged it with her finger, trying to decide whether or not to call Sonny.

He had no business going through her things, damn it. Her secrecy about her marriage was for his own good after all.

She turned to look out the window just in time to observe the arrival of a cab pulling up across the street at the Hudson. She watched Edward, leaning heavily on his crutches, get out of the cab. Furtively, he scanned the street. She followed his gaze until she saw Seamus Flynn scurrying toward the bank.

Oh no, she thought. Maybe they were going to move the suitcases to the vault after all. It looked like Sonny may have been right. She grabbed the ring, threw a few coins on the table and ran out of the diner.

Sonny snatched the note from Sarah's pillow and skimmed it. It said that she'd gone to Mike's Diner. She just needed a little time to herself and that she would talk to him later. Sonny thrust the note into his pocket, grabbed his coat and rushed out of the apartment. He boarded the first downtown bus that came along. He was irritated to find that it was overflowing with loud Saturday shoppers. There were no empty seats available. Much to his annoyance, he seized a strap and stood in the aisle. The constant stopping and starting of the bus began to amplify the stitches and twinges in his back. He needed to sit down before his back went into spasm. He spied a teenager, wearing a smirk on his face and a Beatles shirt under his winter jacket, sitting a few feet away. On the seat next to him was a bag.

"Hey, kid," said Sonny. "You mind moving your bag so I can sit down?"

The kid turned his head and stared out the window.

"I said, 'Hey kid,'" Sonny called to him again, this time louder, "do you mind moving your bag so I can sit down? I have a bad back."

The kid gave Sonny a bored stare. "You have a bad front, too."

The bus lurched. Sonny took the opportunity to step forward and ground his heel into the kid's toe. The kid yelped like a Yorkshire terrier that just dragged its nuts through a briar patch.

"You did that on purpose, you old asshole."

"Sorry, kid. Told you I had a bad back. Sometimes it spasms and I can't control myself." He jerked his arm and caught the kid in the ear with his elbow. "See? Same thing with my arm."

The kid rubbed his ear and gave Sonny a dirty look. "Asshole. Ya still can't have the seat."

Bishop stood in front of the bank checking his watch when he saw Flynn coming up the road.

"Move it," Bishop yelled. "We haven't got all day."

Flynn jogged up to Bishop, grinning ear to ear. "I'm sorry, Eddie," he said, slightly out of breath. "Bit of a late one last night, I'm afraid. You know what the Irish say, 'In heaven, there is no beer, that's why we drink it here.'"

Bishop rolled his eyes. "Look, I'm not in the mood for the blarney bullshit today. We have work to do."

The two of them headed around to the back of the bank. As soon as they were out of sight, Sarah rushed across the street. Her focus on the two of them made her unaware of the city bus that barreled toward her on the slushy street. The bus driver quickly braked, sending the oversized vehicle into a slide. The sound of the bus's brakes caught Sarah's attention.

"Oh my God," she squealed.

Inside the bus, Sonny gripped the strap with both hands. Dozens of passengers fell to the floor like bowling pins. The bus slowed to a stop about ten feet from Sarah. She gave a small wave to the angry driver. He responded with his middle finger and a string of longshoreman-like cursing.

"Fuckin' idiot," seethed the driver.

"What happened?" someone shouted.

"Some stupid broad with a death wish just ran out in front of me." The driver pointed out the window. "Look at her. There she goes."

Sonny followed the direction of the driver's finger and was astounded to see Sarah loping the rest of the way across the street toward the Hudson.

What the hell?

"Hold on, I'm getting off here!" he shouted. As Sonny dashed to the front of the bus, he made sure to give the kid in the Beatles shirt a boot in the shins along the way.

Sarah cast a furtive peek around the corner and watched Flynn unlock the rear door for Bishop. Flynn held the door open for Bishop. They both went inside. As soon as Flynn let go of the door, Sarah sprinted across the slippery pavement. As quickly and quietly as she could, she raced up the steel steps. At the top, her boot slipped on some ice and to her dismay, she fell forward. The fall knocked the breath out of her and her chest felt as if it had caved in. She threw her right arm forward between the door and the jamb, halting its slow, closing arc. Remaining motionless for a few seconds, she closed her eyes tight and listened. When she was sure it was clear, she opened her eyes.

With tremendous effort, she rose to her feet, making sure not to let go of the door. She felt a sharp throbbing near her ribs. Disregarding the pain, she slipped inside the dark and empty corridor. A lone light at the end of the corridor was the only illumination.

Edward moves pretty fast for a guy with an injured ankle, she thought.

She hurried along the corridor until she reached the stairs that led to the main hallway.

With extraordinary stealth, she climbed the stairs until she reached the hallway door. The pane of frosted glass halfway up the door was impossible to see through, so Sarah pressed her ear against it. Hearing nothing, she carefully opened the door and poked her head around it. A warm glow spilled from Bishop's office, lighting up the end of the hallway. She inched her way forward until she was close enough to hear Bishop speak.

"Grab a suitcase, would you? We haven't got all day," she heard him say.

Oh no, she thought. *They are moving them.*

She caught her breath just as a shadow appeared in the doorway. Sarah backed up keeping her eyes on the shadow. She was too far away from the door at the end of the hallway. She knew she couldn't reach it in time. Frantic, she searched for an open door to an empty room. She discovered that the broom closet halfway down the hallway was unlocked. She swiftly stepped inside. Her heart thudded in her chest as Flynn stepped into the darkened hallway.

CHAPTER TWENTY-FOUR

Flynn, with a puzzled look on his face, stood outside of Bishop's office, clutching a suitcase with both hands. Something down the murky hallway caught his attention. He squinted. The hallway was dark but he was certain he saw someone moving in the shadows. With the exception of the guards patrolling the main part of the bank, there was supposed to be no one else in the building. He dropped the suitcase at his feet and reached for the flashlight hanging from his belt. He flicked it on and aimed it in the direction of the perceived movement. Playing the light into the darkest reaches of the hallway, he flashed the beam from corner to corner.

No one there.

Methodically, he moved down the hallway, checking each door along the way. He stopped in front of the broom closet. His lips twisted into a malevolent smile. Now here would be a good place to hide.

He shone the light against the pane of frosted glass and reached for the doorknob.

Inside the broom closet, Sarah held her breath and gripped the doorknob as tightly as she could. With her hands sweaty and trembling, she feared she wouldn't be able to keep it from turning. In horror, she watched the beam of the flashlight through the frosted glass as it increased in size. She felt the doorknob turning slowly in her hand. A loud noise at the far end of the hall stole Flynn's attention from the broom closet. He turned and shone the light toward the end of the hallway. The stairwell door slowly closed.

"I got you now, me boyo," he said with confidence.

He let go of the broom closet doorknob and slowly edged his way to the stairway door.

Bishop grew more annoyed by the second. He was on the phone with Cal Spencer. He gripped the receiver tight, his knuckles white and his face pink with ire.

"Goddamn it, just listen for one second Cal," he growled.

On the other end of the receiver, a clearly tired Calvin Spencer said, "Why are you moving them anyway? You told me that your office was safe."

"It is safe," Bishop snapped. "But I thought about it and I think that it's a lot of money to leave sitting out in the open like this." He cupped his hand over the mouthpiece. "Mob money," he hissed.

"Aren't you worried that someone might see fourteen suitcases filled with millions of dollars sitting in your vault? How do you explain that?"

Bishop let out a long, exasperated sigh and grabbed his bottle of Glen Mhor from off the shelf.

Flynn stood outside the door to the stairway. He decided that the best course of action would be to swiftly shove it open as hard as he could. He would hit whoever was standing behind it. He counted to three in his head. In a single motion, he spun the knob and threw all his weight against the door. Like a ballistic missile, Flynn flew through the doorway. His unfortunate trajectory cleared the top three steps. He hit the fourth step with his shoulder. He bounced upward, his collarbone crushed. Screaming in pain, he flipped over, feet first toward the bottom of the stairs. The back of his head smacked against the rest of the steps as he slid the rest of the way down.

The last thing he remembered before he lost consciousness was the image of a man smiling and waving at him as he sailed by.

Bishop was still on the telephone with Spencer when he heard the awful racket. On the other end of the phone, Spencer asked, "What the hell was that?"

"Hold on," Bishop said. He covered the receiver with his left hand and called out to Flynn. There was no reply. Bishop returned to his call. "It's that idiot Flynn. Who knows what he's done this time. Let me go find out and I'll call you right back."

"Don't screw this up, Eddie. Provenzano will have both of our heads if—"

"Yeah, yeah, I know." Cursing Flynn, Bishop hung up the phone and reached for his crutches.

Sarah opened the broom closet's door a crack and was astonished to see Sonny awkwardly treading down the hallway toward her.

"Sonny? What are you doing here?" she asked.

Sonny nodded toward Bishop's office and put a finger up to his lips as he slipped inside the closet with her. "Someone's coming."

Bishop stepped into the hallway and noticed the suitcase on the floor, but no Flynn. "Unbelievable," he said under his breath. He flicked on the main lights and observed that the door to the stairway at the end of the hallway was ajar. Behind him, he became aware of the sound of running footsteps.

Damn it, he said to himself. The guards. He jabbed at the suitcase with one of his crutches.

"Come on, you son of a bitch, move," he hissed.

The footfalls grew louder. Panicking and with every ounce of strength he could muster, he shoved the bag toward his office.

It moved slightly. "Get — in — there," he gasped.

He managed to get the suitcase inside the office when two guards came sprinting around the corner.

"Oh, it's you, Mr. Bishop," said one of the surprised guards. "Strange to see you here on a Saturday. We heard a noise."

"Hello Carlysle. Usher." Bishop said. "I was, uh — I'm here to pick up some papers from my office when Flynn went to do something — somewhere."

Carlysle raised his eyebrows. "Oh, Mr. Flynn is here too?"

"Um, yes. He's around here — I think," Bishop said nodding slightly. He pointed down the hallway. "I see that the door to the back stairway is open."

Carlysle jogged down the hallway toward the open door.

"It's Mr. Flynn!" he shouted. "It looks like he fell down the stairs."

"I wonder how that happened," Usher said.

Bishop leaned on one of the crutches and pinched the bridge of his nose between his forefinger and thumb. Of all the stupid —

Carlysle hurried down the stairs toward the prone security head. "He's all crooked," Carlysle shouted. He heard Flynn's low raspy wheezing. "Could you send Usher down here to help me?"

"Well, that's just terrific," Bishop mumbled. He turned to Usher. "Could you go give Carlysle a hand, please?" he asked in a flat monotone. As soon as Usher left to help, Bishop reached over and closed his office door. He locked it and limped his way down the hallway, all the while cursing out his incapacitated security chief.

He paused. What was Flynn doing anyway? He thought for a moment. Did that blarney babbling buffoon actually see something?

A few seconds later, Usher breezed past Bishop.

"Where are you going?" Bishop asked.

"We need to call an ambulance," Usher replied without turning around. "Mr. Flynn don't look too good."

Bishop ground his teeth in frustration. At the top of the stairs, he surveyed the scene. He called down to Carlysle. "Is he awake?"

Carlysle snapped his fingers in front of Flynn's face. The security chief stirred slightly.

Carlysle looked back up at Bishop. "I think he's unconscious, Mr. Bishop."

"Ask him what he was doing before he fell down the stairs."

"I don't think he can hear me, Mr. Bishop."

"Goddamn it, Carlysle! Just ask him what the hell he was doing before he fell down the goddamned stairs please!"

Carlysle shrugged and asked Flynn the question but Flynn remained unresponsive. He looked back up at Bishop. "He's out like a light, Mr. Bishop."

Bishop seethed. "Goddamn it," he muttered.

"Look here Mr. Bishop," Carlysle said, pointing to the odd angle of Flynn's shoulder. "I think he may have broken his collarbone."

"Perfect," Bishop responded bitterly. "Usher's calling an ambulance. Is there any way you can drag him up here? We'll need to bring him around to the front."

"Do you think it's a good idea to move him?" Bishop heaved a sigh. "Is he bleeding?"

Carlysle made a quick check. "No, I don't think so. He's got a bump the size of a robin's egg on the back of his head, though."

"Then he's fine. Just bring him up here."

Bishop hobbled back to his office when the third guard, Peterson appeared.

"What happened?" Peterson asked.

Bishop gave him a dirty glare. "Where the hell were you?"

"Having a crap." Peterson stared at Flynn at the bottom of the stairs. "Wow. Is that Seamus Flynn? What happened?"

"He fell down the stairs," said Carlysle. "Pete, come and give me a hand." Usher climbed down the stairs to help Carlysle with the crumpled security guard.

Bishop waved his crutch. "Now, can we please get him to the front door? The ambulance will be here soon."

Carlysle motioned to Peterson. "Let's go." He put his hands under Flynn's shoulders while Peterson grabbed Flynn's feet. The two of them lifted the inert security chief with a collective grunt and carried him up the stairs.

Bishop watched them as they headed down the hallway. Once they disappeared around the corner, he hobbled back into his office. He picked up the phone and dialed Calvin Spencer's number.

"You are not going to believe this," Bishop snarled into the receiver.

Spencer sighed. "What happened?"

"That moron Flynn just fell down the stairs."

"What!"

"I think that maybe he heard or saw someone and went to investigate." There was a pause at the other end.

"Well, was there someone there?"

"I don't know. I didn't see anybody."

Another pause. Finally, Spencer responded. "Is he all right?"

"How the hell would I know? They're taking him to the hospital."

"Jesus —"

"That man would fuck up his own name in a spelling contest. Now I'm not going to be able to get the suitcases to the vault."

"Just leave them where they are Eddie."

"But what if that bonehead did see someone?" Bishop drained his scotch and slammed the glass on his desk. "Can't you just get your ass over here and help me? You know I can't move them all myself. My ankle's fucked."

Bishop heard an exasperated grunt from the other end of the phone. "I can't leave right now," Spencer told him. "I'm helping my mother —"

Bishop interrupted him. "Are you kidding me?" Bishop raged.

"Fine," Spencer grumbled. "If you're so fucking paranoid, why don't I pick you up tomorrow night around eight thirty and you and I will move the suitcases. All right? Will that make you feel better?"

Bishop let out a long, agitated sigh. "Just don't be late, all right?"

"Okay then. Oh, and Eddie?"

"What?"

"Go fuck yourself. See you tomorrow."

Bishop snorted and hung up the phone.

"Asshole," he mumbled. He closed his office door and locked it. Before he turned off the hallway light he took one last look at the door at the end of the hallway.

CHAPTER TWENTY-FIVE

The ambulance was already waiting in front of the bank by the time Carlysle and Peterson struggled through the doors with their prone security chief. Two attendants were in the process of deploying the gurney when they saw the two guards. One of them held up his hands and rushed over to the guards.

"What do you think you're doing?" he demanded.

"We have an unconscious man here," Usher said.

"You should never move an unconscious person," the attendant scolded. "You can make things worse. He could have serious head trauma."

Usher noticed the attendant's nametag — Leonard Kowalski. "He could also freeze to death if you don't get him into the friggin' ambulance, Leonard."

Leonard stood in their way. "No, no, NO. We need to get him on the gurney."

"What's wrong with you?" Carlysle griped. "Let's just get him into the ambulance already."

Bishop stood by the front door watching the scene unfold. His patience was already severely thinned by the morning's events. "Children, please," he snapped. With a crutch, he pointed to Flynn, whose ass was starting to sag toward the snowy pavement. "Please get him out of here."

Even though it was quite cold, sweat coated Peterson's forehead. "C'mon guys. He's really, really heavy." Peterson's tongue stuck out like a dehydrated dog.

Leonard instructed the attendants to wheel the gurney over to the unconscious Flynn. "Get over there before they drop him in the snow."

One attendant grasped the security chief's shoulders and the other took hold of his knees.

They lifted Flynn on to the gurney, wheeled him to the back of the ambulance and shoved him inside. Flynn stirred. A small groan escaped his lips.

"Hey," Carlysle said. "Flynn moved. I think he's awake."

Bishop perked up. He shuffled as quickly as he could to the back of the ambulance.

He jammed his crutch between the doors as Leonard tried to close them.

"Hold on one minute," he said, pointing at Flynn. "I need to speak to him."

"You can speak to him at the hospital when he wakes up," Leonard said.

Bishop whacked Leonard on the wrist with the crutch.

Leonard scowled and clutched his wrist. "Owww. What did you do that for, you jerk?"

Bishop motioned to Carlysle to hold the door open. He hobbled closer to Flynn and leaned in so that his ear was close to the security chief's face.

"Seamus?" Bishop whispered. "Can you hear me?"

Flynn's eyelids fluttered opened, his pupils dilated. "Who's that?" he asked in a weak voice.

Bishop leaned in a little closer. "It's Bishop, Seamus. Tell me what happened."

"What I saw?" Flynn sounded like he had a mouth full of mud.

"What happened to you?"

Flynn blinked. "Who —is it?" he mumbled.

"It's Bishop," he bellowed.

"Ah. Then I am truly blessed." His words were slurred, his voice weak. Bishop cocked his head so that he could better hear what Flynn was saying. After a few moments, Flynn inexplicably blessed himself and passed out.

Bishop sniffed and shuffled away from Flynn. "All right. Where are you taking him?" he asked Leonard.

"Gouverneur Hospital, on Madison," the attendant replied curtly. He then added, "Asshole," and slammed the doors shut.

Carlysle sidled up to Bishop as the ambulance pulled away "Mr. Bishop," he said. "What did he say to you?"

Bishop watched the ambulance drive away. "He confessed his sins to me."

Carlysle's mouth fell open. "He what?"

"Apparently he thought I was a priest," Bishop said. He turned to Carlysle. "A bishop, actually. He wanted to confess his sins to me."

"You're kidding," said Carlysle hiding a smile.

Bishop continued. "No, I'm not. He told me that he often takes the Lord's name in vain and that he masturbates about three to four times a day." Carlysle and Usher exchanged amused looks. "It's no wonder you can't find the ignoramus when you need him," he muttered. Bishop hobbled into the street and flagged down a taxi.

Carlysle opened the door for him. "I sure hope Mr. Flynn is okay," he said as Bishop maneuvered himself into the back seat. "It's so strange that he fell down the stairs though. I wonder what he was doing?"

Bishop's eyes narrowed.

What was he doing, he thought.

"Where to?" asked the cabbie.

"Gouverneur Hospital on Madison," he said. "As quick as you can."

It was twenty minutes since the commotion outside the broom closet subsided. Sonny had his back jammed up against the inside wall. A mop handle was wedged against his already aching spine. He pressed his ear up against the opaque glass of the closet door and listened.

Sarah started to speak but Sonny put his finger to his lips. "Wait a minute," he whispered.

He pressed his ear up against the crack between the door and the jamb. Convinced the hallway was finally empty, he twisted the door-knob. With a tiny creak, he pushed the door open and peeked out.

The hallway was empty.

Sonny motioned to Sarah to follow. "We better get the hell out of here."

"Couldn't agree with you more," Sarah said. She swerved around him and made a beeline for Bishop's office.

"Hey," Sonny hissed. "What the hell are you doing?"

Sarah jiggled the doorknob. "It's locked."

She reached into her purse and fished out her copy of the office key. She unlocked the door and pushed it open. She was relieved to see the suitcases still lined up by Bishop's desk and smiled. "Everything's fine," she said. Sonny tiptoed over to Bishop's office to look for himself.

"Great," he said breathing a little easier. "Now, let's get the fuck out of here before someone sees us." He grabbed Sarah's hand and the two of them made their way toward the rear stairway.

Outside the bank, Sonny and Sarah shivered in the cold February air. Sonny figured it was more from the adrenaline rush rather than the drop in temperature.

"I thought we were done for in there," Sarah said. "It's a good thing you came when you did."

"I got your note and was coming to meet you at the diner. I was also on the bus that almost plastered you all over the pavement."

"Yes, that was a close one wasn't it?"

"What were you thinking? You coulda been killed."

"When I was in the diner, I saw Edward get out of a cab in front of the bank. My heart leaped into my mouth. I thought that maybe you were right about Edward moving the suitcases."

"Jesus, that was crazy. As soon as the bus skidded to a stop, I saw you running to the bank. I figured something was up."

"It's a good thing you followed me. When I saw Seamus coming down the hallway I —"

"Seamus?" asked Sonny. "So that was the guy who took the header down the stairs."

Sarah covered her mouth with her hands. "Oh my God. Seamus fell down the stairs?"

Sonny chuckled. "I saw you duck into the broom closet. Then I saw this guy with a big red mustache and he was sure as shit going to find you. So I had to distract him."

"Distract him?"

Sonny grinned. "I made a noise by the stairway door. I was going to clock him when he came through the door but instead the dimwit jumped through the door."

Sarah's eyes widened. "Are you serious?"

"Bounced all the way down the stairs."

"Oh my God," Sarah said. "I hope he isn't too badly hurt."

"Well, his shoulder was all stuck out like a widow's hump and he was kinda twisted too. He was groaning though, so at least he's not dead."

"After all those times he made my life miserable, I find it a little hard to find sympathy for him," Sarah said. "At least we know that those suitcases aren't going anywhere." Sarah winked. "Until Sunday, that is." She gave Sonny's arm a squeeze and kissed his cheek. "You're going to meet Morrie at Finn's, aren't you?" she asked.

"I was. I was hoping to talk to you about last night first. I feel terrible about what happened."

She kissed him again. "Do me a favor and go meet Morrie. I'll meet you there later," she said. When she saw his confused look she said, "I just need to take care of a couple of things. I'll be there soon. Just relax, okay? Everything is fine." She headed toward the street, quickly making her way along the slushy sidewalk. Within seconds she was gone.

The cold wind nipped at his ears as Sonny turned up the collar of his coat. His back was on fire and the brisk weather that made him shiver was only making things worse. He shuffled through the snow and hailed a taxi. As he got in the cab, he heard the radio blasting out a Beatles song. He turned his head and looked out of the rear window at the bank.

He smiled.

He couldn't wait for Sunday.

CHAPTER TWENTY-SIX

Morrie checked his watch again. He had already been at Finn's for thirty minutes and was starting to wonder when Sonny was going to show up. He signaled the waitress for another cup of coffee. His doctor told him that he drank too much coffee, but he figured it didn't really matter now. Coffee was one of the few pleasures he had in the final stage of his life.

A cough rose in his chest. He tried to stifle it but it was a losing battle. The rattle pushed its way through his throat. The hacking lasted long enough to make the few patrons in the bar stare in his direction.

The waitress returned with the coffee pot and refilled his cup. "Are you okay?"

He pulled out a handkerchief and wiped his mouth.

"Yeah." He held up his water glass. "Went down the wrong hole."

She touched the corner of her own mouth and then pointed at his. He put his hand up to his mouth and felt a slight dampness. When he looked at his fingers, he saw blood on them.

"I bit my tongue. I'm fine."

The waitress shrugged and headed back to the bar as Morrie dumped spoonfuls of sugar into his cup. Stirring his favorite brew, he thought about his last visit with the doctor.

The news wasn't good. The doctor was predicting six months, at best. He didn't tell anyone of the diagnosis, not even Gary, preferring not to burden anyone. He lifted the coffee cup to his lips and took a small sip. The warm liquid was delicious but it burned his chafed throat.

"Hello," a female voice said. "Mind if I sit down?"

Morrie looked up into two of the bluest eyes he had ever seen. She had a short, strawberry blond bobbed haircut. While stylish, it didn't hide the fact that she wasn't in her twenties anymore. Or thirties for that matter. She has a pretty smile, he thought.

"Uh, sure." He was about to stand up but she had already seated herself. She limply held out two fingers. "I'm Chloe."

"I'm Morrie — Morris, that is." He took her limp fingers between his own index finger and thumb and shook them. Morrie thought he could detect the aroma of Houbigant Chantilly Paris perfume. It was the same scent that Gary's wife Louise wore, except that this was mixed with the distinct odor of Gilbey's gin.

"So, Morris," she said, "care to buy a gal a drink?"

Morrie checked his watch again. "It's early for a drink, dontcha think?"

Chloe flashed a smile. "Like they say, it's happy hour somewhere, right?" Morrie thought about that for a moment and nodded.

"Yeah, I guess it is."

"In London, it's like midnight or somethin', so right now they're pretty loaded," she said.

She was also kind of pretty. Sort of.

Keeping his gaze on Chloe, Morrie waved to the waitress. She rummaged through her purse.

"You from New York?"

"Oh yeah. I grew up a few blocks from here."

She took out a pack of Newport cigarettes and slipped one between her lips. Morrie took a matchbook from the ashtray and lit her cigarette. She thanked him and exhaled in his direction, causing Morrie to cough. He prayed that it wouldn't turn into a huge jag.

"Oh, I'm sorry, Morris." She waved the smoke away from him. "Where are my manners? Wouldja like one?" She slid the cigarette pack toward him. "They're filtered."

Morrie shook his head.

"I quit, actually," he managed to say between hacks.

"Really? I tried to quit once. It was really hard. Besides, I kinda like the way I look when I smoke." She took a long drag, sucked in her cheeks and made her eyes pop out. "I think it makes me look like Bette Davis."

Morrie thought it made her look more like Betty Boop. He did find the impersonation kind of cute, in an odd sort of way. When the waitress arrived Morrie ordered more coffee and Chloe ordered a gin and tonic.

"You sure you wouldn't like a coffee or a coke?" Morrie asked.

She shook her head. "Naw, I'm good. Hey, watch this." She took another drag off the cigarette and attempted to blow a smoke ring. It looked more like a fist.

"That's, uh interesting. So, what do you do, Chloe?"

She rested the cigarette on the side of the ashtray and rooted around in her purse again. Morrie wondered why it took so long to find anything in something that was half the size of a shoe box.

"I'm a secretary at Honeyman's Best Bakery," she said. "You know, take dictation, typing, get coffee. All that kind of fun stuff." She pulled a tube of lipstick out of her purse as the waitress arrived with their drinks. Morrie watched in fascination. She was able to apply lipstick across her thick, bow-like lips and speak at the same time. "It's kinda boring, though," she said.

She pulled out a tissue and blotted her mouth. "But, hey, it's work, right? Plus there's the fringe benefits."

"Fringe benefits?"

She tossed the lipstick back into her purse. "Oh yeah. I can get all kinds of pastries and cakes and bagels and things." She winked. "I gotta be careful, though. You know what they say — five minutes on the lips, a lifetime on the hips." She wiggled her rear end in the chair and took a long sip of her gin. "So, what do you do?"

"I'm, uh — " Morrie shuffled his feet under the table. "Actually, I'm retired."

"Really? What did you used to do?"

He glanced up at the small black and white TV over the bar. He noticed that the baseball flick *Angels in the Outfield* was on. "I was, uh, a baseball coach," he said.

"Baseball, huh?" she said. "I really don't know much about baseball."

Morrie breathed easier. The less she knew, the better the story. "Oh, it was just minor league stuff. Some of the guys did go on to make it in the major league, though. "

Chloe's eyes grew wider. "Really? Like who?"

This is fun, he thought.

"You ever hear of Mickey Mantle?"

She sucked in her breath. "You know Mickey Mantle?"

Morrie gave her a boasting grin. "Oh sure," he said, sipping his coffee.

She squealed. "Me too. I banged him once."

Morrie choked. "You what?"

She nodded with enthusiasm. "Yeah. My girlfriend told me he was some big time baseball player, but she told me after we did it. Three times in one night even."

All Morrie could come up with was, "He's a hell of a hitter."

"Don't I know it," Chloe responded with a sly smile. "So, you married or what?" She was very forward.

"No, I'm not," he replied.

Chloe took another sip of her drink. "I used to be. Darryl — that's my husband — he just recently passed on. Two months ago."

"Oh, I'm sorry to hear that."

"It's okay. I'm finally over it, I think. He had a stroke." Not exactly sure what to do, Morrie reached out and put his hand on top of hers. She sighed. "Well, ya see, we were screwing, and I was on top. Normally Darryl's on top, but he threw his back out the week before. Anyways, I was on top and then he made this weird face that I never seen him do before. Kinda like this." She stretched her mouth in an odd up and down slash and bugged out an eye. Morrie's jaw dropped open. "So anyways, he's makin' this face so I thought he was comin', you know, except he wasn't comin'. He was havin' a stroke." She leaned in close to Morrie. "Best orgasm I ever had though." She winked, lifted her glass to her lips and drained it, letting the ice cubes drop one by one into her mouth. She swirled them around for a few seconds and then with a playful grin, let them slip back into the glass. Morrie quickly drained his coffee and ordered two gin and tonics. They were into their third round when Morrie saw Sonny and Sarah come into the bar.

"Hey, look," Morrie said. "My friends are here." He stood up and took the empty chair next to Chloe, allowing Sonny and Sarah to sit together on the opposite side.

Morrie made the introductions. "Sonny, Sarah, this is Chloe."

Chloe held out an unsteady hand. "Howeryadoin?" It came out like a single word. "I'mdoinrealgood."

Sonny glanced at Sarah who was hiding a smile with her hand.

"Sorry we're late," he said. "We had to take care of some stuff this morning."

Morrie wasn't listening. His attention was fixed on Chloe, who was giggling at nothing in particular. Sonny reached over and touched his arm. Morrie made a slow turn toward him. "Hey, Morrie, can I see you for a minute? Over there, by the bar."

"Would you excuse us, ladies?" Morric said as he stood up. "Sonny needs to use the toilet, and I'm going with him. Get it? It's like when women go to the can, they always take a friend with 'em."

Chloe laughed and knocked the rest of her drink on the floor. Sonny sucked in an audible breath and led Morrie away from the table.

At the bar, Morrie ordered two more drinks. "What are you two having, Sonny?"

"Nothing right now. Listen, who's your friend?"

Morrie beamed like a kid who just discovered masturbation for the first time.

"Chloe? A girl I just met."

"Girl you just met? You two are pretty cozy."

"She's very friendly."

"Yeah, I bet she is. Are you sure she's not—"

"Not what?"

"You know — maybe after something else other than friendship?"

The smile dropped from Morrie's face. "Hey, wait a minute," he said in a low voice. "It's not like that."

Sonny held up his hands. "Morrie—"

Morrie's countenance continued to sour. "You're saying she's a pro."
Sonny sighed. "Well? How do you know she's not?"

"She told me."

Sonny rolled his eyes. "She told you she wasn't a pro?"

Morrie shook his head. "No, what I mean is that she's a secretary for Honeyman's Bakery. It's an honest job."

Sonny looked over at where Sarah and Chloe sat. Chloe seemed to be weaving back and forth in her chair. "How many drinks you buy her?"

"Just a couple. What's the big deal? She's a very nice lady and I'm enjoying her company." He sounded irritated. "And what's wrong with that?"

"There's nothing wrong with enjoying a lady's company. I just don't want to see you get screwed. No pun intended."

Morrie exploded. "She's not a pro!"

Almost every head in the bar spun around except for Chloe's. She was in the middle of a rambling anecdote with a thoroughly blank-faced Sarah.

Sonny scowled and put his index finger up to his lips.

"Shhh! Okay, fine. Keep it down, wouldja?" Morrie started to cough. He reached for his handkerchief.

He coughed a few more times and then lowered the handkerchief. Sonny noticed the spots of blood on it. He put his hand on Morrie's shoulder.

"Hey, buddy. Are you okay?"

Morrie lifted his head and nodded.

"Sure," he said. "Just a tickle in my throat." Sonny frowned and removed his hand from Morrie's shoulder. "Yeah. Okay then." Morrie cleared his throat. "Sorry for yellin' at you. It's been a kinda stressful week."

"Yeah. It's been a little crazy," Sonny agreed. He glanced over at Sarah and Chloe. Sarah stared back at Sonny, slowly crossing her eyes. Help me, she mouthed. Sonny turned back to Morrie. "How's about Sarah and I give you two some privacy. I'll talk to you later on."

Morrie nodded. "Thanks, Sonny."

He started to head back to the table when Sonny grabbed his arm. "I'm gonna need you in top form tomorrow night, so you take it easy, okay?" he said with a grin.

Morrie snickered. "Hey, I'll take it any way I can, right?"

Sonny laughed. Morrie never made off-color jokes. He gave Morrie a playful cuff on the arm. "You dirty bastard," he said grinning.

Morrie winked, picked up his drink order and swaggered back to the table. Sonny noted his confident strut. Sarah, who had been patiently listening to Chloe's incoherent yarn about her time with John F. Kennedy and the Peace Corps, noticed Sonny motioning to her. She rose and smiled at Chloe. "Very nice meeting you, Chloe."

"Thepleasure'sallmine," Chloe replied with half closed eyes.

Sarah gave a little wave to Morrie and with a worried look on her face, followed Sonny toward the door.

"Is he okay? I heard him coughing and it didn't sound very good."

"He's fine. Besides, I'm sure he's in good hands."

"Is she a nurse?" Sarah asked with slight sarcasm.

"No, but I'll bet she's got some interesting ways to check his temperature."

Sarah put her hand on his arm. "I told my mother I'd stop in to see her this afternoon."

"Your mother?"

"I meant to tell you earlier. I was going to go after I went to check out the bank. She's getting on and I try to see her at least once a week."

"Okay, you go ahead. I'll see you later."

"Could you pick up something for dinner and I'll meet you at home. We'll have a nice intimate night." Her eyes twinkled. "Just the two of us."

Home. It felt so good to hear her say it. His last home had bars on the windows, no exits and guards ready to crack his head open at any indiscretion.

"Sure," he said. "I'll meet you at home."

"Great." She gave Sonny a small peck on the cheek. "See you tonight."

Sonny watched her walk away and then turned in time to see Morrie and Chloe sharing a laugh.

Maybe it's not such a crazy world on the outside after all, he thought.

CHAPTER TWENTY-SEVEN

Bishop's cab rolled to a stop in front of Gouverneur Hospital. He tossed the driver a couple of bucks and got out. Using his crutches, he limped his way through the main doors. Just inside, a congregation of patients, doctors, nurses and orderlies puffed away on cigarettes as if it were their last smoke. He slowly headed toward the admitting desk through the hazy gauntlet.

Engrossed in a telephone call behind the desk was the admitting nurse.

"No, Stella. It wasn't like that at all." The nurse blushed and giggled. "He was a real gentleman. He showed me a real good time. No, he didn't show me that, although I wouldn't have complained."

Bishop tapped a crutch against the desk and cleared his throat. The nurse turned and put her hand over the receiver, moving it under her chin. "Can I help you?" she asked. Her tone indicated both boredom and irritation.

Bishop laid his crutches against the desk and said, "If it's not too much trouble —" He paused to read her nametag, " — Nurse Stankey, I would like to know where Seamus Flynn's room is located."

She glanced at the list in front of her. "Flynn. Yes. He's not receiving visitors." Without looking up, she returned to her telephone conversation.

Bishop reached over the desk and tapped her shoulder. "Excuse me. I asked you a question."

Nurse Stankey put her hand over the receiver a second time and glared at him. "I told you, he's not receiving visitors."

"That's not what I asked you? I asked you what room Seamus Flynn was in."

"And I told you, he's not —"

Bishop reached over and grabbed the beige colored handset out of her hand. "Hello, Stella? Nurse Stankey will have to call you back later," he droned into the receiver. "She has to get back to her job now or the doctors will have to surgically remove this telephone receiver from her big fat ass. Ta-ta." He dropped the receiver into the cradle with a clunk. He glared at the nurse. "Now, tell me where Seamus Flynn is."

Stankey's eyes burned a hole right through Bishop.

"I'm calling security!" She reached for a microphone under the ledge of the desk and flicked a switch with the nail of her thumb. A blast of feedback reverberated down the hall. "Security. Please report to the admitting desk." Within seconds, two orderlies clad in starched white shirts and black bow ties flanked Bishop. One of them, a large individual with hands big enough to palm medicine balls, took hold of Bishop's right arm. The other one, shorter but with shoulders wide enough to land a small airplane, grabbed his left arm.

"This is Cyrus and Oliver," said Nurse Stankey. "They'll help you out."

"Pleased to meet ya, I'm Cyrus," the larger man said. "Time for you to go." They started to drag Bishop to the main doors.

"My crutches," Bishop yelled. Cyrus nodded to Oliver who picked up the crutches. Cyrus hefted Bishop over his shoulder like a sack of laundry. He carried him like a crying infant through the entrance and deposited him outside by the curb.

"Next time we call the cops," Cyrus warned.

As he watched them go back inside, Bishop raged. "Bastards," he muttered. It was clear he wouldn't be able to get in through the front entrance. He turned his attention to the snowy grounds. He noted footprints trailing small wheel tracks leading around the perimeter of the building. He followed them and discovered that they disappeared into a locked side door. Upon closer inspection, he saw that it only appeared to be locked. He scanned the grounds. Satisfied that no one was around, he sneaked inside. He saw that the trail of snow continued down the hallway. He followed the tracks until he came upon an empty wheelchair with melting slush on the wheels. A thin, gray blanket lay bunched up on a nearby gurney.

Yes, this should do nicely, he said to himself. He placed his crutches under the gurney and slipped into the wheelchair. He covered himself up to his shoulders with the blanket. He rolled himself down the hallway, eyes darting back and forth watching out for Cyrus and Oliver. He spied a pretty young girl about twenty years old, dressed in a red and white pinafore. She was talking with a patient hooked up to an I.V.

A candy striper. Perfect. Bishop pulled the blanket up around his neck and coughed. The candy striper looked over at Bishop. She smiled and approached him.

"Hello," she greeted in a singsong voice. "I'm Candy. Can I help you?"

"A candy striper named Candy," Bishop said in a feeble voice. "How appropriate."

Candy giggled. "Oh, wow. I never thought of that. You're funny."

He gave her a pathetic look and coughed again. "Candy, dear, I do need your help. You see, I have a problem remembering things. I'd like to go back to my room, but unfortunately, I forget where it is."

"You poor man." Candy put a reassuring hand on his shoulder. "You must have magnesia."

"Magnesia?"

"Yeah, you know, that thing where you can't remember things."

"Er, yes. Well, my name is Flynn. Seamus Flynn."

"Well Mr. Flynn, let's see what we can do," she said brightly. Candy positioned herself behind the wheelchair and pushed him toward the admitting desk. He saw Nurse Stankey and immediately grabbed at the wheels.

"What's wrong?" asked Candy.

With a shaky hand, he pointed at Stankey. "That nurse scares me. I don't think she likes me very much."

"Why do you say that?"

"I asked her for an extra blanket and she told me to shut up or she'd give me an enema."

"She's very mean," she said. She patted him on the shoulder. "Don't worry. You wait here."

He pulled the blanket up to his eyes. He watched her rear end swoosh back and forth as she glided down the hall toward the admitting desk.

At the desk, Candy stood patiently in front of Nurse Stanky, waiting for her to finish her telephone conversation.

"No, Stella, I didn't say tall, I said big."

Candy drew tiny circles on the desktop with her index finger. Stankey looked up and saw Candy smiling at her.

"Hold on a minute," she said into the receiver. "I need to do a moron-ectomy."

"Oh, hey there Nurse Stanky," Candy greeted.

Stanky gave her an irritated glare. "What do you want?"

Candy bit her bottom lip and asked, "Do you have a piece of paper?"

The corner of Stankey's mouth lowered into a crooked scowl. "I thought I warned you about getting phone numbers from patients."

"Oh, it's not for me, Nurse Stankey. It's for a patient. He wants to write a letter — to, uh, his grandmother. She's dying and—"

Stankey waved her off. "All right Zippy, spare me the details." Stankey grabbed a pile of papers from the desk and shoved them at the candy striper. "Here, hold this." Candy took the sheaf of papers from the nurse. She saw that the admitting list was sitting on top. As Stanky searched her desk for a blank sheet of paper, Candy lifted the admitting list and waved it at Bishop. Candy noted Flynn's room number and then gave him the "a-okay" sign. A horrified Bishop pulled the blanket higher over his face. Stankey pulled out a long, yellow stenographer's pad. She ripped a sheet from it and slammed it down on the desk in front of Candy.

"Thank you Nurse Stanky," Candy said. She handed the pile of sheets back to the nurse and turned to leave.

"Oh, Princess?" Stankey said.

Candy spun around to see the nurse holding the blank piece of paper she had just asked for by the corner.

"Your sheet of paper," Stanky said. "Patient's dying grandmother, remember?"

Candy smiled and waved it off. "Oh, that's okay," she said. "She's getting better."

Stanky ground her teeth together as she watched the candy striper flounce away. "Idiot," she grumbled.

Bishop witnessed the whole scene unfold from under the blanket. Candy got behind the wheelchair and began to push it.

"You're in room 204," she said. "I'll take you there right now."

CHAPTER TWENTY-EIGHT

Candy wheeled Bishop down the hallway toward Flynn's room. Outside the door, she asked if he was all right to get back into his bed.

"I'm fine dear," he said. "Thank you so much for your help. I can manage from here."

A look of concern crossed the candy striper's face. "Are you sure you're all right? Can I get you anything — some water, or a chocolate bar or maybe some coffee?"

"Thank you, no. I'm quite all right."

"You know, I think a glass of milk would be good for you."

Bishop looked puzzled. "Milk?"

Candy smiled brightly. "For your magnesia."

With a tiny groan, Bishop declined.

Candy smiled one more time and offered a cheery "Toodle - oo."

He watched her curvy bottom and long legs glide away on their invisible skates until she disappeared.

"Incredible," he muttered. He turned his attention back to the room and slowly wheeled himself inside. The room was dark except for some light streaming through the Venetian blinds. Bishop wheeled himself over to the side of the bed and leaned in close to the dozing security chief.

"All right, Seamus," he said in a soft voice. "Wake up."

Flynn lay on the bed, his mustache vibrating from his soft snoring.

"Seamus?" Bishop tapped on the bedside table. "It's time to wake up." Flynn made a slight movement with his left arm. Bishop rapped louder on the table. "Flynn! Wake up!" he said in a louder voice. Flynn's left eye fluttered. Bishop reached over and began to rock the unresponsive security chief back and forth. "Wake the fuck up, stupid!" he yelled. Flynn's left eye opened half way. He stared up at the ceiling and then turned his head sideways until he was facing Bishop. He then opened the other eye half way.

"Well, hello, Eddie," he said in a weak voice. "What are you doing in my bedroom?"

Bishop noted that Flynn's fake accent was noticeably absent. "You're in the hospital, you moron. Now listen — tell me what happened to you."

Flynn looked confused. "What happened to me?"

"You fell down the stairs."

"I did?"

"Goddamn it," Bishop said with exasperation. "You fell down the stairs at the fucking bank."

Flynn started to drift off again. Bishop reached over, grabbed the security chief's shoulders and shook him. Flynn's eyes opened again, this time a little wider than before.

"Oh, hello, Eddie," he said. "What are you doing in my bedroom?"

Bishop violently rocked him back and forth. "Come on, you leprechaun-blowing moron," Bishop hissed.

Flynn rubbed his temples and grimaced. "Oooh, me head," he said, his accent making a triumphant, if unwelcome return. "I feel like I tied one on at McSorley's on a Friday night."

"Seamus, I need you to focus. I need to know what you saw," Bishop said. "It's very important."

Flynn blinked. He closed his eyes tightly, as if in deep thought. "I remember I was takin' the bags to the vault and I t'ought I saw — I t'ought I saw sometin' in the shadows at the end of the hall. I put the bags down." He scowled, taking a deep breath.

"Okay then," Bishop said. He took a deep breath and injected a soothing quality into his tone. "What else did you see?" he asked as if he were speaking to a five-year-old child.

Flynn expelled a long breath. "I t'ought I heard the doorknob by the stairway rattlin', so I snuck up to the door and grabbed it. I pushed the door open and then I went flyin' down them goddamn stairs."

"Did you see someone?"

"See who?"

Bishop smacked his forehead. "Goddamn it Flynn, would you please concentrate? Did you see anyone?"

Flynn closed his eyes. "All I remember was hittin' the bottom and then passin' out." Bishop leaned back in the wheelchair. Flynn was just a clumsy fool after all. All at once, the quiet of the room was shattered by heavy snoring. Flynn had passed out again. Bishop grunted and pushed himself away from the bed. He rolled toward the door. He then remembered his crutches.

"Oh shit," he said. He had left them on the gurney on the main floor. He hoped they'd still be there but if they weren't, he would have to steal a pair.

He opened the door and poked his head out. When he saw that it was clear, he started to roll out into the hallway. At that moment, Flynn opened his eyes and sat straight up.

"Wait a minute," he mumbled. "He was smilin' at me. The dirty, son-of-a-bitch was smilin' at me." He swung his feet out of the bed and on unsteady feet, stood up.

Bishop turned. "What did you say?"

The security chief swayed back and forth. "I do believe I need to sit down, son." He fell back and grasped for the edge of the bed. Instead, his hand found the curtains by the mattress' edge. As he fell, he pulled the fabric from their rings with a staccato popping noise.

Bishop wheeled himself back inside the room and closed the door behind him. "This is getting to be a real pain in the ass," he muttered. He grabbed a pitcher of ice water from the bedside table and dumped it straight into Flynn's face. The ice cubes bounced off Flynn's forehead like ping pong balls.

"Lord Jesus Christ in heaven, I'm drownin'," Flynn sputtered.

Bishop tossed the empty jug on to the bed next to Flynn's head. "No, you're not, blockhead. What did you just say about seeing someone?"

Flynn wiped the water from his face. "I did see someone, Eddie."

Bishop's eyes went wide. "You did? Do you know who it was?"

Flynn shook his head. "Never seen him before."

"What did he look like?"

"He was in his fifties, with kind of a round face and dark hair but with a little gray in it. Big fella. And he was smilin' at me." Flynn's face went dark. "The prick," he mumbled.

"You don't say?" Bishop said. He snatched up the telephone receiver and dialed the bank. "Carlysle," he snarled. "This is Edward Bishop. Listen, I'm coming to the bank."

"Really? I thought you were going to the hospital to visit Mr. Flynn," said Carlysle.

"I just saw him. He's fine. In fact, they're letting him out," Bishop said. "Now listen. With all that damned excitement this morning, I forgot my papers. I'll be there within the hour to pick them up." He slammed the phone down. He pointed to Flynn. "You. Get behind this chair and wheel me out. You're coming with me."

"Oh, I can't leave, dear boy."

"Why not?"

Flynn spun around and showed him the back of his hospital gown. "Me arse is hangin' out of this thing like some cheap tart's titties. I don't have me clothes."

An exasperated Bishop pointed to a chair next to the bed. "Aren't those yours?"

Flynn looked and saw his clothes folded on the chair. "Well, right you are," he said.

As Flynn changed into his clothes, Bishop fumed. So Sonny Carter was at the bank. That son of a bitch.

Once Flynn was dressed, he positioned himself behind Bishop.

"Here we go, my son," announced Flynn as he wheeled him straight into the door jamb.

Bishop grabbed his leg. "Jesus Christ, Flynn."

"Sorry boss. I'm a little dizzy."

Flynn re-aimed the wheelchair and pushed Bishop into the hallway. Bishop held the blanket up to his chin and kept a wary eye for Cyrus and Oliver.

"Flynn!" he hissed. "You just passed the elevator."

"Shhh," Flynn responded. "I'm lookin' for the elevator."

"Meathead! We passed it." Bishop grabbed at the wheels and screamed as the rubber tires burned his hands. "Goddamn it," he hissed. "STOP!"

Flynn leaned against the wall. Bishop looked at his hands. Two red striped impressions ran across his palms. "Back it up, you stupid prick."

"Quit movin'," Flynn said as he reached for the handles.

"I'm not moving, you idiot," said Bishop.

"Well, somebody is," Flynn retorted. He pushed the wheelchair in a wide arc. In the process, he scraped one of the wheels against the wall with a loud screech.

"Jesus, take it easy," Bishop said. At the elevator's control panel, Flynn took a few abortive pokes at the buttons. Bishop slapped his hand away. "Never mind. I'll do it," he said. He pushed the down button. When the elevator arrived, the doors opened and they entered the car.

"Okay, turn me around," ordered Bishop. "Now focus. Just wheel me outside like you work here, okay? And push me in a straight line this time."

"Notta probbem," Flynn replied, slurring his words. The elevator jolted to a stop. "Here we go," Flynn said as he pushed the wheelchair forward. He slammed Bishop into the unopened doors making Bishop howl in pain.

"Fuck." Bishop grabbed his leg. "Wait until the doors are open, stupid."

A low female voice grabbed his attention. "The doors are open, asshole."

Bishop saw Nurse Stankey with Cyrus and Oliver standing behind her. The orderlies reached in and yanked him out of the wheelchair.

Flynn jerked his head up. "So, there are four of you, eh?" he said. He held up his fists. "Is that what it takes? Four of you to take on ol' Seamus Flynn. Well, bring it on, me boyos,"

Cyrus and Oliver exchanged glances. "All right now, buddy, take it easy. You're seeing double. Let's get you back to your room."

Flynn's dilated eyes turned glassy and opened wide. "Not without a fight, son. Are ye prepared to go down?" In slow motion, Flynn shrank behind the wheelchair. His fists slowly opened up like flowers in the morning sun. Seconds later, Flynn was passed out on the floor of the elevator car, wedged behind the wheelchair.

"Please get him out of there, Oliver," ordered Nurse Stankey. She turned to Bishop.

"Well, it seems we can't get rid of you, now can we? If you like it here so much, then perhaps we can help you out."

Bishop recoiled. "You stay away from me," he warned.

Stankey winked at the two orderlies. "I think we need to keep you overnight for observation."

"The hell you will," Bishop said.

"Cyrus, could you help our friend here please?" she asked. Cyrus nodded and grabbed Bishop by his lapels. Bishop tried to escape the orderly's vise-like grip, but it was futile. Once Cyrus had Bishop immobilized, Stankey stepped forward. In her right hand was a large hypodermic needle.

Bishop gulped. "What the hell is that?"

"Something that will calm you down."

"You can't do this. Do you have any idea who I am?"

"I sure do," Nurse Stankey said. "You're the shithead who's ruining my day. Cyrus?"

The orderly yanked Bishop's arm forward. Stankey roughly rolled up his sleeve as Bishop fired off a string of invectives that would have made a teamster blush. She jabbed the needle into his arm. Bishop felt the liquid burn as it traveled through his bloodstream. Within seconds, his cursing trailed off, becoming a jumble of mumbled syllables.

"Put this asshole on a gurney," Nurse Stankey told Cyrus. She pointed to Flynn. "And get Sonny Listless over there back to his room."

Cyrus picked up Bishop and dropped him on the nearest gurney. "What do you want to do with this one?"

He noticed a gleam in the nurse's eye. "Hand me that phone," she said. Just before Bishop passed out, he heard Stankey dialing and then speaking in a faraway voice. "This is Nurse Ethel Stankey at Gouverneur Hospital. Get me the police."

CHAPTER TWENTY-NINE

Sunday, February 9th

Preparations were in full swing for television history. The Beatles, with Brian Epstein and Neil Aspinall, sat quietly in the dressing room. Gary paced up and down the room with Genevieve in tow.

Genevieve was drinking a bottle of Coca-Cola. She took a long pull on the soda and said, "Relax, calisse. You're wearin' out da carpet."

Gary continued to pace. "You know, the last time I felt like this, Louise was about to give birth," he said with a weak smile. "Except there weren't millions of people watching."

"Please sit down," Genevieve implored.

"My throat feels like sandpaper," Gary said hoarsely. Without thinking, Gary snatched the Coca-Cola bottle out of Genevieve's hands. She watched him drain the bottle. He muffled a small burp into his fist.

"Thank you," he said, handing the empty bottle back to her.

Annoyed, she tossed the bottle into a nearby garbage can. "Saint sacrament," she said.

Gary glanced over at the couch. George Harrison lay on the couch with his eyes closed. His skin was sallow and his breaths came out in uneven spurts. Brian poured a large glass of water and brought it over to the ailing guitarist.

"How are you feeling, George?" He handed him the glass.

George shifted into a half sitting position. Beads of sweat peppered his forehead. "I'm fine," he said in a weak voice. He laid his head back. "I'm a little tired, but the show must go on, right?"

Brian turned to Gary. "Where's the doctor?"

Gary pulled at his bottom lip and turned to Genevieve. "Any word yet?"

"He should be 'ere in cinq minutes," she said, fanning her fingers out. "I mean, five minute." She pinched Gary's arm. "Gary, you need to relax, calisse." In spite of her crustiness, Genevieve had a way of calming Gary down when he was on the verge of a meltdown.

She gave the others in the room a reassuring smile. "When da doctor get 'ere, h'everyting will be h'okay. You see." Without warning, the door flew open and a glowering Ed Sullivan tramped into the room.

Sullivan looked exactly as he appeared on television. He was short, with a balding head perched on top of a neck-less pair of hunched shoulders. His bony body was encased in a baggy suit jacket that looked slightly too big for him. His face was as rigid as an Easter Island statue.

Sullivan cleared his throat. "Boys," he said in his trademark nasal tone. "Are you ready to put on a really great show?" John and Paul exchanged glances. It actually sounded like he said "shoe."

John pointed at his feet. "Mr. Sullivan, you'll be happy to know that I've put on a really great pair of shoes."

Sullivan gave him a confused smile. "That's fine, fella," he said. He pointed at George. "Is that the sick one?"

"Yes, Mr. Sullivan," Brian said. "He may have the flu."

Sullivan's scowl deepened. "Goddamn it. I don't give a shit about the flu. Will he be able to perform tonight?"

"We are just waiting for the doctor, Mr. Sullivan," Gary said.

Sullivan aimed his cold stare at Gary. "Where is the doctor, Cooper?"

"We called him an hour ago," Gary said feigning confidence. "He should be here any second now."

Sullivan grunted and glared at George. He turned back to Gary and pointed a crooked finger at the ailing Beatle. "I want that guy on his feet in the next ten minutes, or else I'll put on a goddamn wig and stand up there myself."

Gary wiped his brow. "Yes, Mr. Sullivan."

The rest of the group watched in collective bemusement as the impresario departed in his awkward, stilted manner.

"Nice fella," a dead panned Paul said.

Gary rubbed the back of his neck. "Yeah, he's a real Prince Charming," he mumbled. The arrival of a short, pudgy man in an ill-fitting suit interrupted their discussion. "Are you the doctor?" Gary asked.

He held up a little black bag. "Are you the patient?" he replied.

"No, but I feel queasy," Gary said. He directed the doctor toward the couch-ridden Beatle in the corner of the dressing room. The doctor knelt down beside George and took hold of his wrist as he checked his watch. After a minute, he raised his eyebrows.

He reached into his bag and removed a thermometer. "Say, 'ah', young man."

In a weak voice, George said, "In England, we say, 'Where does it hurt?'"

"Open wide, please," said the doctor.

"I'm just glad you're not taking my temperature the way me Mum used to."

After a few minutes, the doctor announced that George had a one-hundred-and-three- degree temperature. "This man should probably be in a hospital."

A horrified look crossed Gary's face. "Oh, no. No, no, no. He has to perform in less than an hour. Can't you give him something?"

"He has a raging temperature and needs bed rest for a few days."

"You have to do something, Doctor," implored Gary. "There's going to be millions of people watching tonight. He has to perform." He turned to Brian. "Please talk to him."

"Give me a minute, please," Brian said to the doctor. Brian conferred with Neil. Both men whispered and nodded. "Okay," Brian finally said, "can you please do something for him, Doctor?"

The doctor shrugged his shoulders. "It's your call," he said. He opened his black bag and began to prepare a hypodermic needle.

Brian turned and put his hand on Gary's arm. "Is everything arranged for after the performance?" asked Brian. "With George feeling like this, I don't want him bothered by the usual chaos that's sure to follow."

"Don't worry," Gary assured him. "I've arranged for a truck. There will also be two limos that will leave right after the performance. That should fool anyone waiting outside. All of you can then get in the truck and it'll take you back to the hotel."

Brian shook Gary's hand. "I'd like to thank you for all your help, Gary. I can't tell you how much this means to me and the boys."

Gary wished them all luck. To his relief, the color seemed to be returning to George Harrison's face. George managed a small grin. "Shall we do this, Brian?"

Brian smiled. "You bet. Let's give them a night America shan't ever forget."

CHAPTER THIRTY

"I demand that you release me immediately!" Bishop awoke from his sodium pentothal fueled slumber spitting bullets. He perched on his good leg and gripped the steel black bars. His head pounded like he'd been clubbed with a baseball bat. The pain paled in contrast to his fury at waking up in a jail cell.

The desk sergeant, a tall, bespectacled man named Rutherford, looked up from his newspaper. "Pipe down idiot-stick," he barked. "You'll get out when I tell ya and not before."

"What about my phone call? I get a phone call, don't I? I demand my phone call."

Rutherford pushed his glasses up to the bridge of his nose and looked at the clock on the flaxen yellow wall. Bishop looked at the clock as well. It was seven-fifty.

He yelled again. "I want that phone call now!"

The desk sergeant dropped the newspaper on to the desk. He picked up a key and shuffled slowly toward Bishop's cell.

Bishop pounded on the bars. "I know my rights, you know. I'm supposed to get a phonecall."

"If you don't shut your piehole, you'll be using that call for a doctor," Rutherford warned.

He unlocked the cell door. "Pay phone's at the end of the hall." Reaching into his pocket, he fished out a nickel and flipped it to Bishop. Bishop caught the nickel, grabbed his crutches and hobbled as fast he could to the pay phone. He put the nickel into the slot and dialed. After two rings Cal Spencer picked up.

"Cal, It's me. Shut up and listen." Bishop covered the mouthpiece with his hand and peered down the hallway. Sergeant Rutherford was once again lost in his newspaper. Satisfied he wasn't being overheard, he removed his hand from the mouthpiece. "I'm in jail," he said. He grimaced. "Never mind why. Just get over here right now!"

Night covered the city like an inky blanket. Except for a few cars and the occasional pedestrian, the streets were eerily empty. Thanks to Ed Sullivan and the Beatles, New York had become a veritable ghost town.

A block away from the Hudson, the outline of a Honeyman's Best Bakery truck stood silhouetted against the winter moon. Behind the wheel of the truck sat a vigilant Bernie Miller. He let out a low whistle.

"Jesus, I've seen more people at Washington Senators ballgames," he said to himself.

In the back of the truck Al, Morrie and Sarah shivered in the cold. Sonny peered through the small window separating the cab from the rear of the truck. He figured that the streets would be empty but he was still impressed by the calm and quiet. Sarah and Gary were right. It looked like almost every single person in the city was crowded around their television sets at that moment.

Al cupped his hands together and blew into them. "Jesus, this truck is cold."

"Yeah, but it smells good," Morrie said. "I could really go for a doughnut."

Sarah checked her watch. "Okay, guys. It's time." She turned the latch on the door and pushed it open. She hopped on to the snow-covered pavement, closely followed by the others.

Sarah unlocked the bank's rear door. "All right," she said, "there's a stairway with a door at the top. The door leads to the hallway that will take you to Edward's office. Right now, just go inside and wait by that door. I have to open it up from the other side so I need to go around to the front to get in. I'll see you in about two minutes."

Usher and Peterson settled themselves in the lunchroom, waiting for the show to begin.

Usher sat at the table nursing a Coke. Peterson was flopped on the sofa like a beached walrus. A bag of pretzels spilled out on his stomach. Carlysle entered the room and went to the fridge. "Has it started yet?" he asked as he grabbed a Coke.

"Right now," Usher said. He pointed to the TV as the opening of "The Ed Sullivan Show" appeared across the tiny black and white screen.

Peterson tossed another pretzel into his mouth. "Where were you?" he asked.

"Doing the rounds. You know, my job." He grabbed a chair beside Usher, spun it around and leaned on the back of it with his arms folded. "Hey, Pete. Turn it up a bit, would you?"

Without getting up, Peterson reached toward the TV set. After a few moments of unsuccessful flailing for the volume, he said, "Ah, it's loud enough."

Carlysle got up and went to the TV. "I'll do it myself. Just like I have to guard this damn bank by myself."

Outside the front of the bank, Sarah unlocked the door and in silence, stepped inside. The cavernous hall was still and dark, with the exception of certain sections lit up by security lights. As she moved across the floor, she was pleased to note that her boots made virtually no noise in the large chamber. As she passed near the lunchroom, she could hear the sound of a TV. She breathed a sigh of relief. *So far, so good*, she thought. She checked her watch and eyed the front door.

He better be on time, she thought.

Sonny, Morrie and Al waited at the top of the stairs where Seamus Flynn had made his impromptu swan dive the day before. Sonny cupped his hands against the door's window.

"I can't see a damn thing," he muttered. Just then, the light went on in the hallway causing him to spin around. "Oh shit! Nobody move," he hissed. Seconds later, a shadow appeared at the window. They all held their collective breath as the doorknob slowly rotated. When the door opened, Sarah's head popped into view.

"Hello, fellas," she said seductively. "Care to make a withdrawal?"

"Jesus, Sarah," Sonny said. She winked and crooked her finger at them. They followed her down the hallway toward Bishop's office. Outside the office, she held up her duplicate key.

"Here we go," she said. She unlocked the door, pushed it open and flicked the light on, bathing the office with a warm glow.

They all stepped inside. For a few moments, they stood in the room, not moving, eyes completely focused on the suitcases.

"Oh, baby," whispered Al. "Come to papa."

"We'd better hurry," said Sarah. "You guys start bringing the suitcases outside. I'm going to check on the guards."

Sonny nodded and reached for one of the suitcases. "Holy Mother of Christ," he gasped. "This weighs a ton." He turned to the others. "Better grab just one at a time or you'll wind up with a hernia."

CHAPTER THIRTY-ONE

Outside, in the truck, Bernie reached for the radio's volume knob. He tapped the fingers of his left hand in time to the song on the steering wheel. These Beatles guys aren't so bad, he thought. He adjusted the rear view mirror with his other hand and took a look at himself. Moving his head left to right, he groaned.

"Man, I look old," he said wistfully. He decided that the first thing he'd do when he got his share of the loot would be to dye his hair. After taking another look though, he decided that maybe it wasn't so terrible after all. If the gray at the temples thing worked for Stewart Granger, then it worked for Bernie Miller too.

He smiled and re-adjusted the mirror. As he did, he noticed a baby blue Cadillac crawling to a stop across the street. Bernie lowered the volume on the radio and suspiciously eyed the caddy. The caddy's window rolled down and a hand with a cigarette attached to it snaked over the car door. The owner of the hand languidly flicked ashes into the snow. Even from a hundred yards away, Bernie could see a large, gold pinkie ring attached to the hand.

A large pinkie ring. Something about that ring struck a chord in Bernie's memory. *Where did I see that pinkie ring before?* he wondered.

He recalled that when he got out of the joint a couple years back, he looked up his old buddy, Carmine Ciccio. They decided to go out for drinks to celebrate. That same night, another guy they both knew, Jimmy "The Weasel" Calderone, came into the bar. With Jimmy was a young well dressed guy who, according to Carmine, was beginning to make a name for himself in the rackets. Bernie also recalled he sported a large gold pinkie ring on his left hand just like the guy in the caddy. He racked his brain trying to remember the young guy's name. "Jesus, what was it?" he muttered. Gino? Genoa? Genna? Bernie snapped his fingers. Genna. That was it. Renzo Genna. The recollection sent a cold shiver twisting up his spine. He remembered that Renzo Genna was part of Bruno "The Butcher" Provenzano's outfit.

"Ah shit," he muttered. Bruno Provenzano. Tony Ferenza's cousin. The Ferenza family. What the hell was he doing here, he thought.

He immediately went weak. He felt like he was about to throw up all over the truck. He tilted the mirror so that he could keep an eye on the car and its occupant. Although it was a cold February night, Bernie started to sweat like it was the middle of August in Florida. He rubbed the perspiration from his brow and looked into the mirror again. He saw Renzo get out of the car and make his way to the front of the bank.

Bernie's head spun. I gotta let them know, he thought. He waited until Renzo disappeared around the corner before he leaped out of the truck. He headed toward the back of the bank and ran to the rear door. He grabbed the doorknob but discovered that it was locked. He lifted his fist to bang on the door, but stopped. Banging on the door would alert the guards. He paced back and forth, sweat dripping down his back.

"Shit, shit, SHIT!"

Sonny, Al and Morrie hauled the suitcases down the hallway toward the stairs. It was slow going but they were making good progress. Without warning, Morrie dropped his suitcase to the floor and hacked out a loud string of coughs. Sonny spun around to see Morrie collapsing to the floor. He dropped his own suitcase and rushed over. Morrie tried to stifle his coughing but he couldn't stop. Sonny clapped a hand over Morrie's mouth to silence the noisy rattle.

"Damn it, Morrie," Al hissed.

Sonny held Morrie's head against his chest and pressed his hand harder over his mouth.

He felt a slick wetness on the inside of his hand as a trickle of blood dripped down between Morrie's chin and Sonny's palm. Al saw the blood and gasped. "Jesus, what's wrong with him, Sonny?"

"Come here," Sonny said. "Help me get him to his feet."

Carlysle glanced up from the TV. "Hey," he said. "Did you guys hear something?"

Peterson shifted on the sofa and shoved a handful of potato chips into his mouth. "I didn't hear anything," he said after he swallowed.

"Of course you didn't," Usher said. "All anyone can hear is you chewing. I'm having trouble listening to the goddamn show."

"Guys, I'm serious," Carlysle said. "I'm pretty sure I heard something."

"What did it sound like?" asked Usher.

Carlysle shook his head. "I don't know. Like coughing, maybe?"

Peterson shifted on the sofa and farted. He looked up and grinned. "Did it sound like that?"

"God, you're an idiot," Usher said.

Peterson shrugged. "Just trying to help." He turned his attention back to the television set. Carlysle grabbed his cap and flashlight. "I'll be back before the commercial ends."

Sarah was hiding in the shadows behind one of the pillars on the main floor of the bank when she heard the sound of someone coming. Sneaking a peek, she saw that it was Carlysle.

What the hell is he doing? she wondered. *He's supposed to be watching the damned show.*

She snapped her head back into the shadows but Carlysle caught the sudden movement.

He flashed the beam from his flashlight toward the pillar. He drew his weapon. "Whoever is there, you'd better come out," he ordered. Sarah cursed under her breath. She had no choice but to step forward.

"Hello, Carlysle," she said with a smile. Carlysle raised his light up to her face.

"Miss Garrett?" he asked. "What are you doing here?"

"Could you lower the light, please?" Sarah asked.

"Sorry about that Miss Garrett." He lowered the beam. "Can I ask you what are you doing here?"

"Mr. Bishop asked me to come by and pick up some papers for him," she said, disarming him with her smile. "He's still out with an injured ankle."

"Oh that's right," Carlysle said. "He telephoned me earlier and told me he was coming by, but he never showed up."

"I'm sorry about that," Sarah said. "I was with him when he called you. I told him that he should rest and that I would get the papers he needed tonight. See?" She held up her duplicate key. "I have his key."

"That's fine Miss Garrett, but—"

A loud voice from behind them interrupted their conversation. "Hey, Carlysle!" They both turned to see Usher coming toward them. "The Beatles are comin' back on in a minute," he said. "You'd better hurry up and — " He stopped in his tracks. "Oh. Hi there Miss Garrett."

"Hello, Usher," Sarah said. "Are you enjoying the show?"

"Uh — what show?" he asked in a nervous voice. Sarah shifted her gaze from Usher back to Carlysle. Even in the dim light, she noted the flush of embarrassment flooding Carlysle's cheeks.

"Miss Garrett," Carlysle said, shifting from one foot to the other. "I can explain."

"You both can relax," she said. "It's fine. I'll just get the papers for Edward and then I'll leave. It will be like I wasn't even here." She winked. "And I didn't see a thing."

Carlysle offered a weak smile. "Thank you, Miss Garrett. That's very nice of you."

"Yeah, thanks a lot, Miss Garrett," added Usher.

"Just don't forget to put the television back, all right?"

The two guards nodded and headed back to the lunchroom. Carlysle cuffed Usher in the back of the head. "Nice one, dummy," he scolded.

Once the guards were gone, Sarah turned her attention to the front of the bank. She saw someone move but the figure was hidden by the shadow of the pillar.

"Well, that was a close one," Sarah said.

Without a word, Renzo Genna stepped out of the shadows and into the diffused light.

"So," he said with a shady smirk, "how are my little patsies doing with our money, baby?"

CHAPTER THIRTY-TWO

Morrie leaned against the wall and took a few deep breaths. Sonny saw a small smear of blood on Morrie's chin. "Jesus Morrie," Sonny said. He put his hand on Morrie's shoulder and was horrified to see that it was stained with Morrie's blood. He wiped it off on his pants and said to Al "Go have a look and see where Sarah is, wouldya?"

"Is he okay?" Al asked, noting Morrie's ashen pallor. "He don't look too good." Sonny stood up and helped Morrie to his feet.

"Yeah, he's all right." Sonny turned to Morrie. "Are you sure that you can go through with this?" he asked.

Morrie wiped his chin with his sleeve and cleared his throat. "Yeah, I'm fine." He took hold of his suitcase and tried to lift it. "It's a little heavier than I thought, I guess," he said with a weak smile.

"Don't sweat it buddy. I've got it," Sonny said. He reached down to pick up Morrie's suitcase just as Al reappeared. Sonny noticed a strange look on his face. "What's up with you?" Sonny asked.

Al jerked his thumb behind him. A stranger stepped into the hallway closely followed by Sarah. The stranger smiled and gestured to the suitcases. "All right, fellas. You're doing great, let's keep it up."

Sonny took a threatening step toward the stranger, his right hand balled up into a fist. "Who the fuck are you?" he demanded.

The man reached into his pocket and pulled out a pistol. He leveled it at Sonny's chest. "I'm the guy with the gun, so I'm the guy in charge. Everybody pick up a suitcase and carry them out the back."

"Renzo, please," Sarah said in a soft voice.

Sonny stared at Sarah who refused to meet his eyes. "What the hell is going on here?" Sarah looked away. "Just do what Renzo says, Sonny."

"Renzo?" Sonny asked.

Renzo waved the pistol. "Less talk and more work." Sonny made a menacing move toward Renzo but the sound of the pistol being cocked stopped him. "Don't think I won't do it," Renzo said in a threatening voice. "Because I will."

"You shoot me and you'll bring the guards, asshole."

"And what will they see?" Renzo asked. "A couple of dead crooks and a bank employee with her husband who foiled a robbery."

Sonny's jaw dropped. "Husband?"

A flood of emotions swept through Sonny in a matter of seconds. Anger. Frustration. Sadness. Betrayal, more than anything. His insides were numb. Dumbfounded, he glared at her. "You set me up?" Sonny said. "Why — "

Renzo cut in. "That's enough. Let's move it. Now."

"Go fuck yourself," he said to Renzo.

Renzo sighed. "I don't have time for this shit." He moved his pistol from Sonny to Morrie. "If you don't start moving these suitcases right now, I'm gonna put a bullet in that guy's head. Looks to me like he doesn't have much time left anyway. I'd probably be doing him a favor." Sonny placed himself between Morrie and the barrel of the pistol.

"Okay asshole, take it easy," he said. Sonny looked at Al and said, "Grab a suitcase and let's get this over with." He glared at Sarah. "The faster we get this done, the faster we can get the hell away from this place."

CHAPTER THIRTY-THREE

A panicking Bernie frantically tramped back and forth outside the rear door of the bank. Every five seconds he paused his pacing to put his ear up against the door to hear if anyone was coming.

"This is awful," he muttered. "What the hell am I gonna do?"

He jammed his ear against the door again. This time he thought he heard something. He held his breath, straining to listen. Without warning the back door swung open and clipped him sharply in the side of the head. He grabbed his ear and grimaced.

"Sonofabitch!" he yelled. To his relief, when he opened his eyes, he saw Sonny step outside carrying a suitcase.

"Jesus, Sonny," Bernie said. "Thank God, it's you. Listen, we got a big problem."

Sonny stared straight ahead. "I know," he responded, his lips barely moving.

A funereal Al and Morrie followed with Renzo and Sarah right behind them.

"Okay Fatso, Four Eyes," Renzo said to Sonny and Al. "Drop the suitcases right there by the wall." He turned his attention to Morrie. "You. Typhoid Mary. You won't be any fuckin' use, so you wait here with Sarah." He then noticed Bernie. He aimed his pistol at him. "Who the fuck are you?"

Bernie threw his hands into the air. "I'm with them," he said.

Renzo eyed Bernie suspiciously. "Do I know you?" he asked. "You look very familiar."

Bernie's eyes darted back and forth. He shook his head. "I have a very familiar face," he said. "People say I look like Stewart Granger."

"Stewart Granger, huh?" Renzo said sarcastically. "Maybe from the knees down you do." Renzo then noticed Bernie's feet. "Okay, maybe not. Christ, what did you do? It looks like you rolled a ten-year-old for his shoes." He pointed the gun at Bernie. "Okay then. Baby Toes. Go stand over there beside Four Eyes."

Arms still in the air, Bernie hurried over and stood next to Al. Al gave him an annoyed look. "Jesus, would ya put your hands down?" he muttered.

Renzo waved the gun at the foursome. “Okay, then. Baby Toes, Four Eyes and Fatso. Go back inside and get the rest of the suitcases.” He pointed the gun at Morrie. “And no fuckin’ around or Mary here gets it. Got it?”

Sonny’s eyes narrowed. “You call me ‘Fatso’ one more time and I’ll jam that fuckin’ gun so far up inside you, your dick’ll be pissin’ bullets,” he said.

Renzo cocked an ear in Sonny’s direction. “What was that?”

“Nothin’,” said Al as he pushed Sonny inside. “Fatso said nothin’.”

Renzo handed the pistol to Sarah. “Here,” he told her. “Keep an eye on this guy. I’ll go get the car.”

Sarah took the pistol. Morrie leaned against the wall and rubbed his forehead. He gave Sarah a mournful stare.

“Gee, Sarah,” he said. “How could you do this to us?”

Sarah turned her face away, unable to respond.

Morrie sighed. “How could you do this to Sonny?”

Inside Bishop’s office, Sonny berated himself, ten times over. This was all a set-up, he thought miserably. He grabbed a suitcase and started down the hallway again.

What a first class mook. He should have known better. Why the hell would a woman like Sarah be romantically interested in an old relic like himself? She played him like a violin. Fool that he was he fell right into her trap. It was stupid enough to lose ten million bucks, but he was even more of an idiot to lose his heart. It was a sucker’s bet and he swallowed it.

His self-reproach was interrupted by Bernie’s mention of the name ‘Ferenza’. Sonny stopped in his tracks.

“What did you say?” he asked Bernie.

“I was just sayin’ that I think this dough belongs to Tony Ferenza.” Bernie put his suitcase down. “You know that asshole outside with the pinkie ring? I met him about four years ago after I got out. Jimmy the Weasel introduced us.”

“Doesn’t Jimmy work for Bruno Provenzano?”

“That’s right. And Bruno is Tony Ferenza’s cousin.”

"Are you tellin' me this is mob dough?" Sonny asked.

Al turned white and collapsed against the hallway wall, clutching his chest. "Ah, shit," he gasped.

"Now's not the time for a heart attack, Al," Sonny said.

"I knew this was a shitty idea," Al growled. "We're screwed." He slid down the wall and cupped his head with both hands. "Now the Ferenza's will be coming after us. The fuckin'Fer- en-zas."

"Goddamn it," Sonny said. He grabbed Al by the front of his shirt and pulled him up off the floor. Al tried to pull away but Sonny yanked him back like a rag doll. "Nothing's going happen to us," Sonny said. "Just think about it for a second. The only guys connected with this are Bishop and his buddy," Sonny continued. "They're the ones Ferenza will be gunnin' for. Not us."

"You better be right," Al whimpered.

CHAPTER THIRTY-FOUR

Cal Spencer picked up Bishop and zoomed out of the police station parking lot. As the Comet raced along the street, Bishop gnashed his teeth together and fumed. "Gun it Cal. I want to catch Carter in the act. I want to nail that bastard to the wall."

"Good thing the streets are empty," Spencer said as he roared through another red light.

He glanced over at Bishop. "You look like shit."

"You try spending time in jail and see how you look," Bishop griped.

Spencer chuckled. "You were in for one night. It's not like you were busting rocks at Sing Sing."

"Up yours," Bishop muttered.

Within a few minutes, they were a few blocks from the bank. As they neared it, Spencer slammed on the brakes, sending the car into a skid. The Comet slid to a stop, about three-hundred yards from the bank's front door. Bishop glared at Spencer and slammed his hand on the dashboard. "What the fuck, Cal?" he demanded.

Spencer pointed down the road. "Oh shit. Look." Bishop followed Spencer's direction and squinted.

"Right over there," Spencer whispered. "Getting into the blue Cadillac." He shook his head and grimaced. "Renzo Genna."

"Renzo Genna? What's he doing here?"

"Yeah — exactly."

Bishop's eyes went wide. "The money!" Spencer looked at Bishop. "What else?"

"But — wait a minute. Flynn said he saw Sonny Carter on the stairwell."

Spencer guffawed. "Flynn fell down the stairs and landed on his head. You can't be sure of anything that guy saw."

Bishop glowered at Renzo and smacked his hand on the passenger door with a resounding thwack. "That rotten sonofabitch." He reached for the door handle but Spencer restrained him.

"Hold on a minute," he said. "Let's see what's actually going on here." They watched in silence as the caddy moved forward. It then executed a slow u-turn back toward the bank. As it turned, the caddy's headlights lit up the front of the Comet.

"Shit! Duck!" Bishop bellowed, jerking to his left. Spencer immediately dropped to his right. The coconut-like crack of their heads smacking together resonated inside the Comet.

Renzo pulled up to the rear door of the bank and hopped out. He clapped his hands and took the pistol from Sarah. "All right ladies. Let's do this, shall we?"

Sonny, Al and Bernie each dropped a suitcase near the parked caddy. Al and Bernie went back inside to retrieve the last of the suitcases while Sonny leaned against the wall with his hands in his pockets. Renzo winked and gave Sonny a smug look. Inside his pockets, Sonny balled his hands into tight fists.

"Almost ready, baby?" Renzo said to Sarah. He leaned in to give her a peck on the cheek. She flinched. Sonny noticed. She did the same thing to Bishop at the bank the week before.

What gives? he thought.

"Hey, Fats — I mean, uh, Big Guy," said Renzo, tossing Sonny a set of keys. "Be a good fella and pop the trunk, would ya?" Sonny shot Renzo a dirty look and snatched the keys out of the air. He opened the trunk and tossed the keys back to Renzo. They landed at the gangster's feet in a pile of slush with a tiny splash. "Nice throw Nancy," Renzo said with derision. He plucked the keys out of the slush and stood up with a grunt. "Now put those suitcases inside the car. Whatever doesn't fit, cram in the back seat."

In the Comet, Bishop and Spencer rubbed the respective spots on their heads where they'd bashed them together. Spencer winced as he touched his forehead. He opened his eyes and turned his attention to the bank. "Wait here," he said. "I'll be back in a minute."

Before Spencer could exit the car, Bishop grabbed on to his arm. "I want that money, Cal. I don't care what it takes."

Spencer removed Bishop's fingers from his forearm and opened the glove box. He removed a 9-millimeter P-64 pistol. "Not to worry," he said in a low, cool voice.

Sonny cursed as he heaved the last suitcase into the back seat of the Cadillac. Renzo slammed the door shut and saluted the group with a cocky smirk. "Well, fellas, it's been nice." He went around to the passenger side of the caddy where Sarah stood and opened the door for her. "We appreciate all your help. Couldn't have done it without you."

Sarah slipped inside the car without a backward glance. With a flourish, Renzo closed her door and ambled around to the driver's side. He got in and with a little wave of his hand, he peeled out sending a shower of sludge into the air. With bitterness, they watched as the Cadillac drove off into the night.

"Son of a bitch," Bernie sighed.

Al kicked the snow. "I said this was a bad idea."

Morrie coughed. "So close," he said, his voice tinged with sadness.

Sonny didn't speak. He wasn't thinking about the ten million dollars nestled within the caddy.

He was thinking about Sarah.

CHAPTER THIRTY-FIVE

Renzo happily whistled the overture from "The Marriage of Figaro" as he motored along the empty streets. My oh my, what a night, he thought. It could not have gone any better and it went exactly as planned. He looked over at Sarah and grinned. She nailed it, he thought. Those four clueless bozos, the guards watching the Sullivan show - everything. His destiny was finally becoming a reality.

The sound of Sarah's voice interrupted his train of thought. "All right, Renzo," she said, "that's far enough. You can let me out right here."

"What did you say baby?" he asked.

"Stop the car," she said.

He gave her a quizzical look.

"I said, stop the car, Renzo. Now."

"Ah, c'mon baby," Renzo said in a condescending tone. "What's the problem?"

"We have a deal," Sarah said in a low, even voice.

Renzo sighed. He slowed the caddy down and pulled over into an empty lot. "Now turn off the car," Sarah ordered.

"Is all this necessary?"

"Just do it."

Renzo turned off the motor and shrugged. "Happy?" he asked.

"All right Renzo. Let's do this," Sarah said.

"Whatever you say, honey," he said. He reached over to put his arm around her shoulder.

Sarah instantly recoiled, raising her hands in front of her face.

"Don't touch me," she snapped. "I told you to never touch me again!"

Renzo leaned away from her. "Put your hands down," he said. "I'm not gonna do anything to you."

Sarah eyed him through her fingers and then warily lowered her hands.

A smarmy smile spread across Renzo's face. "That's better, baby," he whispered. "Now let's have a —" His voice trailed off. He was surprised then incensed that the barrel of his own pistol was now aimed at his face. She must have picked it up while he was driving. He cursed his own carelessness.

"What the fuck are you doing?" he asked.

"You have what you want," Sarah said. "I held up my end of the deal." She held out her free hand. "Now, hand it over."

Renzo narrowed his eyes. "Put down the gun Sarah."

Sarah gave him a cold, blank look. "Do you like your face? How about if I spread it all over your precious Cadillac?"

Renzo scoffed. "Nice try. You won't shoot."

"Really?" She cocked the hammer. "Try me."

"You won't," he said smugly.

Sarah moved the barrel to the right and pulled the trigger. The gunshot was deafening in the car. The driver's side window exploded as the bullet smashed through it. Renzo's hands went to his ears.

"Jesus Christ! What the fuck Sarah?" he yelled. The acrid smell of the smoke burned his eyes. "Are you crazy?"

Sarah aimed the barrel at Renzo's forehead again. "I'm not kidding Renzo," she said.

"My fuckin' window," he whined.

"You can afford a new one," Sarah said. She held out her hand again. "The papers. Now."

"All right, all right," he said. "Jesus."

He reached inside his jacket and extracted two neatly folded sheets of paper. Instead of taking them from Renzo, she pressed the pistol against his nose. "Open them up. I want to see the signature."

Renzo seethed. "This lack of trust is very disconcerting, you know," he said. He unfolded the papers and showed them to her. She saw the Certificate of Divorce printed at the top of the page and then saw his signature at the bottom of the page. He folded the papers back up and handed them to her. "Happy now?" he asked.

"Delirious," she said taking the papers.

Renzo shook his head wearily. "You know, I actually thought that you and me could maybe, you know, start over. Ten million bucks would sure make it easy. We could…" Without warning, Sarah cracked him just below the hairline with the gun barrel. It left a red, circular impression just above his left eyebrow. Renzo grabbed at his head. "Ow, god damn it! That's gonna leave a mark!"

Sarah's eyes flashed and her jaw clenched tight. "Like the marks you used to leave all over me, you asshole?" she said. "You're lucky it's just a tiny scratch instead of a bullet between your eyes." She opened the passenger door of the Cadillac and jumped out with the gun still pointing at his face. "We're through here, asshole," she said. "Don't even think of trying to find me because if you do—"

He scoffed. "You'll what? Go to the cops?"

"The cops?" She laughed. "Use your head, stupido. Don't you think that Tony Ferenza might like to know what really happened to his money?" She waved the gun at Renzo. "You stay away from me and I'll keep my mouth shut. Understand?"

He snorted. "Quella è vita," he said. He held out his hand and asked, "Can I have my gun back, please?"

Sarah smiled and shook her head. "No, I don't think that would be a good idea. You're a rich man now. Go buy another one." She slammed the door and backed away from the caddy with Renzo's pistol still pointed toward his head. Once she was far enough away, she turned and ran. Renzo watched her in the rear view mirror as she headed for an alley about fifty yards away. As soon as she disappeared down the narrow passageway, he glanced at the suitcases in the back seat.

"Who needs her?" he said aloud as he put the car in gear. "There's plenty of skirts out there for a guy with ten million bucks."

A dejected Al and Morrie sat on the rear fender of the Honeyman's Best Bakery truck.

"So goddamned close," Al wheezed.

"I'm very tired," Morrie said. His voice sounded weak.

Bernie was leaning against the wall of the bank. He shoved his hands in his pockets with his shoulders hunched up to his ears. He kicked at the snow in frustration. "I cannot fuckin' believe we got screwed. Again."

Sonny sighed and rubbed his gut. His ulcer was acting up. "Believe it," he said bitterly. He gave Morrie a pat on the shoulder. "Let's get the hell out of here before someone shows up."

Al slid off the fender and pulled open the truck's back door. A cold gust of wind suddenly came up and Morrie began to cough again. Sonny protectively put his arm around his shoulder. He pulled out a handkerchief and held it in front of Morrie's mouth. Listening to his friend's agonizing hack and watching him double over from the convulsions ripped at Sonny's already ravaged heart.

"Jesus," Bernie said. "Is he going to be all right?"

Sonny nodded solemnly. "Yeah, he's fine. C'mon Bern. Let's get the hell out of here." He helped Morrie into the back of the truck and got him settled in on one of the benches. "Take it easy, buddy," he said reassuringly. Bernie slowly began to drive away.

They had only gone a few hundred feet when the truck jerked to an abrupt stop, throwing Sonny and Al to the floor. Al's glasses flew off his nose and skidded across the floor of the truck.

"My specs," Al yelled. "For God's sakes, nobody move."

Sonny pulled himself up into a kneeling position and crawled to the front of the truck. He banged on the wall. "Jesus Bernie," he called out. "What the hell are ya doin'?"

The unexpected sound of the truck's rear door unlocking diverted everyone's attention.

When the door opened, Sonny's jaw dropped open.

"You," Sonny yelled in utter bewilderment.

Sarah was holding the door open.

"Come on," she commanded as she tried to catch her breath. A look of urgency spread across her face. "We've only got about fifteen minutes."

CHAPTER THIRTY-SIX

At West 58th and 10th, Renzo's Cadillac rolled to a stop at a red light. The wind blew into the car through the driver's side window, causing Renzo to shudder. He cleared away the bullet shattered glass in case any cop on patrol got suspicious. Tonight was not the night to take chances with traffic cops. He whistled and thought about what he was going to do with all that money. For sure he'd buy a new Cadillac. Ah, what the hell, he'd get seven new Cadillacs—one for every day of the week. Gourmet meals at the best restaurants. Hand-made Italian suits. No more off-the-rack crap for him. He glanced down at his pinkie ring. Maybe he'd get one for his other hand. Fuck it, how about one for every finger, like Sammy Davis Junior?

"Hello Renzo," said a voice to his left. He turned and saw Calvin Spencer aiming a pistol at his face. With his free hand, Spencer opened the driver's side door. "Get out of the car," he ordered.

Renzo swore. He glanced over at the passenger side window and saw Eddie Bishop's rage twisted face. "Get the fuck out of the fucking car, you fuck," he bellowed.

Renzo exited the car with his hands in the air. "I highly recommend that you two get in your fuckin' car and get out of here."

Spencer shook his head. "I don't think so, Renzo."

Bishop hobbled around to the driver's side of the Cadillac. Spittle formed at the corners of his mouth. "Do you have any idea who you're screwing with, asshole?" he raged.

Renzo blinked and wiped away a drop of Bishop's saliva that landed under his eye. He turned to Cal and jerked his thumb at Bishop. "Your wife seems to be a bit upset Cal." He turned to Bishop. "I think you need to get laid. Why don't you go fuck yourself?"

Spencer waved the pistol at Renzo. "Enough of this shit," he said. "Open up the trunk."

Renzo crossed his arms. "I don't think so."

Spencer and Bishop exchanged confused glances. "You want to get shot?" Bishop yelled.

Renzo sneered at the two of them. "Blast away killers."

Spencer furrowed his eyebrows. "You don't think I'll do it, huh?"

"Nope."

Spencer moved to the front of the Cadillac. He raised the pistol and without hesitation, put a bullet into the windshield. The gunshot reverberated down the empty street. The glass of the windshield cracked, leaving an intricate spider web design. Renzo grabbed his head in horror and ran to the front of his car.

"What the fuck?" he yelled. "Why is everyone suddenly shooting at my fucking car?"

Spencer moved to the driver's side door and without speaking, fired another shot right beside the door handle.

Renzo rushed toward Spencer and found himself staring down the barrel of the P-64. "Now, for the last time Renzo," said Spencer. "Open up the goddamned trunk."

Sarah was inside the bank by the time a stunned and unbelieving Sonny hopped out of the back of the truck. She vigorously signaled him to follow her. "We have to hurry," she pleaded as she ran up the stairs.

A thousand thoughts bombarded Sonny at once. What the hell was she up to? If this was some kind of joke, he was in no laughing mood. The sound of something heavy being dragged across the floor made Sonny pause on the stairs. *What the hell is that?* he wondered. When he got to the top, he saw an out-of-breath Sarah lugging a leather suitcase across the floor. It looked exactly like the type of suitcase they had loaded into Renzo's Cadillac.

"What's going on?" he asked.

With a grunt, she pushed the suitcase down the stairs where it landed with a colossal thud. One of the latches popped open, sending a greenish piece of paper onto the white snow just outside the door. Even from the top of the stairs, Sonny recognized Benjamin Franklin's unmistakable portrait. His mouth dropped open. A gust of wind grabbed the one hundred dollar bill and sent it flying across the street. A cold chill enveloped Sonny that had nothing to do with the winter wind. He ran down the stairs, two at a time. He flipped open the suitcase. He saw bundles of tens, twenties, fifties and one hundred dollar bills wrapped tightly with rubber bands.

Sonny was dumbfounded.

He reached down and grabbed the suitcase with both hands so that its contents wouldn't spill. He waddled over to the truck and with great effort, tossed it inside. It landed next to Morrie's feet with a thump. Al and Bernie looked perplexed. "What's going on, Sonny?" Bernie asked.

Sonny turned to Sarah. She furiously waved at them with both hands. "We need to hurry," she implored. "We're running out of time."

CHAPTER THIRTY-SEVEN

Renzo loaded another suitcase into the Comet's trunk. Panting, he collapsed to his knees. He rested his head against the taillight and spit. "Fuck you guys. I'm done with this shit," he said. He fished a pack of cigarettes out of his breast pocket. He shook one out and lit it. "You can load the rest."

Spencer sighed and handed Bishop the pistol. "Do you know how to use this?" he asked. Bishop took the gun. He smiled. "I've plugged an animal or two in my day."

"Okay Dillinger," Spencer said. He reached inside the back seat of the Cadillac and grabbed a suitcase. "Christ," he grunted. He dragged it across the seat until it fell to the ground with a muffled clunk. A confused look crossed Spencer's face. "That's weird," he said.

"What's weird?" Bishop demanded.

Spencer kicked the suitcase. "Ow! Jesus Christ!" he yelped. Kneeling down, he flipped open the latches and opened the suitcase. "Well Eddie," he said. "I never would have pegged you as a fantasy fiction fan."

"What are you talking about?"

Spencer reached inside the suitcase. He pulled out a book - *Something Wicked This Way Comes* by Ray Bradbury - and tossed it at Bishop's feet.

"What the hell?" said Bishop. He limped over. He looked into the open suitcase and saw a copy of Alfred Marshall's *Principles of Economics* laying on top of *God's Little Acre*.

The suitcase was filled with books. "Son of a bitch," Bishop yelled. "Those are from my office!"

Renzo glared at Spencer then turned his attention to Bishop. "What the fuck are you guys trying to pull here?" Renzo asked.

Spencer stepped around the suitcase and took the pistol from Bishop. "I think we've all been screwed." Renzo jumped up and ran to the back of his car. He yanked out another suitcase.

Dropping it to the pavement, he ripped it open, revealing more books and Bishop's gold plated desk lamp. "Sarah," he whispered. "That double-crossing bitch!"

Bishop gave Renzo a suspicious look. "What are you talking about?"

"I haven't got time for this shit," Renzo said as he pushed Bishop aside and got into his caddy. He started the car and sped off.

"Get in the car," ordered Spencer. He jumped into the Comet's driver's seat and started it up.

Bishop limped around the car and slipped in the snow. He went down hard on his knee. "Fuck!" he yelled.

"For chrissakes," Spencer admonished. "Get in the damned car, or I'll leave without you."

~

Sarah pushed open Seamus Flynn's office door. "In here," she said. She motioned to Sonny and the rest to follow. She pointed to the open closet. Inside were thirteen more suitcases like the one that she threw down the stairs. "Everybody grab a suitcase," she said.

"I am stunned," said Al. "I am genuinely stunned."

Bernie scratched his head. "I'm confused," he said.

Sarah grabbed a suitcase with both hands and started to drag it across the floor. Sonny took it from her. "Hold on a second here," he asked. "Would you mind telling me exactly what's going on?"

Sarah took a deep breath. "Renzo and I were married," she said. "We separated over a year ago and I've been begging him for months to sign the divorce papers."

"So, you are still married," Sonny said bitterly.

She pulled the signed divorce papers from her coat pocket. "Not anymore." She noticed his suspicious look and sighed. "Let me explain," she said. "Renzo told me that Bruno Provenzano needed to hide mob money. Edward was to facilitate the transaction. Everything was set up - then you showed up at the bank. I knew what you were really up to Sonny, and if you tried to rob the bank that would mess everything up. The police would get involved and they would surely find Provenzano's money. So I made a deal with Renzo."

"A deal?" Sonny asked. "What kind of deal?"

"I made him promise that if I kept you from trying to rob the Hudson, he would give me my divorce."

Sonny's eyes narrowed. "You flirted with me just to keep me from knocking over the Hudson?"

"Please. Let me explain," Sarah said. She dropped her suitcase and grabbed his arm.

"You'd better hurry," Sonny warned as he checked is watch.

Sarah continued. "Provenzano then threw a monkey wrench into the works. Renzo called to tell me that Provenzano wanted him to get the money back. Without Edward's knowledge."

"Why would Provenzano want Renzo to steal his own money?"

"Actually, it's Tony Ferenza's money. You see, Provenzano wanted Renzo to steal back the cash so Ferenza would think that Edward and Calvin Spencer took it."

"And leave those two assholes holding the bag," Al said.

"Right," Sarah said. "Mob wrath would come down hard on both of them."

"Fuck 'em," Sonny muttered as he dragged another suitcase down the hall.

"But that's not all, you see," Sarah said. "Renzo got greedy. He decided that if Edward and Calvin were going to get the blame, why not keep all the money for himself. So he changed our deal."

"That son of a bitch," said Bernie.

"If I wanted the divorce, I had to do what he said," said Sarah. "He wanted me to get you guys to do all the work. All he had to do was show up, force you guys load the suitcases in his car and make his escape."

"You know," said Al, "I really hate that prick."

Sarah continued. "The only time we could get that money out of Edward's office would be on the weekend, but the problem was the guards. It was when I overheard them talking about watching the Beatles on Ed Sullivan, I had my idea. I came up with the plan of having you guys pull the job tonight while they watched the show."

"We take all the risk and he gets all the cash," Sonny said in a low voice.

"But wait a second Sonny," Bernie said as he put his suitcase into the back of the truck. "Why is the money here now? What did we load into Renzo's car?"

Sarah smiled. "After all the crap that Renzo put me through, I decided that there was no way I was going to let him get away with it," she said. "Especially not after—" She paused. "Remember when your boots were stolen, Sonny? That was me. I took them so I could have an excuse to go to the haberdasher to buy duplicate suitcases. I had them delivered to the bank before I met you at Finn's yesterday. I filled them with books, and other heavy things from around Edward's office to give the impression to Renzo that they were filled with the cash."

Al chuckled. "That's incredible," he said.

Sonny grabbed another suitcase from the closet and hauled it toward the stairs. "But why didn't you just tell me what you were planning?" he asked. "Why keep us in the dark?"

Sarah looked down for a moment. "I couldn't risk Renzo finding out. I was afraid that if you knew and something went wrong, Renzo would have us killed." Subconsciously Sarah put her hand up to her face. "He can be very — violent."

Sonny put down the suitcase and took her hand. She looked up at him with the same look she had on her face when he gave her the silver dollar medal at her apartment. Tears filled her large brown eyes. Sonny smiled. "You are a very smart and very beautiful woman, Sarah Garrett," he said. "And very resourceful." He picked up his suitcase and carried it to the truck. As he put it inside, he turned to her. "After what?" he asked.

Sarah gave him an inquisitive look. "What?" she asked.

"A minute ago you said that there was no way you were going to let Renzo get away with it. Especially not after—"

She reached up and threw her arms around Sonny, squeezing him. "I couldn't let Renzo get away with all that money," she whispered as tears started to well up in her eyes. "Especially if we're going to start a new life together."

For the first time in Sonny's life, he had nothing to say.

It had been a long time since he had feelings like this and even longer since someone felt the same way about him. Words caught in his throat. He took her face in his hands and kissed her deeply.

Bernie threw his suitcase into the truck. "But what about when Renzo finds out there's been a switch?" he asked. "You know he's going come after you."

Sarah wiped away a tear and smiled. "He's on his way to Philadelphia tonight. By the time he discovers what happened, he'll be long gone and we'll be long gone. And besides, Provenzano will flip when he finds out what happened. After I make a little anonymous phone call to him, it won't be just Edward and Spencer on the hook. I think Renzo will be too busy trying to stay alive than to look for little old me."

"You know, this is real interestin' and all," Al groaned as he dragged a suitcase to the truck. "But we're runnin' outta time here."

Sonny checked his watch. "I'll go and get the last suitcase," he said. "Everybody get in the truck." Inside the rear of the truck, Morrie rested his head against the wall. His face was very pale and his breathing was labored.

Sarah sat next to him and took hold of his hand. "My God Morrie, your hand is like ice," she said. "Are you all right?"

He managed a reassuring but weak smile. "I'm okay," he said. "It's just the cold air."

"You're looking pretty pasty too, pal," Al said. "You look like a ghost."

Morrie chuckled. "Don't worry. After this, I'll buy myself one of them Pendleton Car coats with my share of the dough."

Sonny returned with the last suitcase and threw it into the rear of the truck. He crawled in and slammed the back doors shut. Al climbed into the passenger seat. "Bernie!" Sonny called out. "Let's get the hell out of here!"

"Roger that, buddy," Bernie said. He threw the truck into gear and pulled out into the road. The truck shuddered in the slush but Bernie was able to straighten it out with a little effort. He had only gone about two hundred yards when he noticed a pair of headlights heading toward them. He spun the steering wheel to the left, swerving to avoid the baby blue Cadillac that seemed to be gunning for them. "Ah shit," moaned Bernie. "Not him. Not now."

In the back of the truck, everyone was thrown against the wall and floor. "Jesus Christ, Bernie," Sonny bellowed. "What the hell are you doing?"

"It's Renzo," Bernie said. "He's back."

Sonny and Sarah exchanged looks. "Goddamn it," Sonny growled. "He must have found out about the switch already."

Bernie's eyes darted from the rear view mirror to the road ahead of him. "He just missed spreading us all over the road."

He hit the gas and swung right. Just then another car, a Comet, ran a red light. It also made a beeline straight at them.

"Hang on," Bernie warned. He spun the wheel again, sending the truck into a semi-circle, closely avoiding a rear-end collision.

"Jesus Christ!" yelped Al.

"It's all good," Bernie assured him. He squashed the gas pedal, but with the extra weight, it was almost impossible to make the truck go any faster. It was like stepping into quicksand. "Holy shit!" he exclaimed. "Al! Did you see that?"

"What?" Sonny asked.

"Renzo just smashed into some poor schmo's Edsel. And the Comet that was behind him just took out his rear bumper. That should give us time to get away." A few seconds later, he groaned. "Uh oh."

"What the fuck is it now?" Sonny asked.

"Renzo just got out of his car and jumped into the fuckin' Comet," Bernie said. "Shit! Now they're following us."

Morrie grabbed Sonny's arm. "What's going on?" he asked.

Sonny gnashed his teeth. "We've got company and we gotta shake them fast.

Morrie thought for a moment and then grinned. "I got an idea."

CHAPTER THIRTY-EIGHT

"Say that again," Sonny said.

"Drive over to CBS," Morrie repeated.

"Are you kidding?" asked Sonny. "That goddamned place will be like Times Square on New Year's Eve."

"Sonny's right," Sarah said. "Every Beatles fan who isn't in front of a TV will be there. It'll be chaos."

Morrie smiled. "That's the idea," he said. "We'll get lost in the crowd." He reached into his coat pocket and took out his press pass from the other day. "Look. I still got it. This can get us inside the building. There's a storeroom inside the rear entrance. We can hide the suitcases there."

Sonny grinned. "Sure. And then move them later when things die down," he said.

Morrie beamed. "I figger they won't think to look for us there."

Sonny clapped Morrie on the back. "Now that's usin' your noodle buddy." He knocked on the little window of the cab. When Bernie opened it, Sonny said "Head over to Studio 50."

"Seriously? That place will be a zoo."

"I know," Sonny said. "That's what we want. But first, we gotta lose these assholes."

"I'll do my best," Bernie said. He wiped the sweat from each palm on his pant legs and gripped the steering wheel tight. The truck shuddered as he hit the gas causing Sonny and the others to bounce like rubber balls. They steadied themselves by clamping on to the shelves.

"Hang on," Bernie yelled as he twisted the wheel.

~

Inside the Comet, the tension was thicker than cold oatmeal. Both Renzo and Bishop were nursing injuries as a result of the Comet's impact with the Cadillac. Bishop's face was a mess. One of his front teeth was imbedded in Spencer's dashboard and his top lip was swollen and bloody. In the back seat of the Comet, Renzo rubbed his nose where it hit the caddy's steering wheel.

Bishop angrily pounded on the dashboard. "Faster!" he shouted. "We're gonna lose them."

The Comet's damaged radiator sent out a dense gray mist into the sky.

"Would you please shut the fuck up?" Spencer yelled over the rattling of the Mercury Comet's motor. "I need to concentrate here."

"Goddamn it," Renzo barked. "Will you two assholes shut up?"

"Fuck you," Bishop yelled.

"Oh yeah," Renzo asked. "How about Bruno Provenzano fucks you instead?"

"Both of you shut the hell up," Spencer said.

Renzo leaned forward, his elbows resting on the front seat. "They're in a fuckin' bakery truck, for God's sake. How hard can it be to catch them?"

"The goddamned fog coming out of the radiator is making it a little tough to follow," Spencer responded sarcastically. In spite of the mist, Spencer floored the gas pedal.

~

Bernie zipped through the intersection at West 60th and Broadway. Spencer followed, scraping two parked automobiles and a lamp- post. Fifty yards ahead, Bernie swerved right, narrowly avoiding a potentially dangerous patch of ice.

~

Spencer, following closely, hit the ice and began to slide. "Fuck!" he roared. He expertly turned into the slide and straightened out the Comet but shot well past the bakery truck. Bernie watched the Comet slide away and smiled. "Time for some evasive maneuvers," he said. Al didn't respond. His eyes were shut tight and his shaky hands held the dashboard in a death grip.

~

Spencer brought the Comet to a halt and threw it into reverse. As he straightened the car out to continue the pursuit, Renzo yelled, "They're heading toward Central Park."

The radiator now spat out a thick cloud of steam that had Spencer practically driving blind. He stuck his head out the driver's side window. "I can't see a goddamn thing." The hot steam and the cool night air wreaked havoc on his eyes. He blinked, trying to focus. When he was able to see, he saw, to his chagrin, that the truck was no longer in front of them. He jammed on the brakes.

"Why are you stopping?" Bishop yelled.

Spencer glared at him. "I lost them."

"Whaddya mean, you lost them?" Bishop used both fists and thumped the dashboard. "Goddamn it. All you had to do was — "

Spencer hauled back and laced Bishop in the jaw with a well-executed shovel hook.

Bishop's head fell against the window with a dull thud. He was out cold.

"You got a nice right hook there, pal," Renzo said. "Very impressive." Without warning, Spencer threw the car into reverse. Renzo flew face first into the back of the front seat. "Ah, shit!" Renzo exclaimed. He gingerly rubbed his nose. "You wanna tell me the next time you're gonna do something like that?" he snarled.

Spencer grunted as he made a one-hundred-and-eighty degree turn and sped off in the opposite direction. "Where are those bastards?"

~

Bernie sped east and spotted an alleyway on his right. He hit the brakes hard, sending his passengers to the floor again. "I don't know if I can take much more of this," Al groaned.

Bernie backed the truck into the small space and turned off the headlights. Except for the low hum from the truck's motor, it was eerily calm and quiet. Squeezing the steering wheel with one hand, Bernie cupped the gear shift with his other sweat-drenched hand. "Here we are, shitheads," he said. "Come and get us." About a minute later, Bernie spotted Spencer's Comet. Shrouded in a haze of radiator fog, it looked like a ghost car. Bernie waited until it passed by. He then counted to five. Throwing the truck into gear, he made a hard left in the opposite direction of the Mercury Comet. "So long, suckers," laughed Bernie.

"Okay Bernie," Sonny said. "Head over to Broadway."

Minutes later, the truck drove by Studio 50. Bernie whistled. "Wouldya look at that crowd? You'd think the Pope was here or something."

Parked by the front doors of the theater were two limousines. The massive mob pushed and elbowed its way for position by the limos to get a peek at the soon to be departing Beatles.

"They'll never find us in this crowd," Al said.

Morrie tapped the window. "Park it right over there Bernie," he said. As Bernie pulled into the rear parking lot, he was surprised to see another Honeyman's Best Bakery truck parked nearby.

"What's that doing here?" Bernie asked. He pulled up close to the second truck and parked beside it.

"Gary was sayin' that there was a problem getting the Beatles to and from the hotel," Morrie explained. "He said he needed a laundry truck or something like that so that they'd be camouflaged."

"Good idea," Al said.

"Yep," Morrie said. "Hey, Sonny — remember Chloe?"

"How could I forget?" Sonny said.

Morrie's upper lip curled in a shy smile. "She works for Honeyman's bakery, right? After we went back to her place yesterday, she made a call and was able to get Gary a truck."

Sonny hiked an eyebrow. "So you went back to her place yesterday?"

Morrie's pale face reddened. "Uh — yeah."

"Are you telling me she provided you with wheels because you greased her wheels? I'm impressed, buddy."

"So am I," Bernie chuckled. "She got a sister?"

"Ignore them, Morrie," Sarah said. She looked at her watch. "We need to hurry."

Morrie held up the CBS pass and winked. He climbed out of the truck and hurried as fast as he could to the rear door of the studio. He knocked on the door. When it opened, Morrie flashed his pass to the page. The page nodded and motioned him to follow, but instead of going inside, Morrie held the door open and waved.

"It's working," Sonny said. "Okay Bernie. Back this thing up to the door."

Once the truck was parked, Al and Bernie each seized a suitcase from the back of the truck. Inside the truck, Sonny pushed two suitcases to the edge and let them drop with a muted thud in the snow.

"Moving these sons of bitches are not doing anything good for my back," Al complained.

"How do you think mine feels?" Sonny said in a sharp tone. "Just hurry it up, wouldya?" Sarah started to push one of the suitcases but fell on the slushy metal floor of the truck.

Sonny turned when he heard the noise and climbed back in to help her up. "I'm fine," she said when she saw the look of concern on his face. "Just slipped on the wet floor."

Sonny took her hand and helped her out of the truck. "Hey Morrie," Sonny said. "I know you're tired, but can you hump one of these suitcases over there? Sarah can watch the door."

Morrie nodded. "I think so," he said. With great effort, he hefted one of the suitcases.

Sonny closely followed behind. They had only gone a few feet when Morrie dropped his suitcase to the ground. It sprang open, spilling several banknotes onto the snow. Morrie bent over to pick them up and started to cough. He covered his mouth but a few droplets of blood escaped, crimson against the pristine snow. Sonny dropped his suitcase and rushed over to him.

"Okay, take it easy," he said.

Morrie straightened up and offered up a half-hearted smile. Wheezing, he held out the fistful of bills. Sonny took them and placed them in Morrie's breast pocket.

"You hold on to those buddy," he said. "Why don't you go inside and show us where to put these suitcases?"

"Okay Sonny," Morrie said. He gave a weak smile and slowly headed up the steps.

"He don't look too good," Al whispered.

Sonny ignored him. "Keep it movin'" he said.

Once inside Studio 50, Morrie pushed open one of the storeroom doors.

"In here," he said with a wave of his arm. "We can put them near the back, behind those boxes."

While Morrie kept an eye out, the rest of them began the arduous task of dragging the suitcases into the room. "I'm too old for this shit," Al said between gasps. "What's the sense of having millions if I have a heart attack?"

"At least you could afford the doctor bills," offered Bernie.

"Fuck it," said Sonny. "Just buy a hospital."

"Honest to God, I think my right arm is numb," Al said.

"That's too bad," Bernie said. "How are you gonna whack off now?"

As soon as the suitcases were piled up against the wall Sonny said, "We'll hang out here for a little while things cool down. Then we'll load back up and get the hell outta this city. For good."

Al heard a muffled cry and turned to see Morrie padding down the hallway waving his arms.

"Someone's coming," he hissed. "Everybody get into the storeroom."

Once inside, Sonny pulled the door shut and turned off the lights. He and Morrie pressed their ear against the thin door and listened as the subdued voices in the hallway grew louder. Whoever was outside the storeroom had stopped right outside the door. One of the voices sounded familiar to Morrie.

"That was the greatest thing I've ever seen," the voice said.

"Hey," Morrie whispered to Sonny. "That sounds like Gary."

Outside the storeroom, Gary, Brian and the Beatles discussed the performance. "I'm so very proud of you boys," Brian said. "A truly excellent performance."

"And we're very proud of you too, Brian," responded Paul.

"Oh yes," agreed John. "Truly excellent manager-ing."

"Mr. Cooper," Brian said. "I'd like to thank you again for your hospitality."

"Mr. Sullivan extends his thanks as well," Gary said. "Thanks to the Beatles and yourself, we had the biggest audience we've ever had tonight."

"Now that we've conquered New York, Brian, what's next?" another of the voices asked. "Japan? South America?"

"Montreal is très bon," said a female voice that Sonny recognized as Gary's assistant said.

"Guinevere's right," Gary said. "You must go to France."

"Tabarnac d'estie — "

"When can we leave, Mr. Cooper?" Brian asked. "We'd like to get back to the hotel as soon as possible."

"Soon," Gary said in an assuring tone. "The studio is surrounded by huge crowd right now. Maybe we should wait until it dies down a bit."

"I could go for a pea wack and a sarney right about now," Ringo said.

"Is that a bathroom thing?" Gary asked. "There's one right this way."

The voices faded and finally the sound of a door closing signaled that they had left.

Sonny waited for a few moments then flicked on the light. "Let's all get comfortable," Sonny said. "Who knows who else is out there right now?" As they settled in, Bernie pulled out a cigarette and put it between his lips.

"What the hell are you doin'?" Sonny asked.

Bernie took the cigarette out of his mouth. "I need a smoke."

"Not in here, you're not," said Sonny. "That's all we need — someone smelling the smoke and finding us."

"Okay then. Lemme go outside for a minute. I can go check on the crowd and keep an eye out for those bastards."

Sonny put his ear up against the door. He cracked it open and had a look. Satisfied that it was clear, he nodded. "Just don't take too long," he said.

Bernie stepped out into the darkened hall. He waited to make sure no one was around and went through the back door. Once outside, he wedged a piece of broken brick between the door and the jamb so he could get back inside.

He wandered past the trucks and went to have a look at the crowd. Rather than getting smaller, it looked like it was actually growing. Bernie leaned against the wall and put a cigarette in his mouth. He searched his pockets for a match.

"Ah shit," he mumbled when he couldn't find one. As he was about to approach someone in the crowd to ask for a light, something strange caught his attention.

The sound of a car with a busted radiator. To his mechanic's ears, it was unmistakable. He poked his head around the corner. He saw Spencer's vapor shrouded Comet heading north. It was probably circling the block, on the prowl for the Honeyman's Bakery truck.

"Oh, you gotta be shittin' me," he moaned. He rushed back inside and burst through the storeroom door. "We gotta get outta here," he said. "I just saw the Comet."

"Goddamn it," Sonny said, grabbing a suitcase. "Go warm up the truck, then get your ass back in here." He turned to the others. "We gotta get these suitcases back into the truck now."

Al groaned. "We just got these fuckers in here," he complained.

"You wanna lose them?"

Grudgingly Al picked up a suitcase.

Spencer fumed as he circled the block. It had been at least twenty minutes since he had last seen the bakery truck and he had no idea where it went. As he drove past Carnegie Hall, he glanced over at Bishop. The bank president was still unconscious. In the back seat, Renzo scrutinized the streets through the rear window. As Spencer rounded the corner, he was immediately blocked by the teeming multitude in front of CBS Studio 50.

"Goddamn it," he said.

~

Renzo turned around and saw the crowd. "Goddamn Beatles," Renzo sneered. "They're no Frankie Valli and the Four Seasons, that's for sure."

"Not a fan?" Spencer mumbled as he put the Comet into reverse.

Renzo blew a raspberry. "Fuckin' fad. I give 'em a month, two tops."

Spencer observed two limousines in front of the building. "This crowd must be here waiting for the Beatles to leave."

Renzo scoffed. "Jesus, every asshole in this city was supposed to be at home tonight in front of their stupid TV sets. Sarah and I were talking about it the other night. That's why she wanted to —"

He paused. Spencer noticed that Renzo had a faraway look in his eyes. "What is it?" Spencer asked.

"They're here," Renzo said. "I know it."

Bernie started up the truck. He decided to take another look for the Comet. He hurried toward the crowd and poked his head around the corner of the building. To his horror, he saw the Comet slowly navigating its way through the crowd. Cursing under his breath, he rushed back to the others. As he passed by the truck, he heard someone with an English accent call out to him. Confused he looked over at the truck and was surprised to see five young men seated in the rear.

"What the —"

Someone sitting in the passenger seat said, "Hello there. Are you our driver?" Bernie saw a well-dressed gentleman holding out his hand. "How do you do? My name is Brian Epstein and these fellows in the back are the Beatles and their road manager Neil Aspinall. I believe you have been hired to take us to the Plaza Hotel."

"'Ere John. This is not so bad," said one of the Beatles, looking around at the inside of the truck.

"At least it's not a laundry truck," John replied. "George. Remember the soiled nappies?"

"Don't remind me," said George. "At least this one smells like jam buttees and not me grandma's knickers."

"If you could hurry," Epstein said, "I'd like to get the boys back to the hotel as quickly as possible."

"Hotel?" Bernie was about to protest but an idea suddenly dawned on him. "Sure. I'll get you to the hotel," he said. He slammed the truck's rear doors shut and ran to the driver's side. "Hold on to your asses," he said as he threw the truck into gear. "It's gonna get bumpy."

CHAPTER THIRTY-NINE

The bakery truck shot out of the lot like an intercontinental ballistic missile. "Jesus Christ!" shouted Renzo. "Look out!" he yelped. Spencer, blinded by the headlights, instinctively hit the brakes. The truck shot forward. It missed the Comet by inches.

"Goddamn it," Spencer hissed. He spun the wheel and gunned the Comet in the direction of the escaping bakery truck.

~

In the parking lot, Sonny dropped the suitcases where the truck used to be. "Where'd it go?" he asked.

Morrie pointed to the second Honeyman's Bakery truck. "I thought it was parked next to that one," he said.

"Are you sure this is not it?" Al asked.

Sonny shook his head. "No way. Ours was parked closer to the door. Also, that one over there is missing the "O" in Honeyman's." He quickly scanned the parking lot. "Where's Bernie?"

"Yeah, where is he?" Al asked.

"We haven't got time for this," Sonny said. "Al, go and see if those bastards are anywhere nearby."

As Al dashed to the front of Studio 50, Morrie walked up to the passenger side of the second truck. "Hey," he said, "there's someone in here."

The driver's side window rolled halfway down. A cigarette butt flew out before the window went back up. Sonny jogged over and knocked on the window.

The driver turned and gave Sonny a questioning look. Sonny motioned to the driver to roll the window down.

"Hey, can I ask you a question?" asked Sonny.

The driver shrugged his shoulders. "Shoot," he said.

"There was another Honeyman's truck, by the door over there. Did you see the driver?"

"Yeah, I did. I saw him jump into the truck that was parked by the door. He shot outta here like Parnelli Jones at the Indianapolis 500. It was crazy, man."

"Did you see anybody else?"

"Nope. Nada man."

Sonny thanked the driver and went back to see the others. "So apparently Bernie took off with the truck like a bat outta hell."

"Why the fuck would he do that?" Al wondered.

Sonny rubbed his chin. "Maybe he saw those guys. Maybe he took off, hoping they'd chase him away from here."

"What do we do about all the suitcases, Sonny?" Morrie asked. "We can't leave them here."

Sonny jogged over to the other truck again and knocked on the window. "What's up?" asked the driver.

Sonny stepped up on to the truck's running board so he could get closer to the driver.

"Listen pal," he said. I know you're waiting to drive the Beatles to their hotel —"

The driver looked surprised. "That's supposed to be a secret," he said.

"Yeah, well the cat's outta that bag. How much are you getting for this little job?"

The driver shrugged. "Fifty-five bucks. Why?"

Sonny held out a fistful of cash. "How'd you like to make a hundred and fifty instead?"

Inside the Beatles' bakery truck, Bernie coaxed more speed from the heavy vehicle's engine. "C'mon, baby," he purred. He sped through another intersection, spraying slush and snow everywhere. He checked his mirror and saw the lights of the Comet a few blocks behind. He leaned into the next curve, taking it wide. The tires clipped the curb and for a moment they lifted off the pavement — only an inch, but they were airborne. "Just like the old days!" he exclaimed.

In the passenger seat, Brian Epstein clutched the dashboard. "Do you Americans always drive like this?"

"Nah," Bernie said. "Only the real good ones."

In the rear of the truck, the Beatles jolted, jerked and jostled against the walls of the truck. Ringo Starr gripped one of the shelves and blurted out "How much did we pay for this ticket to ride anyway?

"Ticket to ride?" John repeated. He smiled. "Oh, that's good. Who has a pencil?"

Bernie took another look in the mirror and saw that he was actually further ahead of the Comet than he planned. His intention was to lead them away from Studio 50, not to lose them. He eased up on the gas, allowing his pursuers to close the gap.

A persistent tapping on his right arm made him turn. "Excuse me," Epstein said in a small voice. "Don't red traffic lights mean stop in America?"

Bernie saw the red light and watched two, slow moving cars motoring through the upcoming intersection. "You better hold on to something," he warned as he slammed on the brakes.

~

The truck's brake lights flashed. In the Comet, Spencer swore and slammed on his own brakes. It smashed into the rear bumper of the truck, sending both vehicles sliding into the intersection. The truck missed the first car but slid into the path of the second, a DeSoto station wagon. The DeSoto, unable to stop in time, piled into the side of the truck. The Comet continued its own treacherous trajectory toward the station wagon. It struck the DeSoto, sending an explosion of steam into the air. In the back seat, Renzo shook his head and winced. "Christ all mighty," he muttered. "I can't take much more of this crap."

Bishop stirred in the front seat. His eyes fluttered open. "Are we home yet?" he asked in a quiet voice.

Renzo pushed his shoulder. "Just get out of the damned car," he said.

Spencer leaped out of the driver's seat and sprinted toward the bakery truck. He grabbed the door handle and wrenched it open. Instead of suitcases full of cash, he found five disheveled young men, wearing buttoned-up overcoats and somewhat dazed expressions.

"Who the hell are you?" Spencer demanded.

One of them crouched on his haunches and waved. "Hullo. We're Randy Fellows and the Winchester —"

"Sonofabitch," Spencer bellowed as he slammed the door shut. He kicked the side of the truck and strode back to the Comet.

Bishop was still trying to get his bearings when he slipped and landed hard on his back.

He looked up to see a priest standing over him.

The priest, the driver of the DeSoto, spoke to him. "We seem to have had an accident." Bishop slowly and with much pain pulled himself to his feet. He sneered at the priest.

"Get lost, churchy," he growled.

The priest took a step back. "I'm sorry, but we've had an accident. We need to discuss this," he said.

Bishop pushed the priest backward. "What we need to discuss is you fucking off."

The priest's eyes narrowed. "Forgive me, Lord," he said and kicked Bishop in the shin.

"God damn it." Bishop clutched his leg and fell face down onto the road.

The priest tutted. "Such foul language," he scolded.

Spencer and Renzo both watched Bishop writhing in the snow. Renzo smiled at the priest. "Nice job, Padre."

"I tried to speak to him like a civilized human being but he was rude. I was —" The priest stopped talking. His attention was riveted on the pistol in Spencer's hand.

"You don't want another accident, do you, Father?" Spencer asked. The terrified priest shook his head. Spencer looked at the demolished Comet and sighed. He pulled open the door of the DeSoto and got in.

"What do you think you're doing?" the priest asked. "That car belongs to the church."

Renzo hoisted the moaning Bishop and led him to the back seat of the DeSoto. As he passed by the priest, he remarked, "God helps those who help themselves, Father."

Once they were settled inside the priest's station wagon, Spencer slammed the car into gear and spun out in a one hundred and eight-degree turn. "They're not getting away this time," he said. Renzo turned around and surveyed Bishop lying on the back seat. The bank president, not only looked like what the cat dragged in but after it had eaten it and thrown it up.

One of Bishop's eyes was swollen shut. He returned Renzo's stare with his good eye. "What the hell you looking at?" he demanded.

"You know what?" Renzo said. "You look like Lon Chaney."

Spencer shook his head. "Both of you shut the fuck up." They were now only minutes away from Studio 50.

~

Sonny backed up the borrowed bakery truck to the rear door of Studio 50. Sarah and Al lugged two of the suitcases outside and went to get more. Morrie walked around to the front of the building to keep a lookout. He took a deep breath. The cold air burned his cough-ravaged throat. The soreness in his chest was getting worse and his hips felt like they were on fire. The doctor had warned him that the cancer would spread. And it had. However, the pain that wracked his body was nothing compared to the torment he felt that he couldn't pull his own weight anymore. He felt as useless as an infant. The idea that he was letting the others down was something that he didn't want to accept.

Outside the front of Studio 50, the crowd was still going strong. It looked to Morrie like they didn't realize that their idols had already departed. He saw one car, a green DeSoto station wagon with a big dent in its side, having trouble navigating through the sea of teenagers. The driver impatiently leaned on his horn and gunned the engine.

What a jerk, Morrie thought. He's gonna hurt someone. He squinted, trying to get a better look at the driver.

Sonny's attention to the task at hand was broken by the sound of frenzied shouting. He looked up to see Morrie holding his chest and running toward him as quickly as he could.

"They're coming!" he wheezed. "I just saw them, Sonny. They're right out front."

Sonny turned. "Sarah! Al!" he called out. "They're back." As he ran to warn the others, the slamming of the truck's cab door caught him by surprise.

"Morrie," Sonny shouted. He rushed around to the front of the truck and saw Morrie in the driver's seat. Sonny pulled open the door. "What are you doing?"

Morrie sighed. "You know what I gotta do."

Sonny tried to grab his arm but Morrie managed to shut the door. "Please Morrie," Sonny pleaded, "don't do this."

"We don't have time for this Sonny," Morrie said. "They're right out front." He smiled. "It's okay. I need to do this."

Sonny tried to grab his arm again but Morrie blocked him, knocking Sonny off balance.

He fell backward on to the snowy pavement. His back spasmed and for a few seconds, he couldn't move. Morrie stuck his head out of the window. "You're my best friend, Sonny. Thanks for everything," he said. "I mean it. Everything."

He gave him a little wave and pulled away.

~

Spencer leaned on his horn as he slowly maneuvered the DeSoto through the crowd.

"Why don't these idiots go home?" he growled.

He inched the car forward. He bumped into one surprised teen, sending him into a slow motion sprawl across the top of the hood. He pressed his face against the windshield.

"What the hell, man?" he yelled. "You tryin' to run me over?"

Spencer rolled down the window and stuck his head out. "Get off the goddamned car," he yelled.

The kid slid off the hood and slammed his fist on the hood of the car. "Up yours, asshole," he said.

Renzo gnashed his teeth and punched the dashboard. "Just drive over them if you have to," he seethed.

Spencer blasted the horn again accompanied by an impressive string of cursing. He poked his head out of the window. "Get out of the fucking way," he shouted. "Goddamn it, you morons, you need to move your asses now." He kept leaning on the horn until a little gap in the crowd finally opened up. Spencer nudged his way through the gap, widening it slowly but aggressively. Just as they managed to squeeze through, a Honeyman's Best Bakery truck shot forward. It sent up a wall of slush, covering the DeSoto's windshield.

Renzo jammed his finger up against the window.

"There they go," he roared.

Spencer floored the gas pedal. He kept his eyes on the truck, careening along East 47th. Despite the DeSoto's boxy shape, it was powerful enough to keep up and Spencer was determined not to let them get away this time. He managed to keep the gap between them tight. The truck made a quick turn on to Third Avenue, heading north until it hit East 56th. Spencer followed close, his eye on the prize, barreling through all the intersections. They raced along East 56th toward the East River, sending waves of sludgy snow into the air.

Renzo leaned over, his chin almost brushing Spencer's shoulder. "Bump 'em. Knock 'em on their asses."

In the back, a wobbly Bishop sat up. He leaned against the window, his head foggy and his eyesight blurry. The sound of a siren made him turn his head. He blinked, trying to focus. "Shit," he said. "We got company." Renzo jerked his head around and saw the lights of the police prowler car getting closer.

"Fuck 'em," he said. "We get the money, then we'll take care of them."

"Take care of them? What are you talking about?" Bishop asked.

Renzo flashed him a malicious smile. Bishop reached over the seat and grabbed Renzo's arm. "Are you out of your mind? You can't kill cops."

Renzo slapped Bishop's hand away. "No, you idiot. We'll throw them some cash and they'll fuck off, nice n' sweet." He shook his head disdainfully. "You're a banker. Don't you know how anything works in this city?"

At the intersection of East 56th and Sutton Place, Spencer narrowed the gap. "Everybody hold on," he warned.

"What are you going to do?" asked Renzo nervously.

"Hold on," Spencer repeated. He gunned the engine. The DeSoto shot forward and smashed into the truck's rear bumper. The impact caused the truck to swerve to the left and then to the right.

"Holy shit," Renzo said. They watched in horror as the zigzagging truck sped toward a Pure Gas Station.

"This is not good," Bishop said.

The truck hit the gas station's price sign, sending it flying over both the top of the truck and the DeSoto. It smashed into the police cruiser's windshield, causing the cruiser to hit the curb and flip on to its roof.

The truck continued its momentum toward the gas pumps.

"Shit," Spencer gasped. The truck crashed into the pumps at a terrific velocity. In an instant, there was a massive explosion. A bright orange fireball lit up the night sky. Spencer slammed on the brakes. When the Comet skidded to a stop, Spencer and Renzo jumped out. They stared helplessly as the Honeyman's Best Bakery truck, completely engulfed in flames, rolled under the Franklin D. Roosevelt Drive overpass and down the embankment and into the East River.

With a resounding splash, it went into the water, followed by a loud hiss as the waves snuffed out the flames. Spencer and Renzo rushed to the edge of the river. They arrived just in time to see the rear end of the truck slip below the river's murky current surrounded by smoke and bubbles.

Renzo dropped his head into his hands. "Un-fucking-believable," he muttered.

A strangled yelp behind them caused them both to turn. They saw Bishop limping down the embankment toward them. "The money," he squawked. "The money!"

Spencer let out a long sigh. "It's gone," he said.

"The hell it is!" Bishop hopped on one foot as if he was about to wet his pants. "Ten million dollars!" Thick blue veins popped out of his neck. He pointed to the water. "Look. It's floating to the top!"

A few charred one hundred dollar bills floated on the water's surface close to where the truck disappeared. Bishop reached out to snatch the bills from the water. Spencer grabbed Bishop's coat collar. "Listen to me, you dumb fuck. I've had enough of your shit. You wanna jump in the river, then go ahead. I won't stop you."

"But the — the money—"

"The money's gone. Capiche? It's at the bottom of the goddamn river." Spencer shoved Bishop away in disgust. "It's over. It's fuckin' over."

~

By the time Sonny, Sarah and Al arrived, it was pandemonium. There were police cars and fire trucks as well as a large crowd of rubberneckers pointing and whispering amongst themselves. Sonny saw the tire tracks and the black ashes covering the snowy embankment near the water. A wave of nausea hit him and made his head spin. He fell to his knees.

"Jesus." Al gasped. "It looks like —" He couldn't finish the sentence.

Sonny fixed his eyes on the churning dark water. His chest tightened when he saw the charred hundred dollar bills floating on the surface.

A tiny moan caught in his throat. "Morrie," he whispered.

Two firemen standing by the edge of the river discussed the events. "The truck smashed into the pumps before it went into the river," one of them said. "It's lucky the whole block didn't go up."

"No survivors?" asked the other.

"No way," the first fireman said. "The damn truck was on fire and then sank into the river. I doubt they'll find anything until they dredge the bottom."

Al sat down in the snow and put his head in his hands. Sarah knelt beside Sonny and put her arms around his shoulders.

Amidst the noise of the fire trucks and the din of the crowd, Sonny cried.

CHAPTER FORTY

"What?" Marco cupped the receiver with his left hand. "The river? Good Christ." He rubbed the bridge of his nose and stole a glance at Provenzano who's attention was fixed on the small television above the bar. This is going to be ugly, he thought. Marco placed the receiver into its cradle and cleared his throat. "Um, Bruno? I gotta tell you something and I don't think you're gonna like it."

Bruno continued to stare at the tiny black and white television. "Spit it out. I'm watchin' 'Bonanza'."

"Yeah, okay then." Marco took a deep breath. "Somethin' happened to Tony's money," he said.

Provenzano turned his billboard-sized face toward Marco. His eyes narrowed. "What did you say?"

Marco cleared his throat. "Somethin' happened to Tony's money."

"Whattya mean sumpin' happened to Tony's money?" he asked. "What happened to Tony's money?"

"That was Freddie on the phone. He said that the money was in a truck that got burned up and sank in the East River."

Provenzano looked at Marco like he just said that he fucked his sister. "What?" he bellowed. "How the fuck did dat happen?"

"I don't know Bruno. You'll have to talk to Renzo about it."

Provenzano gave Marco a cold, grim smile. "This is a joke, right? I mean this better be a fuckin' joke because —"

"It's no joke boss. It's all gone."

Provenzano gripped the edge of his little wooden table in his two beefy fists. Marco could see the wood vibrating between his fingers. In a low, menacing voice Provenzano said, "Find Renzo. Get him here right this fuckin' second."

Marco shrugged. "Nobody's seen or heard from him all day."

With a loud war cry, Provenzano pulled the table apart. He then punted his chair across the room. It smashed into the wall with a loud thwack and fell to pieces on the floor. Marco couldn't ever remember seeing Provenzano this angry before. His face was bright crimson and his mouth foamed like a rabid dog. Marco was convinced that the big man was about to have a stroke right in front of him. Provenzano waddled across the room until he was standing a few inches from Marco. A trail of the foamy saliva dribbled its way down the folds of his chins until it made a bubbly home on the dark blue lapel of his Italian suit. As Marco watched, a crazy grin started to spread across his face. "I see now what's goin' on," he said.

"What are you talking about boss?"

"Don't cha get it?" Provenzano asked, his dark eyes burning, his raptorial smile chilling. "Renzo's fuckin' wit' me. He's fuckin' wit' me and wit' Tony. He's got Tony's dough."

"What dough Bruno? It all burned up in the crash."

"Bullshit!" he screeched. "He's got dat cash! I know it!" Provenzano moved in even closer to Marco. He could smell the cacciucco the gargantuan gangster had for lunch. "I want you to find him, Marco," he wheezed. He shuffled across the Jersey Club's wooden floor. "I want you to find him and like John da fuckin' Baptist, I want his head on a silver fuckin' plate."

"Easy Bruno," warned Marco. "You'll have a heart attack."

Provenzano shook his head, causing his meaty cheeks to shake violently. "Renzo's pullin' sumpin' here. I know it. He prob'ly planned it wit' dat Spencer pal of his and dat banker piece of shit. Dey got my — I mean, Tony's dough. So listen ta me." He was so close that his sweat dripped onto Marco's patent leather shoes. "I want dat sonofabitch Renzo and dose two fucks — now."

Marco headed for the door. "Leave it to me, boss." Before he stepped out of the room, one of Bruno Provenzano's chunky mitts grabbed on to his upper arm.

"And Marco." The mobster twisted his lips in a menacing grimace. "You make sure dat you bring 'em back to me alive."

CHAPTER FORTY-ONE

August 20, 1964

Sonny and Sarah drove through the beautiful Genesee countryside in silence. Sarah stared out the window. She watched the greenery blend into a warm wash of jade, harlequin and teal. For a long time she suggested they take this trip, but Sonny always resisted. Until today. Much had changed over the last year. Sonny had changed too. He was calmer, more at peace and less willing to take on the world. He glanced over at Sarah and smiled. He had a lot to be thankful for. They continued to drive in silence until at last they arrived at their destination.

"We're here," Sonny said in a quiet voice. Sarah took Sonny's hand in hers and squeezed it.

The entrance was a large winding brick and stone driveway. It was landscaped on both sides with manicured shrubs, and augmented by blue and white scilla. The driveway led to a large one story building with white porticos on either side of an ornate door. Sonny pulled the car into a spot under the shade of an ancient elm. They both got out and walked around the building to the rear. In Sarah's hands was a bouquet of white roses, Asiatic lilies and Monte Casino asters.

Sonny paused by a bench under an oak tree. He sat down and said, "I don't know if I can do this."

Sarah gently placed the bouquet of flowers on the bench and sat next to him. She wrapped her arms around his neck and felt his shoulders tremble. "You can do this, honey," she said.

Sonny started to weep.

"Here," she said as she reached into her purse. She pulled out a handkerchief and lightly dried his tears. When she finished he closed his eyes and lifted his face to the sun. The tranquil warmth bathed his face, calming him. When he opened his eyes, Sarah was standing with her hand held out to him. "Are you okay now?" she asked. Sonny took her hand.

They walked among the flowers and the markers until they came to the spot they were looking for. The headstone was simple yet elegant.

Sonny was sure Morrie would have approved. Sarah knelt and laid the flowers in front of the stone. She stood up and kissed Sonny on the cheek. She sat down on one of the benches near an expansive oak tree leaving Sonny with the privacy he needed.

He stared at the headstone for a few moments. He lowered himself to the grass and sat cross-legged at the foot of the grave. He read the words carved in the marble as he thought about what he wanted to say.

"Hey, buddy. It's been a while, huh?" he said. "Sorry that I haven't been here since the funeral, but you know me." He swallowed back a lump in his throat. "I miss you, Morrie. I miss you a lot, actually. I never thought I'd ever miss anybody, you know? It's funny. I can almost see you smilin' at that." His eyes became moist again.

"I sure wish you were still around. Lots of good things are happening. Al's kid is getting married. Now he can afford one of those big splashy affairs and help the kids out too. Yeah, Carrie is marrying Robby. Remember that guy whose jaw she busted? Al still worries about her though, but this guy Robby, he's a real good kid. He's aces. He'll take really care of her." He chuckled. "If she doesn't wind up puttin' the poor bastard in the hospital, that is."

He raked his hand through the green grass. The lush softness comforted him. "Bernie's doin' good too. He got his dad in a nice nursing home upstate. He goes up there every week to visit him. His dad, well, he doesn't know who Bernie is anymore. Ain't that sad, Morrie?" He plucked a blade of grass and flicked it back and forth with his finger. "Can you imagine? A guy spends his life making friends, experiencing stuff, falling in love and fills up a whole boxful of memories. Then it's like some bastard comes along and steals the box. He empties it out until there's nothing left but the scratched up insides and a whole lot of nothing. And then you can't ever find them anymore 'cause they've all blown away." Sonny sighed. "It's not really fair, if you ask me. Sometimes, memories are all you got in this stinkin' life. I'm lucky though, buddy. I got good memories of you."

Sonny swallowed hard. His voice was quiet but it was strong and steady. "I know I could be a jerk to you sometimes, but you know I never meant it, right?" He smiled. "We had good times, you and me, didn't we? Sure, there was bad stuff, but I like to remember only the good stuff. Like that last job. I'll admit, I wasn't sure if we'd be able to do it, but one thing was for sure — we wouldn't have wanted to do it without you, Morrie. I mean, without you, we wouldn't have been able to pull it off at all. Nobody ever figured out it was us. Everyone thought that all the dough was lost in the river. All they found was a couple of hundreds floatin' on the water. Those musta been the bills I stuffed in your pocket, remember? Nobody knew that you took off before we had time to load the truck. You fooled 'em all, buddy." Tears started to fill his eyes again. He rubbed them and sniffed. "You wanna know the best part? Those bastards Bishop, Renzo and Spencer got whacked for it." He reached into his pocket and took out a folded up clipping from the New York Times. "Listen to this." He unfolded it and started to read.

"Authorities are investigating the discovery of three oil drums tied together, floating in the East River. New York City Police retrieved three mutilated bodies stuffed tightly inside each drum, missing heads and hands. Investigators have a few leads in the case. Police are not talking but a source close to this reporter says that one clue they are tracking down involves a man's gold pinkie ring stuffed inside one of the bodies."

Sonny put the clip back in his pocket. "They don't say where the ring was stuffed, but I have a pretty good idea." He chuckled. "Hey, do me a favor, would ya? If you see that prick Bishop floating around up there, kick him in the balls for me, okay? And don't worry about your share of the loot. I made sure Gary got it. I told him you socked away some cash over the years, and you wanted him to have it. At first he couldn't figure out how you managed to save so much, but I told him not to ask too many questions, you know? I told him he probably wouldn't like the answers anyway. He's a good guy, Morrie. You'd be proud of him."

Sonny turned his head to look at Sarah. He smiled. "And me and Sarah? Well, it's not like we're talking marriage or anything." He winked. "Yet," he whispered.

He inhaled a deep breath and got up. He stood next to the headstone and rested his hand on the warm sun-kissed marble. "You're my closest pal, Morrie. You'll always be in my head and in my heart. Yeah, I know, it sounds sappy, but it's true. I may not be religious, but I'm sure that, if there is a God, you're up there with him right now." Sonny leaned in close to the headstone. "And if you are, could you do me another favor?" he whispered. "Could you put in a good word for me? Just in case."

Sonny ran his fingertips over the top of the headstone and wiped his eyes again. He was aware that Sarah had come over to stand next to him.

He marveled at her beautiful smile and her dark brown eyes as they sparkled in the sun. She made his heart thump like a high school kid on his first date. All the money in the world never gave him as much happiness as one smile from her could.

Sonny tapped the gravestone. "See ya, buddy," he said. "I promise to come back real soon."

Sarah took Sonny's hand in hers and squeezed it. "Sonny Carter, I want to hold your hand."

Sonny squeezed back.

"You know," he said, with a wide grin. "I'm starting to really like the sound of that."

The End

www.ingramcontent.com/pod-product-compliance
Lightning Source LLC
Chambersburg PA
CBHW071355100726
47908CB00004B/1000

9780987735720